SCHOOLHOUSE DANCE SHOWDOWN

"Never mind," Tom Sebastian warned Buffalo Galt, voice steady and hard. "You're a yellow dog and you don't lay your hands on my guests. Go back to Tumpah for your women."

"That's rich, from you," ground out Buffalo Galt. "That baby on your ranch—who's the father of it, friend Tom?"

One moment of stinging silence followed and was broken by the flat, curt sound of Sebastian's hand slapping Galt full in the mouth. "You've been making war talk lately, Buffalo. I hear you have said I was afraid of you personally. Let's see about that now."

Then body struck body with a solid, meaty reverberation. Buffalo Galt locked his arms about Sebastian's waist and his head plunged into Sebastian's chest until the latter's body was broken acutely backward. Then Sebastian's shoulders rose and his knee smashed upward into Galt and the latter yelled out his pain and let go and recoiled.

Ernest Haycox

SIGNET BRAND WESTERN

THE SILVER DESERT

by

Ernest Haycox

A SIGNET BOOK
NEW AMERICAN LIBRARY
TIMES MIRROR

Published by arrangement with Mrs. Ernest Haycox

SIGNET, SIGNET CLASSICS, MENTOR, PLUME AND MERIDIAN BOOKS
are published by The New American Library, Inc.,
1633 Broadway, New York, New York 10019

FIRST SIGNET PRINTING, FEBRUARY, 1980

1 2 3 4 5 6 7 8 9

PRINTED IN THE UNITED STATES OF AMERICA

THE SILVER DESERT

by

Ernest Haycox

A SIGNET BOOK
NEW AMERICAN LIBRARY
TIMES MIRROR

Published by arrangement with Mrs. Ernest Haycox

SIGNET, SIGNET CLASSICS, MENTOR, PLUME AND MERIDIAN BOOKS
are published by The New American Library, Inc.,
1633 Broadway, New York, New York 10019

FIRST SIGNET PRINTING, FEBRUARY, 1980

1 2 3 4 5 6 7 8 9

PRINTED IN THE UNITED STATES OF AMERICA

was slim. His hands folded across the horn were heavy, and his shoulders moved now and then with a faint restlessness. Physically, quiet as he was, Lily Tennant felt the impact of a willful personality drastically curbed behind the grave cheeks. She saw her words hadn't penetrated his guard and she ceased to regret them.

"I wasn't trying to be personal," he added. "Only stating a fact. But maybe I might as well commit the sin I've been spanked for. From California, aren't you?"

"As the license plate will tell you."

"I don't need to see the license plate. Your temper—which is accustomed to being obeyed—tells me." The soft, spurious urbanity at once reached its mark; she felt herself being put in place. His sudden grin only ground the injury in. He removed his hat. "I apologize for blocking your royal signal." The second rider appeared from the alkali fog again and shut off the stream of cattle.

Lily kicked on the engine and moved the car forward, abreast the tall man. "Thank you, Moses," she said succinctly, "for commanding the waters to divide." Her head bowed with an exaggerated respect and then the long delayed roadster roared out of the confusion into the full punishment of that burning Nevada afternoon. She struck the junction of the Reno-Virginia City road furiously, spewed a storm of shoulder gravel behind and pressed her shoe against the foot throttle with nothing less than manslaughter in her heart. Reno's buildings, just ahead, were outlined against an atmosphere that seemed to flow like liquid glass. The smell of the earth was tinder-dry. Inside the town limits, she drove more sedately across the Truckee, stopped in front of a house pleasantly surrounded by locusts, and left the car.

Even on this hot day she went up the walk with a stride that had in it the faintest touch of a swagger, with a quick rhythm that synchronized and turned utterly graceful the supple members of her body. She was a slender girl, somewhat above the average height and her shoulders, small and straight, were presented squarely at the world in a manner that flaunted serene confidence like a banner. Four years of fighting her way up through the Hollywood extra ranks had given her that; but the unquenchable vitality so apparent in every motion was her birthright.

Hannah opened the door—Hannah being a dark, plain woman with a slightly resigned expression—and Lily let out a long sigh as she passed into the shaded coolness of the living room. She removed her hat impatiently and threw it on a divan; and her heavy brown hair, thus released, fell turbulently down across a white forehead.

"Hannah, I'm wrecked. Fill the tub."

"Yes, ma'am. There's three telegrams."

"Is Kit Christopher here?"

"No, ma'am. Mr. Timmy Akin called about an extra guest. May I know how many there will be for dinner?"

"Oh, eight or ten. It doesn't matter. You can handle them. And mix me a glass of iced lemonade, Hannah. A tall one."

Hannah contrived to put sorrowing patience into her "yes, ma'am," and went from the room in soft-shoed silence. Hannah's manner, Lily knew, was purely fictitious; for Hannah could rise to any crisis. At the living room table, Lily Tennant looked down on the three yellow telegram envelopes lying there and wondered if she had ever sufficiently thanked Jay Stuart. For when the days of cooking her own breakfast over a gas flame had come to an end—only two weeks ago she had walked from Superb's office with the contract that meant stardom in her pocket—it was Jay Stuart who had brought Hannah to her with the briefest explanation. "This is your personal maid and your cook—the only one in California you want." Jay Stuart knew so much about the good things in life.

Standing there, Lily delayed opening the telegrams, her expression faintly darkened by thought. Her face was not extraordinarily beautiful; it had not the possibilities of mystery or graphic storminess of the great stars. The even contours of her features did not lend themselves to the creation of glamour, to shadowed subtleness. Lily Tennant, as far as Hollywood was concerned, was a type—and that type was definitely the American Girl. But the odd, deep powder-blue coloring of her eyes lifted her completely out of the commonplace definition of type; for in those eyes was a directness as true as the flight of an arrow and a depth that suggested many things. It was Sam Wein, foxy old press agent, who had defined Lily Tennant. "You ain't Continental. You ain't the face that launched a thousand ships. That stuff's dime a dozen now. You're Lily Tennant, see? You're what the American man dreams of. Get it? You've got fire and laughter, you're loyal and you're straight. You could carry a water bucket on a ranch or move through a palace and never miss a step either way. You're a good scout. But get this, Lily. Beyond all that, when you look at a man you're a woman all the way through. A full-blooded woman—and it gets into the gelatin—and you'll be as great as the greatest of them some day. Am I telling you?"

She ripped open one of the envelopes and pulled out the message. It was from Jay Stuart, who had so swiftly assumed a major share of her attention these recent days:

PLAY YOUR GAME WITH THE STUDIO AS YOU THINK BEST NEVER LET THEM TAKE YOU TOO MUCH FOR GRANTED BUT DON'T OVERPLAY YOUR INDEPENDENCE RIGHT NOW WAIT TILL YOU'VE MADE YOUR FIRST PICTURE YOU HAVE BEEN GONE A WEEK AND I HEAR SUPERBS GETTING RESTLESS ABOUT IT IT ISN'T GOOD POLITICS TO GUM UP THEIR SCHEDULE BETTER COME BACK ANYHOW I MISS YOU HOLLYWOOD IS PRETTY EMPTY FOR THIS OLD TROUPER WHILE YOU ARE AWAY REMEMBER I SAID YOU WERE GOING A LONG WAY IN PICTURES AND THAT I WANTED TO TRAVEL AS FAR DOWN THAT ROAD WITH YOU AS YOU WILL LET ME

JAY

It was a perfect projection of his personality—discerning, very smooth, gently insistent. She laid the message back on the table and pursed her expressive lips; she let her glance touch the platinum bracelet on her right wrist. Hannah spoke from the hall.

"Your tub's ready, Miss Lily. Was there any particular dessert you wanted served tonight?"

"Anything cold," said Lily, and went instantly to the tub. Relief sailed through her when she stepped into the water and she felt regret again for having lost her temper on the road. Sam Wein would have disapproved, and when she thought of Sam's fat and homely face beaming through the smoke of an ever present cigar she wished he were in Reno to give her counsel she so desperately needed. Four years of bitterest struggle lay behind. She had what she wanted, a contract that meant stardom. She wasn't afraid of failure—never of that. But stardom meant the end of all her security and it meant the beginning of something she saw vaguely, and dreaded as she saw it. It was why she had fled Hollywood. Here in comparative quiet she had hoped to think it out.

The phone rang. Hannah's soft tread shuffled down the hall and Hannah's voice, without any expression said: "She's busy, Mr. Akin. Wait a moment." Outside the bathroom door Hannah said: "It's Mr. Timmy Akin wanting to know if he may bring another guest."

"Of course. That makes nine, doesn't it?"

"Ten," said Hannah sadly and went away.

Out of the tub, Lily Tennant studied herself candidly in the panel mirror. It had been a mistake to suppose that one could think any more clearly in Reno than in Hollywood. Something happened when you stepped up from the ranks and became an individual personality. People surrounded you. Camp followers and self-seekers and strange new friends. There wasn't any privacy any more.

Kit Christopher's amused tones came through the door. "I'm home, darling. People who sing in bathrooms always come to bad ends."

"Have I been singing?"

"Perhaps it was a soliloquy."

"I seem to discover I've already come to a bad end, Kit."

"Well, sin is such a comfort when you get to know it."

Lily slid into mules and a wrap, poked the edges of her thick brown hair carelessly back from her forehead. Coming out of the bathroom she found Kit Christopher limp on the divan, blowing smoke circles at the ceiling. Lily settled in a chair and sipped at her waiting lemonade.

"Been slumming?"

"Reviving old memories. Bob Nesbitt and I were divorced here three years ago. Bob came up just before the final decree. We had a wonderful week—and we parted better friends than ever. I wasn't his property any more and he treated me as though I were a desirable woman again. Love's got some funny angles, honey."

She was, Lily thought, representative of all that Hollywood stood for—an urbane, truly sophisticated woman with a gleam of humor in her eyes that covered a very quick mind. In a way she was hard as nails, unsentimental and unafraid of anything. What affection she possessed was saved for her few friends. Tall and quite slender, and not more than thirty, she did better than any other character actress in Hollywood, the civilized, ultra-modern drawing room type. All her keen, faintly dusky features were quizzically alert; and two pearl drops displayed on ears from which her black hair was pulled partially back lent the last immaculate touch. She was a smiling worldling, seeming to possess an ironic wisdom too definite ever to be disturbed.

"What've you been brooding about, honey?"

Lily rose and went to the table, handing Kit the telegram from Jay Stuart. As an afterthought she took up the others. One was from Sam Wein:

IF THIS ABSENCE IS AN ACT GIVE ME MY CUE IF YOU ARE MAD ABOUT SOMETHING WHY DON'T YOU LET OLD SAM KNOW SUPERBS MAKING FUNNY NOISES AM I ASKING SAM

The other, from Rex Gilman, Superb executive, was more brief and pointed.

LITTLE GIRLS CAN'T AFFORD TEMPERAMENT WE HAVE A PICTURE TO SHOOT TAKE TONIGHTS PLANE REX

She passed these to Kit and went back to her chair. But she didn't sit down. She stood in front of Kit.

"I'm not putting on an act, Kit. I'm not going temperamental."

"Of course not. You got stage fright and ran away."

"More than that, Kit."

Kit Christopher's expression reminded Lily then of Jay Stuart. It held the same bland, material wisdom. "I knew something was bothering you," said Kit. "But, of course, I wasn't asking."

"Look, Kit, as long as I was an extra girl, nobody paid much attention to me. I was just Lily Tennant. I could do what I pleased and act as I pleased without being watched or criticized. I was a normal person. I'm not now."

"Didn't you see that coming?" queried Kit gently.

Lily's answer was slow. "No—I guess not. I was so busy fighting for a place in the sun that I never gave it a thought. Well, overnight I've become Lily Tennant, a possible star. I have lost all my privacy. If I go on I'll never get that back."

"No—you never will."

Lily, impelled by an energy that seldom let her remain inactive, moved around the room. "That isn't frightening me so much. It's another thing. Let's not fool ourselves, Kit. I'm saying good-bye to something else—whether I want to or not. Decency, Kit."

Kit Christopher's lips made an enigmatic curve. Lily went hurriedly on.

"There's a lot of fine things and fine people in Hollywood. But there's a lot of rottenness too. And when any girl becomes a star it is the rottenness the world thinks of. Hollywood has been kind to me. But Hollywood can be very cruel. People there will put the worst implication on every word I say, every step I take. I'm just common property for everybody to share. All the same old dirty stories, the same sly winks, the same raised eyebrows—that's what's ahead, Kit."

Kit Christopher looked across at Lily Tennant's platinum bracelet. "By any chance are you thinking of that?"

Lily lowered her eyes. "I took it from Jay because he was very kind to me. Because he seemed to get so much pleasure from giving it."

"Also," said Kit Christopher, with a faint dry drawl, "because it was flattering, because when Jay Stuart passes out a platinum bracelet to a girl it means she is definitely on the way up."

"Yes," agreed Lily, quite candid. "But I didn't see the other side of it until a day ago."

"What other side?"

"As far as Hollywood is concerned I became Jay's woman when I put this bracelet on."

Kit Christopher bent to crush her cigarette in a tray. She didn't look directly at Lily. "It's a game with Jay. He's been in pictures since the ark—once he was a star in his own right. He's seen them all come and go. What means more to him now than anything is his reputation for picking the girls who will be tomorrow's box office hits. When he gave you the bracelet he was laying his bet on you."

"Yes?" said Lily, openly skeptical.

Kit's smile was ironic. "I'm not defending the animal, darling. He'll take whatever he can get from you. He'll be insistent about that, for he is a lady's man. If you see it his way, that's his luck. He hasn't any scruples there at all. But if you stick by your guns he'll admire you all the more and still plug for you."

"Until a new girl comes along."

"Certainly," said Kit equably. "It's his fun and his money, isn't it? It's a game with him and he'll play it either way you insist. I suppose many people would call Jay a thorough-going scoundrel. I have always thought him a gentleman after his own lights. Take what you can get from him. He expects you to. As for the other—keep whatever standard you wish and never mind what Hollywood says."

"Kit," said Lily, "I'm afraid."

"Of what?"

"I hate to get mud on me. I hate to think that some of the

dirt may creep beneath my skin. I know what I am now but I don't know what I may become. If I go on, Kit, I'm leaving one Lily Tennant behind. We'll never see her again."

Kit Christopher's answer was abruptly impatient. "If you are going to be a star you have got to believe in yourself utterly. You'll have to be cruel at times, and calculating and egotistical. Some things aren't going to be pretty—that's the price of being a star. Above all you'll have to be completely indifferent to the abuse the public throws at you. Even when you know they think your private life is a scandal you've got to smile back."

"I don't like that," said Lily with an extraordinary sharpness.

Kit Christopher smiled. "Did anyone tell you your eyes glow beautifully when you're roused?"

"I don't want to be pulled out of shape. I don't want to be an abnormal human being."

"Lily," said Kit, "why are you worrying? You are one of the few women as lovely off the screen as on it."

Lily Tennant's shadowed gravity dissolved. She couldn't help smiling. "Kit, you're a smoothie."

Kit reached out to touch Lily's arm. "It's hard to sit by and watch innocence get its first shock, Lily. But you'll become hardened to it."

"Should I?"

"We won't go into that, darling. Who's coming for dinner?"

"Just people. Kit, are you at all serious about Timmy Akin?"

Kit Christopher thrust a half-amused glance at Lily and rose and turned to her bedroom. It was a complete answer and didn't need any added definition. But at the door she swung her shoulders slantingly on Lily. "How can you discourage an airedale?"

"Don't be cruel. Timmy's nice."

The older woman's face was utterly smooth; but there was a reluctant sadness in her tone. "The day will come when you'll be just as cruel. Because in self defense you'll have to be. More cruel than I am now—for you are going higher than I can ever go."

There were seven people enjoying cocktails in the living room when Lily turned to the kitchen to see how the dinner looked; Judge Sillavan and his wife, two young unmarried couples of the town and Kit Christopher whose smile lay unchangeable and enigmatic on her lips. When Lily returned, the party was made, for Timmy Akin had arrived with his guest. Seeing that guest, Lily suddenly put down her cocktail glass, a deeper color tinting her cheeks. She straightened, though she did not realize it, and her chin lifted. She went quietly over.

Timmy, whose chief effort was always to please people, grinned happily. "You wanted to know an authentic cattleman, Lily. So here's one. May I present Tom Sebastian of the Barrier ranch? This is Lily Tennant, Tom."

For one small moment neither moved. Looking up to him, Lily saw his features tighten and she instantly guessed he was wondering how best to handle the awkward situation—this man who had held her up with his cattle on the Reno-Carson road. Beside Timmy, who was small and neutral-colored, he was strikingly solid, arrestingly alive. Actually he was tall, taller than she had first noticed. He was dressed in a finematerialed gray suit and there was a looseness about the coat to accommodate that restless motion of his big shoulders which she had noticed before. Against the whiteness of his shirt his skin was quite dark; and she felt the steadiness of his glance. Timmy stirred, not understanding the stretch of this silence. The rest of the people in the room had ceased speaking.

"It was a pleasant thought, Timmy," said Lily, matching Sebastian's own even calm. She extended her hand to the man. "And it was nice of you to come."

As he bowed she caught a quick and vanishing streak of humor in his gray eyes. He said, taking her hand: "That reassures me, temporarily."

He had finesse, Lily decided, and turned to introduce him to the rest of the party. But Kit Christopher smiled frankly on the man and said, "Timmy introduced me to Mr. Sebastian the other day." And it was immediately obvious that the Reno people knew him well. Judge Sillavan spoke with a heartiness she could not miss. "That's good-looking beef you drove in today, Tom."

"It ought to be," Sebastian observed. "I'm paying for the privilege of raising it—according to the market."

"Why don't you get out of the business then?" suggested Kit.

"Cattlemen don't change—they just die."

Lily moved to the table where the glasses were and paused, watching this Tom Sebastian as talk went idly on. He stood with a balanced straightness, as though ready to whirl, and behind his calm she detected once more that recklessness of spirit which colored his ironic words. He was talking to Sillavan but his glance went over to Kit Christopher and remained there a moment; and then it turned and touched Lily with the same careful attention. He was, she guessed, analyzing what he saw. She picked up a cocktail glass and crossed to him, handing it over. The judge retreated. For a moment Lily had Sebastian to herself.

He said: "If the situation is embarrassing to you I'll be glad to duck out."

Lily matched his cool, blunt manner. "I am not embarrassed."

"Cattle," he said, "sweat off flesh rapidly in hot weather. That's why I seemed so anxious to get them across the road. I'm sorry about it."

"Why apologize for an honest impulse? You were irritated. So was I. Let's not lie about it now."

He drank his cocktail and his eyes showed a quickening interest as they studied her. It was, she thought, the dangerous gray color that made the impact of his glance so much like a jolt of electricity. "Just water under the bridge?"

"That's it."

His grin was a quick break of light across watchful reserve. "Good enough."

Hannah announced dinner and the party trailed into the dining room. Lily, standing at the head of the table, indicated the seats. At the other end of the table Kit Christopher lifted her wine glass. "To all good sinners."

It was a pleasant beginning and Hannah had done well with the meal. The talk, touched off by the cocktail, held a light and urbane gayety and Lily, isolated a moment by her own thoughts, wondered at the strange contrasts of this Nevada land. In the afternoon Sebastian had been a figure from the Old West, herding his cattle through the incredible heat; and here he was, a civilized being, perfectly at ease in sophisticated surroundings. She turned to him.

"Why is it called Barrier ranch?"

"That dates back," said Sebastian agreeably. "In my father's day, 1871, it was about the only piece of civilization up in the north."

Judge Sillavan cut in dryly. "You wouldn't exaggerate if you said it was still about the only piece of civilization there."

"The wild and woolly West still lives," murmured Lily with a faint skepticism.

"Our tourists are very wise," was the judge's amused observation.

"Perhaps," retorted Lily, "we should be prepared to defend our doors tonight against the Indians?"

"No, the Indians are gone," said Sebastian.

"Other things remain?" she challenged him.

"Maybe," he said.

Timmy Akin broke in. "I heard this today. A man was shot dead at a waterhole last night, not far from here."

"The romantic West in best tradition," murmured Lily Tennant. "Timmy, you are incurable. The rustlers and stage robbers are practically all in Hollywood now, doing pictures."

But Akin's information did something to the Reno people. Judge Sillavan bent toward Tom Sebastian. He said: "Did you know about that?"

"Yes. It was Pete Rice."

"At Crockford Wells, then?" said Sillavan, quietly.

"Yes."

Sillavan's talk was obscure to Lily. "That's hitting close to home."

Tom Sebastian said: "Didn't I tell you all cattlemen were dumb? They don't change—they die." But he shifted from that topic casually, turning to Lily. "You don't have much faith in the traditional West, do you?"

"I think you cling to sentimental memories. You are a modern man, but you wish to believe you are a part of the old times. I have seen the gambling tables and the long mahogany bars in Reno. They are picturesque. They're good theater for the tourists. But they're old-fashioned now."

"Let us grieve for the lost innocence of this irreverent generation," complained Sillavan.

"Not irreverent," corrected Lily with a faint smile. "But unsentimental."

"There you have it," applauded Kit Christopher from the end of the table.

"You are hard people, you youngsters," said Sillavan. "You don't believe in anything. Maybe my generation was a little too given to weeping in its beer when the professor played Home Sweet Home. But we believed in our tears. You people forbid yourselves the luxury of honest emotion because you're afraid of it. So you are all turning brittle and transparent."

"We are being spanked," intervened Kit Christopher.

"And don't tell me you're a realistic generation," went on the judge, amiably severe. "You're novices at that. My generation could step over dead men on the way from church to Sunday dinner and never turn a hair. We could put a school at one end of the town and a public crib at the other. That's realism, my infants."

Lily said with extreme quietness: "What should we believe? What is there to believe?" She looked at Tom Sebastian. Hannah, moving quietly around the room, touched the light button and the sudden crystal gush from the chandeliers set off in quick fire the copper glints of her chestnut hair. Her firm, full lips remained steady. Her chin tipped upward and her round and actually beautiful shoulders were caught in a still straightness.

Tom Sebastian spoke with some brusqueness. "That's an empty question. You don't mean it."

"I am puzzled by a great many things that seem unanswerable."

"Maybe there are no answers," said he. "Why bother? Live the day out and let it go like that."

Judge Sillavan said unexpectedly: "I love all you youngsters. Because you are young and full of hell. You can be reckless and take your spills and still laugh. That's important."

They were finished with coffee. Lily said, faintly restless: "Let's go somewhere."

Kit Christopher's hands expressed despair. "Lily, can't you ever stay put?"

But Tom Sebastian had risen promptly, his white grin once more breaking. The party adjourned to the living room and the women went for their wraps. Judge Sillavan's ruffled silver head bent down; he clipped a cigar with a gold pen knife attached to his watch chain. His quiet talk was for Tom Sebastian alone. "Pete Rice was a gentle soul. But he was one of your friends."

"They are hitting me through my friends," observed Tom taciturnly. "Men can't afford to be my friends any more."

"Certainly—certainly. Nevada politics. Been so since the very beginning." Sillavan looked up and his very old and very shrewd eyes glittered with some of that ruthlessness that had been his long ago. "It will get worse for you. Well, you are as rough and tough as any of your enemies and you have but one weakness, which is a set of scruples against deliberate murder. The other side doesn't have any such scruples. Do you know what it's all about?"

"Freeze-out."

Judge Sillavan's smile was very thin. "Come see me at the

office tomorrow." He stopped talking and bowed to the approaching ladies with a gallantry that held the flavor of a distant past. There was something in the manner of this old-type Westerner that reminded Lily of opening an attic trunk and finding there the crinoline and linsey-woolsey of a dead age. The party trooped out toward the cars at the curb but Lily touched Sebastian's arm and they went walking on through the fragrant dusk of the quiet street. The people behind were cheerfully in argument. These two were silent, and remained so all the way into the brightness of Reno's center. Orchestra music flowed from a hotel and couples in evening dress casually and gayly passed them. Along the curbs men in boots and broad hats watched this parade without emotion. Many of them spoke to Tom.

Lily said: "You know a lot of people."

"In Nevada everybody knows everybody else. You want to remember—" He ceased speaking and Lily, following the turn of his head, saw a great mass of a man idly posted against a building wall. He had a chest so extraordinarily deep and broad that it made the rest of his body seem thin, and his features were queerly flattened against a brick-brown skin. His eyes, of a muddy opaque color, clung winklessly to Tom Sebastian. And then, in spite of the utterly desolate expression of his face, a smoldering dislike flashed plainly across it. Her glance whipped back to Sebastian and she noticed at once how friendless was his own expression. Afterwards, when they went on, that unforgiving tautness around Sebastian's lips remained in her mind. She spoke.

"Who was the grotesque giant?"

"A half-breed by the name of Star Humboldt."

"Not a charming personality."

He looked down at her, not quite smiling. "He's not in the tourists' guide, Lily."

The party swung into the Goldfield Club into the sudden confusion of sound and smoke. Down the long room stretched the successive gaming tables, well patronized; and through it moved that queer stream of people which gave Reno its particular color, cowhand and prospector and townsman rubbing shoulders indifferently with the sightseer in his crumpled clothes and the divorcee in evening dress. The party eddied slowly along, propelled by the players drifting from table to table. Five men in white duck served behind a long polished bar.

Kit Christopher wanted to try roulette and Timmy Akin obediently found a place for her. The Reno people were chatting with others who had come up. A man passing by touched Sebastian on the shoulder and said: "Want to see you later, Tom," and went on without waiting for an answer. Turning back to Lily Tennant, Sebastian found her regarding the roulette table with an amused indifference.

"Not interesting to you?"

"Not very."

Kit Christopher had tried her luck and found it bad; she came away from the table with an expressive shrug and the party went into the street again, Lily and Tom bringing up the rear. Tom Sebastian spoke with a strange bluntness.

"What interests you?"

Her face rose, showing a queer liveliness. "Anything. Anything that is real."

"You're not bored. You're troubled."

"How would you know that?"

"You're too much alive to be bored."

"Thank you, Tom." The party turned into an alley and entered a doorway overhung by a single light. But Sebastian put a slight pressure on Lily Tennant's arm and stopped; and his head turned back to the main street. Looking in that direction, Lily presently saw the great figure of Star Humboldt cruise across the mouth of the alley. Humboldt threw one glance down the alley, toward Sebastian, and then passed on.

"What is it?" asked Lily.

Sebastian only shook his head, his cheeks holding an oblique and secret humor. They followed the party into another of Reno's clubs, this one smaller and quieter than the Goldfield, with its crystal chandeliers throwing off a faint air of elegance. Kit Christopher was again trying her luck, but Lily Tennant stood fast in the center of the room and looked about with a cool curiosity; and then the curiosity died and left her aloof and indifferent. Tom Sebastian turned a little to catch the straight, level effect of her glance. He bent toward her, reserve going from his manner.

"How long are you going to be in Reno?"

"A day—a week. I don't know, and it doesn't matter."

He said: "You haven't seen—" He broke off the sentence and folded his two hands in front of him. His cheeks went keen and perceptibly reckless; he spoke quite brusquely. "You're a lovely woman, Lily."

Her eyes held him. Her voice was serene, speculative. "You are a man of extremes."

"You've seen Reno. But there's another side of Nevada you don't know—"

The party was retreating from the roulette table. Kit Christopher said: "I'm the world's worst gambler." A man came through the doorway with a swift swing of his shoulders and stopped quite suddenly beside Sebastian.

"Tom," he said, "how are you?"

Sebastian's answer fell short of friendliness. It was nothing more than acknowledgment. "Hello, Buffalo."

He was a smiling man, this newcomer. His eyes were lightest hazel and his yellow blond hair—he had at once removed his hat—curled carelessly down his forehead. He was as young as Sebastian, with quite bold features across a lightly florid skin. In the muscular roll of his shoulders and the glinting liveliness of his glance was a visible hint of animal magnetism. A pointed silence fell as he stood there, half faced toward Lily Tennant. Sebastian, coolly polite, said: "Miss Tennant, may I present Buffalo Galt?" and plunged his hands into his pockets. Then he added: "And Miss Christopher, and Timmy Akin."

Buffalo Galt's bow was deliberately gallant. "This," he said, "is a pleasure I deliberately sought."

Lily said, "Thank you." The man was so smilingly aggressive, so obviously traveling through life at a top stride. Kit Christopher murmured gently: "It is a nice philosophy, Mr. Galt—to go after what you want."

"It's done well for me," said Buffalo Galt. His grin exposed the whiteness of his teeth; his eyes raked Tom Sebastian and there was in them a lurking malice. "But Tom wouldn't agree to that. Tom sticks to traditions."

"As I've said before," drawled Sebastian, rather dry, "cattlemen are a dumb lot." He seemed to dismiss Buffalo Galt then from his mind. He looked at Lily. "You have never seen the Nevada lying beyond Reno."

Lily tipped her head upward, toward him. They were at that moment quite alone—all others excluded from their talk. The sense of a challenge lay between them, quite definite. Tom Sebastian's mouth cut a solid line across the darkness of his face. Lily Tennant spoke out of her deep calm.

"Is it something I should see?"

"Come to Barrier with me."

"When?" she asked.

"Tonight."

"What an abrupt sort you Nevadans are," observed Kit. But nobody answered and Kit's eyes, at once sharp, raced to Lily Tennant and remained there. Faint color touched Lily Tennant's cheeks; something disturbed her inner calm. Her shoulders rose and became straighter. Studying Tom Sebastian, she said: "What shall I see on Barrier?"

"Does that matter?"

"All right."

Sebastian looked up to the rest of the party. "That includes all of you, of course."

"Me?" interposed Buffalo Galt.

Sebastian stared at the man. "Would you feel comfortable on Barrier, Buffalo?"

"I'm always willing to take my chances," retorted Galt with a minute accent of arrogance.

Judge Sillavan's white head reared. The smoke of his cigar didn't quite conceal the harsh brightness of his glance. "You always are," he said, quietly. The silence returned then, and remained until Kit Christopher was prompted to speak by some obscure impulse.

"Come along, Buffalo. I think I should enjoy your company."

Buffalo Galt laughed, and looked at Sebastian with an ironic triumph. "You will find me at least entertaining, Miss Christopher. I never do the expected thing."

Sebastian's black head was inscrutably bowed toward the floor. Lily Tennant felt the thick quality of his reserve, noted the quick streak of pressure down his jaw muscles. The party slowly eddied into the street. Buffalo Galt turned with the obvious intention of stepping beside Lily, but she had already joined Sebastian. Kit Christopher, who missed nothing, laughed a little and touched Galt's arm. When he dropped back to pair off with her his burly shoulders brushed Timmy Akin aside very carelessly and Timmy was forced to the rear, among the Reno people.

Sebastian's car headlights glowed down a road as straight as a transit line. The speedometer needle oscillated gently at 65 miles, but the flat blankness of the surrounding land gave no indication of the rapid traveling. Sebastian's hands merely steadied the wheel. Here and there a lone pinpoint of light from some shanty accented a night so black as to possess a kind of velvet shine; the stars were like crushed and loosely strewn crystals. Lily Tennant beside him had said very little during the first forty miles. Judge Sillavan and Timmy, sitting on the humps, only now and then spoke; but Buffalo Galt, riding the rear seat with Kit Christopher, kept up a steady good-humored talk.

Timmy Akin said, in a muffled voice: "Am I stepping on a rifle, by any chance? Something's under my feet."

Sebastian slowed the car for a sharp turn and Buffalo Galt's laugh was abnormally loud and ironic. Then the car, gathering speed, began to beat up a more violent sound from the rougher road they had taken. One tall water tower loomed and died and a cabin nearby thrust out its single splinter of lamp light. Sebastian dropped his hand to the horn, leaving a long halloo behind. The glow from the instrument board fell down on the blackened butt of a .45 protruding from the side pocket of the car.

"Lily, what troubles you so much?"

"It is quite obvious?"

"In you—yes."

She looked straight ahead, but her shoulder fell against him, so that he might hear. The rush of the car made whirlpools of sound inside the tonneau; speech came faintly from the people in the rear. She said: "When you come to a blind jump and you don't know what lies beyond, what do you do?"

"Jump it."

"As easy as that?"

"If you've got to make the jump why stop to think about it?"

"Suppose I can jump or stay behind?"

His shoulders swayed over the wheel; there was a howling echo beneath, a hollow roar bounding away from a plank bridge. Far, far ahead one faint light began to wink intermittently. "You're not the kind to refuse a jump."

"Are you so sure?"

"You're a high-powered girl, Lily."

"I'm not sure that's a compliment."

"It shouldn't matter. I'm being truthful."

"You waste no time."

"Not with you," he said, and stopped talking. His profile was a hard, keen silhouette. It was unsentimental, and touched by a distant bitterness. Without warning he added: "With some people it isn't a question of time. You and I are as good friends as we'll ever be, right now."

She straightened a little. "Why?"

"Friendship is a mild emotion. I'm not mild, and neither are you. We're the sort that pushes on to the logical end—which is either dislike or love."

She sat silent, thinking. The car passed into the shadows of a hill on the left hand. The road curved and the wink of the light far out on the desert died. Beyond the curve another light began to send its signal forward. The air turned chilly and a sense of tremendous emptiness began to press against Lily Tennant. Farther on the headlamps touched a coyote standing in the middle of the road, its tail down and its starving body gone taut. It slid into the desert without hurry.

"It would be silly," she said, at last. "But it might be true."

"It is true—and for us it would be disastrous. What is this jump you've got to take and can't see beyond?"

"Fame—of a sort."

The distant light grew stronger; another light appeared beside it, and then a cluster of them. The stark, irregular shape of a series of corrals flittered by, and in a moment they had left this solitary habitation to the rear. Sebastian looked aside at her. "You're afraid of what you've got to give to get it."

She put her hands together and let out a quick breath. "Yes."

"Is it what you want—fame?"

"Perhaps."

"Then give what you've got to give."

She spoke with sudden energy. "That's a little bit brutal."

His answer touched gentleness. "Maybe. But you can't be Cinderella and Madame Pompadour at the same time. When we reach the ranch I want to show you what the down payment on fame amounts to."

The car drummed on under a more blackly brilliant sky, devouring the distance by its ceaseless rushing. The talk fell off for long periods of time. Away ahead another light made a thin point through the emptiness, toward which Sebastian pointed. Presently they had reached this ranch and had sped by. It seemed to Lily then that they were racing across a pure emptiness, guided only by these faint beacons, sighting them, straining for them, roaring past them. Once they skirted the margins of a small lake, their lights shining on its lonely silver surface; another time they seemed to rise and pass into a narrow canyon, beating up ancient echoes as they traveled.

Considerably later Sebastian spoke again. "How far do you think you've come from Reno?"

"Fifty miles."

"A hundred and ten to be exact. We're almost home. Thirty miles more."

"Almost?" she murmured. "You don't take your distance very seriously, Tom."

"We can't afford to. Barrier is about as far from Reno as New York is from Albany."

"It's such a lonely feeling land."

They slid into a denser darkness, running again along the foot of a low range of hills. They kept to it, mile after mile; over in the east was a flatness that had no flaw. Sebastian said, "That's desert you're looking at. We're paralleling the Moonstone range. Barrier's southern boundary begins here. Up yonder in the north is the Oregon line."

"Just a little ride to settle one's meal," called Kit Christopher. "I should be a lost soul if I lived here."

They left, at last, the hovering shoulder of the Moonstone range, and lights met them again, not far ahead. The speed of the car fell off, the road slowly turned. Pulling herself from a dark tangle of thoughts, Lily Tennant found fence posts flickering by, pale against a solid night. There was a long low ranch house to the fore and the silhouette of lesser buildings surrounding it. Sebastian let the car coast as far as the porch of the main house and stopped by the steps. His arm went to the latch of the car door and halted there; and Lily, mildly curious, saw his long frame turn still. A man moved away from the porch shadows and other men came quietly across the yard. Someone called distinctly: "Put out the lights, Tom."

Sebastian cut the switch. Obvious hurry got into him. He opened the side car door and stepped out and said to the others, "Into the house, please. Matt, where are you?" A slow, utterly cool voice answered him from another angle of the porch, and Sebastian moved away.

Lily got out and waited for the rest of the party. Silence and a cold excitement gripped them all; Timmy Akin cleared his throat nervously, and the clack of an electric plant somewhere made abnormal echoes. A tall shadow appeared before Lily and touched her arm. When he spoke she identified Sebastian. "Come into the house as fast as possible," and he guided her up the steps. He waited on the porch until they had collected around him, then he opened the door swiftly and reached inside to cut off the room lights.

Only for one moment had the porch been visible. But in that moment Lily's eyes, turned aside, had struck the shape of a man lying a few feet beyond them, face down. Blood glistened along a ragged rivulet on the boards.

Lily swept in startled breath into her lungs and allowed herself to be pushed into the room by the others so quietly and urgently behind her. Kit Christopher's voice sibilantly arrived. "What on earth is this about?"

The door slammed shut and the room lights came on again. Tom Sebastian stood with one hand on the switch, gray and cold, a dim shadow of fury breaking through his cheeks. "There's been a little trouble here," he said, very soft with his words. "One of my men was killed by a party of riders out on the desert—"

A strong yell sailed across the yonder yard; and instantly afterward a burst of rifle fire broke the uneasy quiet. There was a small, spitting sound on the wall, and a star-pointed hole bloomed in a window directly behind Tom Sebastian. Men ran across the porch. Somewhere out on the desert—whence this firing seemed to come—a long shout rose and sailed forward. In one startled glance, Lily saw the party with a frozen camera clarity—standing closely together, all pale and strained.

Something happened then that she did not clearly understand. Buffalo Galt pushed Timmy Akin and Judge Sillavan roughly aside. His florid cheeks were quite flushed as he stepped to the wall, knocked Sebastian's hand from the light switch, and snapped the room into full darkness again. A moment later he had opened the door; and his chesty command went rolling across the yard, out to the party firing from the desert. It was violent enough to hurt Lily Tennant's ears and it carried a wicked authority.

"Ben—Duke! Stop that, you damned fools! Stop it!"

The miracle was that the firing stopped. The echo of the last shot died out with the sound of his voice, and afterwards the silence was almost painful. Cold air flowed through the doorway. The breathing of the party scraped irregularly across the black. Afterwards she heard hoof-beats tremble over the desert and grow less distinct.

"Turn on the lights," said Galt.

Somebody turned them on. Galt stood with his back boldly exposed in the doorway. He was grinning at Tom Sebastian with a malice too open to mistake; and presently his raking eyes went to Lily and she saw the over-mastering pride in them—the flame of conscious power.

Chapter 2

There was confusion outside, the scuff of boots charging across the porch and the bitter rise of men's voices. A gun in the yard smashed its echoes at the night with a spaced and calculated wickedness and stopped after the fifth shot. But all that harsh anger had no effect on the room's stillness. The group had retreated from the door, leaving Buffalo Galt and Sebastian near it, confronting each other. It was strange, Lily thought, to see so much malign scorn on a man's face as was on Galt's; it was rather dreadful to watch Sebastian's cheeks freeze out all expression. His solid lips crushed together, his eyes turned from gray to black—or so it appeared to her then.

He intoned his careful words. "That makes things pretty clear, Buffalo."

Buffalo Galt flung back his reckless retort. "I never beat around the bush."

"You were pretty sure about those men out there."

"Who else would be trying to shoot up Barrier?"

"You had no trouble stopping them."

"They know better than to not mind me," said Buffalo Galt.

Lily saw Sebastian's glance eat its way through this blond, rough-and-tumble figure; she actually saw the wild temper coiling and threshing behind Sebastian's reserve. Yet his talk remained barren. "You're certain of yourself."

"I wanted you to see these men eat out of my hand. I'm a power in this part of the state, friend Tom. In the future, don't forget that."

The door was thrust open and a very tall young man hurried in. He was incredibly redheaded; his eyes, jade green against a brick-bronze skin, flashed wickedly. "What are we waiting for?" he challenged Sebastian.

"There's always another day, Matt," said Sebastian, soft as the wind.

"Like hell there's another day!" ground out the redhead. "Tip Hagan's lyin' dead on the porch! Come on!"

Sebastian spoke evenly. "Barrier is seventy years old. It can bide its time. It has before." And Lilly saw how swiftly Sebastian's words disciplined the tempestuous redhead. Sebastian turned to the crowd, inflexibly courteous. "This is Matt Strang, Barrier's foreman."

Matt Strang scarcely acknowledged the introduction; his eyes clung to Buffalo Galt and were violent. Sebastian's iron calm again bore down on his man.

"Buffalo is not staying with us tonight. He wants to ride over to Tumpah. Saddle a horse for him."

Matt Strang said: "I won't guarantee his safe arrival into Tumpah."

"I will," countered Sebastian, at once cold.

The foreman wheeled discontentedly out of the doorway. Buffalo Galt showed a thin smile. "Thanks for the transportation, Tom."

Sebastian said: "Don't touch Barrier again at any point, at any time."

Buffalo Galt shrugged his husky shoulders. "I'll be back some day."

"Not in my time."

Galt's half-handsome face mocked the other man. "How long will your time run?" He turned toward Lily. "I hope to see you again." After that the ironic amusement returned to him and he walked through the doorway, without hurry, and vanished from their sight.

Sebastian closed the door, speaking to the group. "I'm sorry if you have been upset."

"Imagine that—in America in this year of grace," breathed Timmy Akin. Lily turned and found the shine of atavistic pleasure in this harmless little man's eyes. Shock still chilled her.

"Was this the Nevada you wanted me to see?"

"I regret the scene," apologized Sebastian.

Judge Sillavan's bright eyes swept the disturbed group. He smiled with a perceptible skepticism. "What's the matter with this realistic generation? I expect more from you than fright."

It jolted them out of silence. Kit Christopher laughed uncertainly. They all moved toward the cheerful blaze of a fireplace and Lily for the first time observed the sprawling old-fashioned room with its handhewn furniture. A stairway went up to a balcony circling three walls, off which the doors of a dozen other rooms opened. It was like a Western inn, yet the touch of somebody's hand kept it from being impersonal. Above the fireplace was a framed map in which certain sections had been colored.

"That's Barrier," explained Sebastian.

"How big?"

He said, carefully: "Two hundred and fifty thousand owned acres, I suppose. With probably another hundred thousand acres of government graze." He seemed conscious of the general disbelief. "It has been seventy years in the making, you understand. That's not much land when you consider the size of this country." He watched Lily. "We were speaking of fame. Well, Barrier's famous in its own way. The cost of such fame has been about forty-five dead men since 1870. My own father, Henry Sebastian, is one of those. And my grandfather, Dan. And the man lying on the porch out there now."

"But, what on earth!" murmured Kit Christopher. "Why?"

"Because," answered Judge Sillavan, openly enjoying the scene, "this is a choice spot and men fight for land now as they did in the time of Moses."

Sebastian seemed increasingly aware of the disturbance to his guests. He chose his words carefully. "It's a matter of viewpoint. You're accustomed to living in a region where there's a street full of people in front of you and a police station in the next block. It's different here. The county Barrier's in is more than a hundred miles long and better than sixty wide. Our nearest town is Tumpah, twenty miles east, with seventy-five inhabitants. Outside of that you could ride this whole region for a month and never see more than an occasional shanty or a solitary horseman. Or maybe a few Indians straying across the Black Rock range from the reservation. This is desert country, and almost empty." He stopped and smiled. "I think you'd all appreciate a rest."

Somebody walked along the balcony and came down the stairs; and then Lily saw a girl reach the living room and advance with a straightness of carriage that suggested a weight balanced on her small, gloss-black head. Sebastian's voice lost all its hard resonance and became instantly gentle. "Charm, this is Lily Tennant, from Hollywood. Charm Michelet, Lily."

Charm Michelet inclined her head. "It is nice to have you on Barrier," she said. Lily smiled her answer, and from a corner of her vision caught the flash of interest in Kit Christopher's glance. Sebastian continued the introductions, leaving Lily to study the girl with a queerly aroused attention. She was not more than twenty-two, that was plain. But her serene self-possession was something to silently marvel at. Slim and quiet as she appeared before them, Lily got the reflection of a hidden vigor of emotion. She was a dark girl with a glowing, faintly olive skin—the survival of some distant Spanish blood, Lily guessed. She wore a dress as good as to be found in any Los Angeles shop; and at her belt hung a cluster of house keys which her fingers now and then brushed. Her eyes rose toward Sebastian and remained a moment on his face, reading his will. Afterwards she said to the women: "If you will come."

Lily and Kit followed her up the stairs and went along the balcony to a corner room. Charm Michelet snapped on the lights. There was a big bed and a few pieces of furniture, a bathroom, and a fireplace.

Charm said: "May I lend you nightgowns—or anything else you wish?"

"And a comb and some cold cream—if it isn't too much bother," suggested Lily, once more admiring the girl's graceful carriage. Charm went to the open door and called below with a quiet touch of command. "Gath—bring some wood for this fire." She turned and smiled back at the two women and walked along the balcony. Somewhere a child cried with a quick, startled irregularity.

Kit Christopher stood in the center of the room with her chin risen, with her expressive mouth turned amused and skeptical. "So," she murmured, "what have we here? Her name is Michelet and Sebastian is obviously very fond of her. And there's a baby—"

"Don't, Kit."

Kit said: "Aren't you the girl who insists on realism?"

"Realism, but not scandal. Do you realize she's quite striking?"

"The type that goes primitive. All for love. No reservations."

"As many of the rest of us might do."

"You? Don't be sentimental. You couldn't endure messy things."

"But you'd approve of whatever relations Jay Stuart and I might establish."

"That's something practical. This other thing—going the whole distance for great love—is merely romantic nonsense."

Lily listened remotely to Kit, drawing into herself. "I hadn't known that pure giving, without thought of return, was nonsense."

"You've got to see things much clearer than that, darling. This is a brutal world."

"So Tom Sebastian's mentioned tonight."

Kit Christopher spoke with a degree of sharpness. "Don't, by any chance, let yourself go on that man."

"Now who is being silly?"

"You could, you know," insisted Kit. "Very easily. He happens to be the sort over which women usually do make fools of themselves. He's a rough, hard, and dominating man. You'd ride down his road or you couldn't ride at all. He'd make you thoroughly miserable—and for a while you'd think it was love. Until the novelty wore off. Don't I know? That's the way it was with Bob Nesbitt. He had all the old-fashioned ideas about women and home and children."

"So now you prefer the deferential ones like Akin?"

Kit shrugged her beautiful shoulders. Her certainty abandoned her and left her less firm, less pleased. "It's weird. We want more power in our men than Timmy possesses. But if we get a man with power, we're nothing but mere wives and that isn't to be endured. It's so mixed up. I guess if we wish to be in the picture business, and be independent, we've got to take the weaker sort of men and be unhappy about it."

"I don't like that bitter, unmoral mood of yours at all, Kit."

Kit was dimly smiling. "You can go very far in pictures—if you don't make the mistake of letting a man interfere."

An elderly fellow in boots and overalls walked in with an armload of wood. He went to the fireplace, not looking at the women, and arranged his load on the hearth; he lighted a match, kneeling piously while the flame took hold. Kit said:

"I seem to hear a baby. Whose is it?"

The man drawled: "Charm's."

"Really? How old?"

"About three, I guess," said he, and rose. He stared at the doorway. "Ain't that right, Charm?" he asked and then went on. Charm Michelet came softly in. She laid the extra nightclothes on the bed and walked to the dresser with the few toilet articles Lily had asked for. There was embarrassment here for Lily, but Kit Christopher's talk was smoothly natural.

"A boy?"

"A boy," answered Charm Michelet, returning to the door. She swung there, facing the other women with an unbreakable dignity that struck Lily Tennant hard; it was something so much deeper than acquired manners, so much more real. "Is that all?" Charm asked, and Lily understood then that this girl was out-facing Kit; that she was at the moment superior to the worldly Kit. Kit only said, "You're very kind," and afterwards Charm enigmatically closed the door behind her.

"I think," said Lily, quite frank, "you got the worst of that."

But Kit walked around the room with an aroused interest. "There's something very odd about all this. I shall have to ask Timmy in the morning."

Lily got ready for bed. Steps shuffled along the balcony; Judge Sillavan's slow, sleepy talk struck through a partition. A moment's silence came and was presently broken by the sound of a great many men moving around the room below. Kit Christopher stopped roving. "Does it strike you Tom Sebastian was trying to conceal something from us tonight?"

"The dead man lay at our very feet," remembered Lily, and felt cold.

Kit crossed to the door and drew it slightly open, looking through. She whispered: "Come here if you want to see something."

Lily went over and put her head beside Kit's to catch the scene below. Sebastian stood with his back to the fireplace, arms clasped behind him. The redheaded Matt Strang was at his side. In front of these two the Barrier hands were silently ranked. There were thirty or more of them, with the firelight reaching out to brush saturnine color across their faces. One thing struck Lily powerfully: Barrier was more than a ranch—it was a military establishment, with the feeling of iron discipline quite clear to her. She drew back and gently pushed the door shut.

"I think we may be eavesdropping."

Kit looked at her, lips half-parted. "Actually, it's feudal. Reno's a hundred and forty miles away—and we've dropped back about four centuries. Imagine!"

Sebastian pulled his arms back of him and stared at the tough faces of his men. The heat of the recent fight still simmered sullenly in their eyes; the rage that comes from spilled blood was there.

"How did it happen?" he asked.

Matt Strang moved away until he could turn and face Sebastian. "Rex Meeder was riding north of the Moonstones. DePard and his bunch ran into him and chased him home. They stayed out there. Tip Hagan just happened to come from the house. They caught him as he stood in the doorway—a clean shot through his ticker. We threw a little lead back at 'em. Then you came up." Matt's raw-red cheeks were bitterly furious. He was a canny, cool man but he was also a natural fighter and this delay rubbed him the wrong way. "It ain't like you, Tom, to pull your punches. Tip Hagan's dead and, by God, he deserves more than pious regret!"

Strang's temper was the temper of the crew. He could see his foreman's fiery talk sway these hard, unforgiving men. He had picked each one of them for strength and toughness, because he knew he would one day need them. He said quietly: "So, then?"

"They've gone back to Tumpah. That's where we should go."

"No," decided Tom Sebastian. "We won't follow."

Matt Strang drew a heavy breath. "It's your ranch. But Tip Hagan was a friend of all of us. Regardless of what you say, we may do something about this killing. As friends of Tip."

Sebastian went leaner and taller. His talk struck out with a physical effect. "No more talk like that. Barrier's got plenty of enemies waiting for us to make a bad break. The DePards didn't do this on their own hook. They were told to do it by somebody who wants us to go wild and hit back. But we'll hit back in our own time and fashion—and I'll tell you when that is to be. Get that clear in your minds. Do as I say or quit the ranch."

Matt Strang shifted his weight irritably. "That's puttin' it strong, Tom."

Sebastian stared severely at him. "When I made you foreman, I put the power of Barrier in your hands. If I can't trust you with it, tell me now."

"It's hell to think of Tip Hagan killed!" groaned Matt.

"It would be hell to think of more boys killed on a fool raid to get even. Are you with me, Matt?"

Strang said moodily: "Of course—but it's Buffalo Galt who's behind this."

"You sure?"

Matt looked swiftly at Sebastian. "Anybody else?"

"Maybe. That's all. I want guards put out tonight."

The crew filed through the doorway. Sebastian turned and climbed the stairs, going into his own room at the head of the landing. As he did so, Charm Michelet appeared from a lesser hall leading off the balcony and followed him, closing the door behind her. On the lower floor, Matt Strang had lifted a lighted match to his pipe but he saw that incident and he flung the match from him and made a violent turn. He stopped in front of a chair and sat down, bending forward to clasp his long palms tightly together; and he stared up to Sebastian's room, strain stiffening all his features.

Charm Michelet crossed to where Tom stood looking through the window at the shadowed desert. She touched his arm and drew him around, and for a long interval her dark eyes studied him. Her breathing quickened. When she spoke it was with gentleness. "Is it very bad, Tom?"

"I think it is going to be, Charm."

"Something I don't know about?"

"Something none of us know about."

Her voice lifted with partisan loyalty. "There aren't enough crooks in northern Nevada to drive Barrier men off Barrier."

"Charm," he said, almost sadly, "there are other methods of running a ranch nowadays than by using gunmen. Big business has a way—and politics has another way."

She said: "You knew it was the DePards. But you refused to chase them. Did you refuse because you were thinking of Tommy and me?"

"Perhaps."

"Do what you've got to do—and don't think about me!"

He said: "Did the shooting wake him?"

"No." She stayed there, one hand touching his arm through the long silence, until her eyes drew a smile from him. He said: "We have guests, Charm. The women might be a little shocked to know you were in here."

She retreated to the door and turned and looked back to him with an obscure expression. "Lily Tennant is a beautiful woman."

"Is she?" murmured Tom—and never observed the swift emotion flash out of Charm's eyes. She slipped quietly from the room.

Matt Strang, seeing her return along the balcony to her own room, at once straightened from his crouched, cramped position in the chair. He let his arms fall; and the tenseness left his face. He fumbled around for his pipe, fingers unsteady, and rose and strolled to the yard.

There had been one other interested observer. Kit Christopher, sitting in front of the bedroom fireplace, heard Charm's heels tapping down the balcony. She promptly got up and opened her door a mere fraction, thus observing Charm go into Sebastian's room. Later she saw Charm come out. Closing the door, Kit stared significantly at Lily. "She went into his room. There's a wifely air about that young lady."

"Don't be so full of malice."

"I'm interested in the contemporary morals of Nevada's strong, silent men. There's a funny feeling about this house. I must ask Timmy in the morning."

Lily only half heard. The desert's spiced, cold air crept through the window opening; and something of the desert's hooded mystery crept in as well. Out of utter silence floated the wail of a coyote, mournful and wild beyond her power to describe. It was a faint note in vast, timeless space. It was something primitive, something that had neither beginning nor ending—like the shine of the stars in the infinite sweep of this black Nevada sky. The thought of it was unreal and disturbing. "Something unchangeable in a world full of change," she murmured.

"Novelty," said Kit, really sharp. "I shall get you away from here in the morning."

"A lonely land," said Lily softly, "where anything might happen."

Standing beside the open grave wherein the fresh pine box enclosing Tip Hagan lay, Lily thought of how blunt and final the events of this land were, of how simply these people accepted the accidents of the day. Tip Hagan was dead and they were giving him a moment's respect before they buried him; and then they would pass on to other things. In a way, she reflected, it was beautiful—because it was real and natural, because there was here none of that artificial delicacy or exaggerated grief of her own Hollywood world.

Poplars surrounded the four sides of this cemetery which held, she had noticed, the three generations of Barrier. Tom, at the head of the grave, was reading the twenty-third psalm: "The Lord is my shepherd; I shall not want." And as his voice rose and fell, she studied the men of the crew opposite her as they stood ranked against the penetratingly clear light of early morning. Some were quite gray, and some young. She felt the solidity of all. They were not individuals. They were part of Barrier. And they were not, she decided, soft men.

Sebastian ceased speaking. The silence hung on a short moment, then two hands stepped forward and began shoveling the mounded earth down against the pine box. The small crowd turned down the gentle incline toward the ranch quarters now freshly bathed in sun. Corrals and barns covered the foreground. Past these a series of shops and sheds and bunkhouses formed a plaza; beyond the plaza sat the main house, looking out upon a southern desert all bronze and yellow. In the distance a lone occasional water tank broke the monotony, and that was all. It was, Lily thought, immense and empty beyond description.

Kit gravely walked beside her. Seldom did this smiling, aloof woman ever permit the world to disturb her, but she was plainly disturbed now. Looking behind, Lily saw Tom Sebastian still standing at the grave, his bare head lowered. Charm Michelet walked in front, every motion of her lithe strong body aflow with a natural grace that reminded Lily of a spirit as free as the winds. It was something intangible, like the perfume of wild rose.

Crossing the plaza, Lily noted how deliberately the buildings of the place enclosed and barricaded it—a memory of the turbulent days of 1870 when Barrier had been, in Sebastian's words, "the only piece of civilization on the northern range." Going on through the house to the living room, Lily remembered Kit Christopher's descriptive word. Feudal. How queer a thing in these modern days.

Kit Christopher smoked a cigarette with a strange nervousness. Sebastian came in.

"I don't want to be inhospitable," he said. "But I know you want to get home—and we had better drive it before the sun gets any higher."

He turned to the porch. Kit rose and followed. Sebastian stopped on the steps, by the auto, his eyes roving the eastern distance. Fresh sunshine poured out of a cloudless sky.

Kit said: "Well, you showed us something different, which was your wish."

He didn't look at her. "I regret it."

She moved over to a porch post and put her slim back against it; and made an immaculate, self-sure picture. "You regard us as soft weak people from whom the bitter truth should be concealed. It isn't a very high opinion."

"You came to Nevada for a little pleasure. Not to get your clothes dirty."

She said: "Yes. That's why Lily will be going back to Hollywood tomorrow."

"Is she?"

Kit Christopher narrowly studied his face. "Reno romance is like shipboard romance. Only illusion. Lily's going to the top in pictures. She mustn't nurse any silly dreams."

He went down the steps, betraying no feeling. Sillavan and Timmy and Lily came out of the house. For a moment Kit stood beside the front door of the car, but Lily came up and got in beside Sebastian. Kit shook her head faintly and turned into the rear seat with the other men. Sebastian drove away.

Dust rose in heavy clouds behind and the ranch posts began to flicker like fast film.

"Tip Hagan," Lily thought aloud, "really died for the ranch. Did he have to?"

"Men like Tip stay on Barrier as long as they live."

"Loyalty," she said in a gentle voice. "Something that doesn't change, and can't be destroyed."

He didn't take his eyes from the road. "Yes."

"Loyalty to Barrier. Well, you are Barrier. So—loyalty to you."

He didn't answer. Looking aside then she wondered if it were that sense of responsibility which laid so strict a reserve across his eyes, which made his lips so solid. He wasn't a laughing man.

The land flowed past, yellow and hot, mile blending into mile. The smell of scorched earth was quite pronounced.

"If you want something bad enough," he spoke suddenly, "you'll pay whatever you've got to pay to get it. It isn't a matter of reason. It's something in your body that drives you on and never will let you alone."

"Supposing I go ahead, and find out too late I paid too much?"

"You will."

"How do you know?"

His glance remained on the thin ribbon of road; his heavy-knuckled hands gripped the wheel willfully. "Barrier is a great ranch. My people made it famous throughout Nevada—and now it is mine. Whatever it means, I mean. When I act it is for all the people on Barrier, who trust me." He paused. "It leaves a man pretty lonely. That's the power of fame. Someday you'll regret the way it has affected your own life. But nevertheless it will drive you on."

Her answer was for Sebastian alone; but the words sang with sudden rebellion. "I don't want such a thing to happen to me!"

They came by a lake whose water had receded a quarter mile or so from a cracked and bitter white alkali bed glaring under the sun. Beyond the lake they passed over a low-lying mass of iron-gaunt hills. Two hours from Barrier they came upon a ranch surrounded by a few poplar trees and stopped by a tub of water by the roadside. Another car stood beside the tub, its ancient hood steaming; an elderly man bent and dipped water with a lard pail. The sound of Sebastian's machine pulled him around.

Sebastian got out. He said: "I thought you'd weaned that flivver, Lot."

"Just so, Tom, just so. I'm merely foolin' around. You're the second car I've seen today. This country's gettin' crowded."

Sebastian grinned. He turned to the car. "You should know Sheriff Lot McGinnis. These are some folks from Hollywood, Lot."

McGinnis removed his hat and made a grave bow. The desert had weathered him to a uniform bronze shade, against which the silver whiteness of his hair and long mustache made an extreme contrast. He was a tall, spare man with a broad jaw and a pair of deep blue eyes that seemed to contain remote humor. He said, "I'm pleased," very courteously and let his glance touch each person in the car. "Matter of fact, I was over in the desert and saw your dust coming. So I thought I'd head this way. I want to see you sometime, Tom."

"Be back from Reno tonight."

"That's all right. Take the bucket. I ain't goin' anywhere."

Sebastian filled his radiator and settled behind the steering wheel. "I've got some news for you, Lot."

The sheriff said mildly: "I expect you have. I've heard it. Now I think I'll point this leapin' Lena of mine in the general direction of Winnemuc and see what happens, if anything."

"Why that direction?"

"She don't seem to want to go in the other directions," stated the sheriff. "But it's all right. I'm not particular. Happy to have seen you folks. Leave a little dust on the road for the next man, Tom."

Sebastian shot the car out of the poplar shade, into the insistent flash of the sun. Kit Christopher was talking: "Is he as guileless as he looks?"

"A good many men have wondered," said Tom. "The answer is no."

An hour and ten minutes later the endless road had its ending at last, curling past a water tank and shanty into a broader highway that swooped over a dry, sun-scorched hill. At the top of the hill they saw Reno, one fluff of smoke standing over it. Sebastian, still thinking of what had been said far back on the road, spoke almost harshly: "What is it you really want?"

She delayed her answer a long while. Her voice fell. "To love—be loved."

They flashed across the flat lands and into the town. Sebastian stopped and when Lily looked out at her rented bungalow sitting between its pleasant locusts, a feeling of uncertainty shot through her. Kit Christopher and Timmy got out. Sebastian turned to Lily.

"You can't have both. When you fall in love you surrender a great deal. You give as well as take. If you're going on to fame you can't give anything. Fame is all taking."

She said, in wonder: "How would you know that?"

"I have had plenty of time to think," he said, very quietly.

Kit Christopher came up, her discerning eyes on them. "So," she said, "this is the end of another buggy ride."

Lily left the car, but stood with one arm touching its door. "Shall I see you again?"

"I'll be going back to Barrier in an hour."

She said: "I'm sorry."

He drew a long breath. "So am I."

There was a silence then. Kit Christopher, more watchful than ever, touched Lily's arm. "Let's get out of this sun."

Lily said, "Good-bye," and walked to the bungalow porch. But she didn't go in until she saw Sebastian's car, carrying Sillavan, turn a corner and vanish.

"There's been a long distance call from Mr. Stuart," said Hannah. "He wants you to ring him back at Hollywood." Then she added, "There's letters."

Lily went in with a brusque swing of her shoulders, Kit and Timmy Akin following. Kit said, with a touch of urgency, "Call Jay. He may have something important to tell you." Then she stopped, for Lily turned and looked at her directly. All the ease was gone from this fair, slender, womanly girl; all the laughter was out of her. She didn't speak, but Kit said, "I'm sorry, Lily."

Lily opened the first telegram:

I MUST INSIST YOU TAKE THE NEXT PLANE BACK REX GILMAN

She threw it aside and took up the other:

WHAT HAVE YOU FOUND OVER THERE IN SUCH A WILD PLACE THAT LOOKS BETTER THAN GOOD OLD HOLLYWOOD I HAVE GOT SUPERB PICTURES BREATHING DOWN MY NECK SAM

Restlessness possessed her. She dropped the telegram and faced the two people looking on. "Probaby I'll go back. But I won't be pushed, Kit."

"Starlight and romance—in Nevada," murmured Kit. "You've got to grow up, Lily."

"Perhaps. But I'll have to find that out for myself."

Kit said: "I told you there was something queer about that ranch. Timmy discovered it. Charm Michelet isn't married. She grew up on the ranch as an orphan. The child is hers, but only Sebastian knows who the father is. Does it throw any light on the morals of a Nevada ranch? Did you observe how gentle he was with her?"

More aroused than she had been before, Lily said: "I don't believe it!"

"It's hard to put away your dreams," was Kit's soft answer. Timmy Akin, very sensitive to things unspoken, turned and left the room.

Tom Sebastian dropped Sillavan at a downtown street corner. "I'll be back at your office in fifteen minutes," he said, and drove on. He parked before a bank, went in and sat down by a flat desk, beside George Grannatt. Grannatt was around forty and he looked very tired; his eyes warmed a little when he saw Tom.

"There ought to be a credit exchange through from 'Frisco tomorrow," said Tom. "For the cattle I shipped yesterday."

"How much?"

"Around eleven thousand, I suppose, if the market hasn't changed much." Tom took a check from his pocket and laid it on the desk. "I need five thousand."

Grannatt beckoned a cashier over, handing him the check. "You're carrying a lot of men out there."

"I need a good many men."

"Better cut wages."

"They've been cut."

Grannatt minutely scowled. "You could do with less men, but you're proud about it. Your dad ran that big a crew and you can't see the way clear to do otherwise."

"Those fellows have been on Barrier a long time. Where would they go if I turned them loose?"

"Sentiment. All Sebastians have been full of it. Your grandfather and your dad both died because a sentiment for Barrier trapped them. You've got to handle Barrier on a straight business basis or you'll sink."

"George," said Sebastian, "you know better. If running Barrier was a business I wouldn't need all those men. What I've got over there is an army of defense. You know why."

"Perhaps," admitted Grannatt uncomfortably. Then he added with an increase of vigor: "Don't get pulled into any trouble." The cashier came back and laid a half dozen packets of bills and a sack of silver in front of Sebastian. Grannatt said, very casual: "Is that all the money you need?"

"I think so. How's things in the bank?"

"No better than they should be."

"That bad?"

"Tough times for all of us, I guess. I'm not crying any more than the rest."

"You'll pull through." Sebastian tucked the bills into various pockets and stood up with the sack of silver under his arm. Grannatt, not looking up, said: "You sure you've got enough spare change to carry you over until next time?"

"Yes," said Sebastian. His eyes watched Grannatt carefully a moment. Then he repeated: "Yes. See you later."

Grannatt walked as far as the gate with Sebastian. He was openly concerned. "Don't get drawn into trouble. That's the second time I've said it. So I must be saying it for a reason."

"I know."

Sebastian left his car where it was and crossed the street to Sillavan's office, which was up a flight of stairs. There wasn't any anteroom. If people wanted to see Sillavan while he was busy with others they stood in the hall and waited. The walls of his quarters were solidly lined with books; and Sebastian found him in an accustomed attitude, half lying in his chair, feet on the desk, cigar smoke turning the atmosphere blue. Sebastian put his silver sack on the table and sat down. The phone rang and Sillavan bent perilously in his chair to get it. He listened a moment, then said, "I'll be over in a little while," and hung up. Afterwards he resumed his sprawled position.

"What do you think you're up against now, Tom?"

Sebastian curled and licked a cigarette. "A big ranch always has enemies. Barrier's a big ranch."

"My boy," said Sillavan, "I'm sorry to tell you it isn't simply that."

Sebastian got out of the chair and braced his solid back against the bookcases. "Go ahead, I want to hear this."

"I'm pretty old," said Sillavan. "I rode with your grandfather. I knew your dad. So when I hear of some quarrel popping above the surface now I can go clear back and remember where that quarrel started. Things like that don't die in this state. They're passed from one generation to the next."

"Go ahead."

"Your grandfather Dan was a laughing man," mused Sillavan, "who never gave an inch of ground. But your dad was different. I never saw him smile. Henry was one of the great men of my time, Tom, and you can be proud of that. He had a feeling about Barrier—like religion. He never sold an acre of land in his life. He wasn't happy unless Barrier's boundaries were spreading out. He didn't give a damn about the money. It was the idea of a great ranch."

"He got it," observed Tom.

"He did. But when you're powerful you make enemies of

other powerful men. Your father was an influence in this state. He was honest, but he could kill either physically or politically when his back was against the wall. Some of the greatest fights in the West centered around your father. Your dad is dead. Some of his enemies are not. That's what you inherit."

"That's why I keep a strong crew."

"Shooting? Sure, that's coming. But it isn't the whole thing. Range wars are fought other ways. Politics—and money."

"You're not mentioning any names."

Sillavan's deep-lined face momentarily vanished behind cigar smoke. "No," said Sillavan. "I wept over Henry's grave when he died. And if I were younger I'd kill the man that shot him. I know that man. He's still alive. But I can't speak secrets. They concern too many people and they're better buried with me. All I wanted to tell you was that there's a fight coming up against Barrier that will be worse than you think, because the roots of the quarrel go farther back than you know, and the sources are higher up than you imagine. I'll try to help in my own way. Only, I'm getting old."

Sebastian said: "All this sniping by the DePards doesn't fool me. I'll wait. When I know where to hit, I will."

"Be careful," adjured Sillavan. "The whole campaign of your enemies is to put you in a bad light, to get you to commit an error. Then they've got you."

"I can wait. A lot of crooks have broken their hearts on Barrier."

"You've got your father's patience."

"That ranch is my life."

"Whether you've got your dad's power to destroy remains to be seen," added Sillavan. The phone rang and he lifted the receiver and listened. Then he said, with a fine, soft courtesy, "Yes, of course," and hung up. "Lily Tennant wishes you to call before leaving town," he said.

Tom only nodded. He got his sack of silver and passed from the judge's rooms. Leaning back in the chair Sillavan continued to smoke for a matter of minutes, then abruptly he got up, clapped on his hat and went over to the bank. Just before going in a very tall, fat man in a wrinkled cream-white suit passed. He murmured, "How are you, Judge," without breaking his stride. Sillavan said, "How, Ed," and his cigar tipped upward between his teeth. He crossed the lobby to Grannatt's corner.

Grannatt said: "I've got to run to 'Frisco this afternoon to see the Fleishmann brothers. They may take over some of our frozen paper. I want you to go along."

"Me?"

Grannatt said wearily: "I haven't got a single decent business argument why they should buy this junk. You know them. I want you to put it on a sentimental plane. They made their money in Nevada silver. It's their home state, and if this bank busts it's going to hurt a lot of their old friends. By the way, did you say anything to Sebastian?"

"This bank is my client. How can I mention its affairs? But I wish to God he could be warned."

"I dropped a hint," said Grannatt, "which he refused to take." Then the rawness of his nerves showed. "I guess he'll have to suffer with the rest of us."

Lily Tennant waited for Sebastian on the bungalow porch. She wasted no words. "Would you mind if I imposed on you? I want to go back to Barrier. For a day—or for a week. With Timmy and Kit, of course."

He said: "Why?"

"Just consider I'm running away from something I don't want to face yet."

"I'll guarantee you isolation—but not quiet."

She said: "Will I be a bother?"

"I told you last night you and I were as good friends as we'd ever be. There is some risk involved, Lily. But I'd like to have you."

"Risk?" she queried.

He only looked at her; and then she understood. "I'll take my chances on the moonlight, Tom."

"Come along."

She returned to the house while he went out to the car. In a moment she reappeared with a small fitted case, Kit and Timmy following. Kit got in the back of the car with Timmy. Lily took her place beside Sebastian. Sebastian put the car down the street.

"Moonlight," he said quietly, "is for adolescents. It may be something more real than that, Lily. And you and I are flesh and blood people."

"I told you I was a realist, didn't I? Why do you suppose I'm going back?"

"Why?"

She drew a long breath. "Never mind—now. But I can take whatever comes to me without crying. I don't ask favors."

They were in the center of town. Kit said: "I'd like to do a little errand here, if you don't mind."

Sebastian drew over to the curb. Kit got out, going into the telegraph office near by. Her wire was to Jay Stuart. It said:

LILY HAS GONE NATIVE ONLY YOU CAN STOP THAT SO COME IMMEDIATELY KIT

She returned to the machine. Sebastian drove on, reached the open country and raced across it, underneath the burning sun.

Chapter 3

Tumpah, spawned by a mining boom, had lived through its hurdy-gurdy days. It was nothing now but a frowsy, disintegrating settlement with a dirt street that began in the desert and ended in the desert slanting between an irregular collection of paintless buildings. A restaurant and card room, a store and a school and a garage, a blacksmith shop that was also a stable, and a scattering of shanties—these were all. These and Madame Belle Gilson's two-story saloon and rooming house which sat somewhat apart from the town proper. When Buffalo Galt cantered out of the night from Barrier headquarters on a Barrier horse, Madame Gilson's lights made the only cheerful show in that dismal town.

He racked his horse beside other horses already in front of the place, and stepped through the door. Four men playing a desultory game of cards at one of the tables looked up—and the game stopped. Two prospectors turned to watch him from the bar; and one other man stood at the end of the bar by himself and unobtrusively enjoyed a drink. Galt walked to the table and stared at the seated four—at Duke and Ben DePard, at Star Humboldt, at Dode Cramp. He helped himself to their bottle of liquor. He said:

"Where's the rest of the party?"

"Split up for the night," answered Duke DePard. "Didn't want 'em, did you?"

Galt watched Duke DePard. "You damned, ignorant saddle bum!" It was wickedly spoken.

"Nuts," grumbled Duke DePard. He was a small and dark and lithe man, with a dangerous temper of his own. "Don't get sore, Buffalo," he added. "We had to pull that stunt at Barrier."

"Who said so?" rapped out Galt.

The rest of the men weren't speaking. Star Humboldt was quite evidently lost in smoldering, violent thoughts; Dode Cramp remained silent because he was afraid. As for Ben DePard, the meaningless grin of the simpleton covered his vacant face as it always had. There wasn't anything in his head but a dog-like devotion to his brother, Duke; that and a sly ferocity when roused.

"It had to be done," repeated Duke DePard. "I'll tell you why—"

"Don't talk here. Go on up to the house."

The four rose. Buffalo Galt turned his severe attention to Humboldt. "I thought you went to Reno."

"Yeah, but I saw Sebastian there—so I came right back."

The four turned out of the place, shoulder to shoulder. Nick the Greek came down a flight of stairs. "Belle wants to see you," he told Buffalo.

Buffalo finished his drink. He made a quarter turn, toward the tall and mild figure alone at the end of the bar. "What you doing in here, Sheriff?"

Lot McGinnis looked up as though surprised. "Evenin', Buffalo. Just payin' you folks a visit."

Buffalo continued to stare into the bland countenance across the room. He said, "You're a soft-footed old scoundrel, Lot," and went up the stairs, following a hall to its end. He opened a door without knocking, thus coming into a room cluttered badly with ornate furniture. A crystal chandelier lighted the place. In a corner divan sat a woman, who, thirty-five years before, had been beautiful. A portrait painting on the wall testified to that. But she was a big, rawboned creature now with an outlandish pompadour overhanging rough and brilliantly crimson cheeks. Her voice was as strong as a man's.

"Buffalo," she said, "you're a fool."

Buffalo removed his hat and stood beside her. Madame Belle Gilson waved a homely, jewelled hand. "Never mind your manners. You're still a fool."

"I had nothing to do with that shooting on Barrier, Madame," he said quietly. "It was Duke DePard. I don't know why, but I'll find out soon enough."

"Don't lie, Buffalo. It's your doing."

"No," he answered, still soft with her. "It wasn't. But I don't regret it."

"Give me a cigarette," she said, and waited till she had lighted it. "Buffalo, I'm sixty-three and I never knew a man to buck Barrier who didn't die or disappear. Wilder men than you have tried to beat that ranch and broke their hearts on it."

"Times change," he said. He stood almost at attention and his voice never lifted.

"Times may change. Sebastians don't. I knew them all. Old Dan Sebastian was a slant-eyed pirate with a red beard. They had to shoot him in the back to kill him, but he left Henry Sebastian thirty-thousand acres. Henry built it up. Only three people in the state weren't afraid of him." Madame Belle's strident voice went suddenly soft. "He was a great man, Buffalo. And Tom Sebastian's like him. As long as a Sebastian lives don't fool with Barrier."

"Maybe the Sebastians won't live forever, Madame."

"Buffalo," was the Madame's loud retort, "if that idea is in your bonnet you'll end up either in the death house at Carson or in a dry gulch."

"I'm not afraid to try."

Madame looked long and straight at him. "No, there's something in you that won't stay down. You were a cheap cattle thief. Now you've tied up with some political influence. You progress, Buffalo."

He showed his open surprise. "How do you know, Madame?"

Madame's answer was ironic. "I'm a disreputable old woman, but in my day I knew all the young sports. They're respectable citizens now and they run the state. But they still remember old times. When I want information I go to the top for it. What are you after, Buffalo?"

Galt went dogged. "What do you think, Madame?"

"Buffalo," rapped out the old woman, "leave Barrier alone."

"What do you care?" demanded Galt, resentfully.

"Because," said Belle Gilson bluntly, "as much of a scoundrel as you are, you are nevertheless my son."

"Thanks," said Buffalo, and made a short, stiff bow.

"I'd regret seeing Barrier hunt you down as it has others. Don't cross Tom Sebastian. You got started off wrong in this world, but there's something in you nevertheless—and I guess I know where that came from, too."

Buffalo Galt stiffened. "Madame, there is only one thing in

this world you can do for me. I have asked it before. Who was my father?"

Madame's eyes were enigmatic. "Some day I may tell you."

"Good God, Madame!" he burst out. "Why not now?"

"I don't want to dig up skeletons, Buffalo. I play the game square, which is something you need to learn."

"It happens," said Buffalo, thickly, "I know who my father is."

"You're just guessing."

Galt swung violently. He walked the length of the room, then wheeled back, his heavy lips cruel. "Madame, I'm not blaming you for my being born illegitimate. But you want to know what I'm after. Well, I'm after all I can get. I don't care how but I'll get it! I've got power in this country and I'll have more! Then we'll see what Nevada's got to say about the bastard son of a dancehall girl!"

He stopped talking, his big fists clenched together. But he thought of something else to say. "I'll make my money out of Barrier, Madame. Because Henry Sebastian was my father and that ranch is half mine and I'll get my share of it one way or another."

"Buffalo!" snapped Madame. "Keep your dirty tongue off Henry Sebastian! He was a good friend of mine—but he wasn't your father."

"I don't believe you, Madame."

"No, of course not. You want some excuse to steal from the ranch and so you'll use that one. But he wasn't your father, my boy."

"Who was?"

She said: "Some day I'll tell you."

He looked at her, a throttled rage swelling the tissues of his face, and abruptly turned from the room.

Madame got up and made a wry grimace. She stared at a wall mirror whose decorative cupids had shed most of their gilt. She said, gently, dispassionately: "Damn, I'm an ugly woman." But, turning her eyes toward that picture of herself in youth, she added: "You were wise and didn't know it. You had your fun. I regret nothing you did."

Somebody knocked. She said, "Well, come in." Sheriff Lot McGinnis entered and casually shut the door behind.

She said: "Hello, Lot. Sit down. You're getting sort of old. My God, your hair's clean white."

He let himself into a chair, looking around with his slow

blue eyes. "Been about five years since I came up here last. You ain't moved anything as I can note."

"Saw Buffalo didn't you?"

Lot McGinnis smiled faintly. "He saw me first and didn't like my presence none."

"He's gone bad. Always was a little crooked, but he's whole hog now."

"I have observed him change," remarked Lot McGinnis. He had relaxed his narrow body and his hands lay on his knees. "I don't like to come up here, Belle. It takes me back too much to the younger days. I keep rememberin' the fun—and the mistakes. It's the mistakes that bite worst."

Madame remained standing. She shook her head. "He wanted to know who his father was, Lot."

"Tell him?"

"No."

He sighed. "That's a mistake we both made. He should have been told when he was a lad."

"We were a little too proud then, Lot. You were an ambitious man and I didn't want to hurt your reputation. Now it's too late. You've had a fine life. It wouldn't do to let the country know you had a crook for a son."

His voice descended to soft sadness. "It's the mistakes beyond repair that stick in a man's mind to the end. I should have acknowledged that boy twenty years ago—and rode with him all this time. His life would have been different."

"I don't believe that, Lot. He's got my blood in him—and that always was wild. What's to be, will be. It was written in the book that way, from the beginning."

"It is hard to think," he mused, "that one day I shall have to lay my hands on him. He's gettin' pretty bold. I'm waitin' for some evidence."

"It's Tom Sebastian he hates, Lot. Stop that before somebody's killed."

"I'm seeing Tom tomorrow."

Buffalo Galt cantered up the wholly dark street to the stable. He went inside and said to the hostler: "Next time a Barrier hand comes to town tell him to take this animal back where it belongs." Then he saddled another horse and swung out of the stable.

A man's voice issued from the opaque side of a building wall. "Want to talk with you a minute."

"Not here, Blagg. Come up to the shack." Buffalo Galt spurred his pony out along a road that began climbing the side of a hill. A few minutes later he reached his place and unsaddled and threw his pony into a corral. Other men had reached the house before him, their voices coming through the open door, but he stopped briefly on the porch. The few lights of Tumpah were at his feet. Far beyond, the twinkle of Barrier alone broke the wide-flung western vastness. Buffalo Galt stared that way, his big shoulders rearing. He lighted a cigarette, the match flame saturninely etching the rebellious details of his cheeks.

He went inside. He said to Duke DePard: "What the hell did you do?"

"We were west of the Moonstones yesterday," explained Duke, cool and casual. "Up near the woodcutters' camp. A Barrier rider saw us and began banging away. What the hell? We went after him, and he streaked for home. We followed and stood out on the desert and slapped a little lead at the house. This guy in the doorway—whoever he was—we dropped him."

"It was a dumb stunt."

"Yeah? Well, now you tell us why you happened to be so chummy with Sebastian tonight. And what was the idea of yellin' out Ben's name and mine?"

"Don't get tough with me," warned Buffalo.

Duke DePard's black and narrow visage hardened. "Trying to make a big shot out of yourself?" he asked, falsely soft. "Usin' us as suckers?"

"That's enough."

"It won't do," grunted Duke DePard. "Stay in your own class or—"

Buffalo slapped his words brutally back. "Shut up!"

Duke DePard rose half out of his chair. Ben DePard's silly smile vanished. "Don't talk to brother Duke like that," he complained. Star Humboldt was lost in his sultry thoughts. Dode Cramp stayed discreetly outside the quarrel.

The silence turned thick. But presently Buffalo spoke. "Never mind. I've got something up my sleeve—and it's all right. What's eatin' you, Star?"

Humboldt dragged his eyes from the table. "Nothin'."

Buffalo's glance speculated on this enormous lump of a man. "We'll get nowhere wasting lead on the Barrier ranch house. Only two ways are any good. One's to keep right on nibbling at Barrier's beef. We're making a good living at that, ain't we?"

"What's the other?" Duke DePard rested on arm across the shoulders of his brother.

"Nothing," said Galt, again watching Humboldt, "keeps Barrier alive but the man that runs it. All Sebastians are alike. They're gunslingers—and the law protects 'em. Ain't that so, Star?"

"What law?" said Star.

"Same law that took your land away from you when you got drunk too much and went busted. As far as courts are concerned or men like Sebastian are concerned, you're just a bum to be kicked around. Don't forget it, Star." He added one ironic jab. "So be properly respectful of Sebastian when you meet him."

Star Humboldt sat dumbly by the table, the temper in him heating up. Dode Cramp laughed uncertainly. Ben DePard didn't understand. But Duke DePard knew the purpose of this barbed talk. The telephone rang, and a car coughed up the hill in front of the house. Buffalo went to the wall and lifted the receiver. A man's voice said: "Galt?"

"Yeah?"

"Wait a minute for Reno." The wire crackled and then another man's voice came along.

"Buffalo?"

"Yes."

"You know who is talking?"

Buffalo said, in a softer, more alert way, "Yes, I do."

"Come and see me this week."

"Yes," said Buffalo. He hung up and turned. Blagg stood in the doorway, listening. Blagg ran the weekly paper at Tumpah. He said, "Who was on the wire?" His severe, intolerant face was a warning in itself; his pen was venomous and he had no known scruples. He was here because Buffalo wanted him, but nobody trusted him, and none of the others bothered to look at him.

Buffalo said to Duke DePard, "There's a dance at the Parral school night after tomorrow."

Duke said, "Fine," and got up. The others, all ignoring Blagg followed Duke out and in a moment the echo of their horses died down the hill. Buffalo Galt turned to Blagg. "I've got a chore for you, Blagg," he said, and began to talk.

Ten minutes later Blagg left. Buffalo Galt walked to the porch and stood there, alone and bitter, a relentless ambition clawing its way through him.

The impressions of this land were all strange and strong. Sitting at the supper table in Barrier's long dining room, Lily watched the changeless ritual of eating. You came in and sat down and reversed the capsized plate and cup. You filled your plate and ate with the least possible delay. You stacked your dishes and went out.

It was no place for dawdling; these people ate only to quench hunger. There was little talk except at the head of the table where Sebastian sat and she had the feeling that this little was really a concession to Kit and Timmy and herself. Charm Michelet was on his right at each meal, maintaining a silence more vocal than words. In this girl's eyes when she looked at Tom Sebastian was something hard to define, hard to forget. This particular evening, Lily noted, the men present seemed dressed beyond their usual limits. After the meal, she happened to mention it.

"I completely forgot to tell you," remarked Sebastian. "There's a dance at the Parral school. Most of us are going—you people will want to come, of course."

Kit said: "You don't look like a dancing man to me."

"I only stand in the doorway and watch the show."

It was queer to Lily how insistently Kit Christopher maintained her antagonism toward Sebastian. Kit murmured, "The king must make his appearance."

"Just so," Sebastian grinned. But Charm Michelet turned a half indignant glance on Kit.

Around eight-thirty the party strolled out to Sebastian's now familiar touring car—Sebastian and Lily, Timmy and Kit, Charm and the redheaded Matt Strang. Charm was delayed. When she finally appeared on the porch she had on a black taffeta dress, full and swirling with a silver jacket and a cerise comb slanting in her jet hair. She paused there, womanly instinct seeking man's approval. Obviously it was Sebastian's approval she wanted but Lily saw which man was hardest hit. Matt Strang, whom Charm never saw at all at this moment, straightened to his full height, his whole expression startled and stirred.

They got in the machine, Lily beside Sebastian, and drove comfortably down a ranch road. Nothing much was said and when, twenty minutes later, they reached a single building on the treeless desert, Lily roused herself from what had been a kind of thoughtless peace. Not since childhood could she recall a similar sensation of irresponsibility.

A sagebrush orchestra was already playing. They walked through parked buggies and cars and hitched horses toward a doorway clustered with cheerfully talking men. There was an immense hallooing as the Barrier horsemen came storming in; and just before entering the schoolhouse she turned to admire them. In the saddle, released from the dusty earth, they were arresting, masterful figures.

Sebastian said to those around the door, "A little room here, boys," and a good many people spoke to him. There wasn't any ceremony. When they got beyond the stag line Sebastian threw his hat on a chair and wheeled away with Lily. Benches had been piled together in one corner to make a promiscuous bed for a dozen or more babies. Older people formed independent circles along the walls. Lily's discerning eyes saw how weatherbeaten some of the older women were, how soon middle age seemed to print its marks on them, and a dark question formed itself in her mind. Was the desert so merciless?

"This," said Sebastian, agreeably, "has all the earmarks of another brawl. There's enough liquor here to float a submarine."

"Here or Hollywood, all dances are the same."

It made him chuckle unaccountably. "Wait a while."

The music stopped and they walked back toward the doorway to rejoin the other Barrier folk. Kit Christopher came up with Timmy, less assured than usual, and cast a silent signal of help at Lily. Men and women squeezed them together and Lily found herself in a barrage of introductions. There was the same formal patter, "Miss Tennant, Mr. Gaines. Miss Tennant, Miss Farrell." It went on and on, until a man yelled out of the stag line; the music started and the partners were shuffled. Timmy—faithful, obedient Timmy—took Charm away from Matt Strang. Strang scowled and swung to Lily. She got a glimpse of Sebastian wheeling Kit past the stag line, and then beyond him, the broad figure of Buffalo Galt. Galt's eyes were on her.

Matt Strang's dancing was increasingly poor as he swung Lily from side to side in his effort to keep his eyes on Charm Michelet. Suddenly he said:

"Miss Tennant, don't believe anything you hear."

"What, Matt? And why?"

"Just don't," he said earnestly.

A whistle screamed, the music stopped again. Going back to the meeting place, Lily got the heavy reek of whisky. A man staggered into the middle of the hall, quite drunk; two others caught him under the armpits and dragged him off the floor. The crowd yelled its approval and the room grew warmer. A young woman going past lifted her eyes to Sebastian and let them stay there with a long inquiry. Her partner pulled her away.

Matt spoke to Sebastian. "I want to see you a minute. I've heard something."

They were interrupted. Buffalo Galt came through the jam of people, cutting a trail with his big shoulders. He stopped, bowed to Lily.

"May I have this dance?"

The feeling of trouble seemed to blacken the light of the room. Matt Strang's long lips turned violent and bitter and people near by stared. Some breach of habit or manners had been clearly made. Lily's glance went to Sebastian; such pleasant humor as he had shown tonight was quite gone. He said distinctly:

"Buffalo, you're on the wrong foot."

The music started. Buffalo's voice lifted. "I'm not asking you. I'm asking Miss Tennant."

"You are asking me," Sebastian told him curtly.

Couples dancing past stirred them in their places and the room was at once quite hot to Lily. Sebastian wasn't moving, but she felt his will and his hidden anger rising. Buffalo Galt's lips curled with amusement. It was, she told herself swiftly, an impossible situation. She looked at Sebastian. "If you don't mind," she said, and offered her arm to Galt. His laugh rose distinctly as they danced away.

He said: "Put this down in my favor. I'm never afraid to try."

"No," she said without friendliness. "But is that a virtue?"

"What's virtue? Some sort of rule? Listen, Miss Tennant, rules are made by the rich and powerful to keep others out of the gravy trough. When I'm rich and powerful I'll live by that set of rules, too. But meanwhile, I play my own game. I break rules. And I get what I want. People at the top of the heap are cowards. I know that because I scare them so easy."

"Your system works very well," she said. "For a time. Then it doesn't work any more."

"Why not?"

"Because sooner or later you run into some man more ruthless than you are. And because some things aren't gotten by bluff or force."

He grinned. "Maybe I'll reach that stage, and get my nose knocked back. But I've had the fun of trying, haven't I?"

Something happened then. The music stopped before they had quite circled the floor. Looking over that way she saw Matt Strang standing in front of the orchestra, his arm commanding silence. Galt's smile as he escorted her back to

Sebastian was tight and not pleasant to see. Sebastian inclined his head at Galt.

"I want to see you outside a moment," he said, and turned through the doorway. But Galt remained to say one more thing to Lily in a level voice:

"I wish I could get that idea across—the fun of taking chances and seeing them work out. It's like drawing four cards to a king and coming out with a full house. Think it over, Miss Tennant, and thanks for the dance. When I see you in movies I'll say, 'I danced with that girl.' That's something for a saddle bum in the Nevada desert, ain't it?"

He plowed his way through the clustered stags, his great shoulders deliberately striking men aside. Matt Strang strode past them, also leaving the hall. Men began to hurry out of the place. Timmy said, "Excuse me," and followed. Kit called sharply, "Timmy, don't leave us so rudely alone," but he never heard. The smell of trouble was as distinct as the smell of liquor here. Lily saw Charm Michelet's fear overflow her expressive eyes. The music started but there wasn't much dancing. All those left in the hall were waiting for something to happen, faces swung toward the doorway.

Out in the school yard a man's hand lifted a lantern high in the velvet black and lowered it to the ground. Sebastian stood alone, a half-circle of watchers back of him; then Buffalo Galt came forward at a lunging gait. The circle instantly closed around them and they were brutally locked inside the inexorable walls of desert opinion. Matt Strang shouldered his way through the ring and spoke one cursing word as he halted. Buffalo Galt's breathing was sharp; there wasn't any laughter on his face now.

"No man," said Sebastian, speaking with a frozen clarity, "imposes himself on a guest of mine, Buffalo. Your character stinks clean across the state and you know you have no right whatever to force your attentions on any decent woman in that hall."

"Miss Tennant seemed to think it was all right," sneered Buffalo.

"Miss Tennant danced with you to avoid a scene. Miss Tennant doesn't know you."

"You made the scene, by getting tough. This schoolhouse acre doesn't belong to Barrier. So you're off the reservation."

Timmy Akin nimbly climbed into a wagon and looked directly down into the circle. He put his hand over his heart and when he felt its unhurried beating he muttered in a wondering, half-pleased way: "Well."

"Never mind," Sebastian warned Galt, voice steady and hard. "You're a yellow dog and you don't lay your hands on my guests. Go back to Tumpah for your women, which is where you belong."

"That's rich, from you," ground out Buffalo Galt. "That baby on your ranch—who's the father of it, friend Tom?"

One moment of singing silence followed and was broken by the flat, curt sound of Sebastian's hand slapping Galt full in the mouth. Galt stumbled backward against the tight circle of men. Timmy Akin clutched the wagon seat. Matt Strang started forward, toward Galt, but Sebastian's voice hit Strang with a warning flatness. "Get back there, Matt. Don't interfere." Timmy saw Sebastian's face clearly at that instant and didn't recognize it. What made it the more lurid was that ring of enclosing men, each motionless and waiting for the kill, each faintly savage from anticipation.

Sebastian said: "You've been making war talk lately, Buffalo. I hear you have said I was afraid of you personally. Let's see about that now."

Timmy, watching Galt just then, experienced morbid dread. For Galt's broad body was so crouched as to make him seem abnormally powerful. Sebastian's dead-still speech chilled Timmy. "I'll repeat it, Buffalo. You're a yellow dog and you belong back in the brush."

Prepared for trouble as he was, Timmy didn't quite catch the slashing leap Buffalo Galt made at the Barrier man. Body struck body with a solid, meaty reverberation. For a little while it was entirely dark and all Timmy could discern was two shadows wildly plunging; then somebody deliberately lifted the lantern to illumine this lurid scene.

It went straight back to abysmal, primitive depths. Buffalo Galt locked his arms about Sebastian's waist and his head plunged into Sebastian's chest until the latter's body was broken acutely backward. Fascinated by what he saw, Timmy yet was detached enough to note that no sound came from the watching circle. Nothing rose up but the rasping breath of the two fighters, the scuffling of their feet, the rip of cloth, the moaning guttural noise in Galt's throat.

Then Sebastian's shoulders rose and his knee smashed upward into Galt and the latter yelled out his pain and let go and recoiled. Sebastian jumped forward. He struck Galt's broad, exposed face with his right and left fists once and again. Galt's face turned red. Blood gushed out. He rushed Sebastian and got his arms about the man again. His skull hit Sebastian's chin with a clean, hollow echo that sailed definitely across the night. Liquor and dust smell lifted on the air. Timmy Akin brushed his hand across his mouth. His own lips felt smashed.

Galt's head was once more jammed in Sebastian's chest and his huge arms were crushing Sebastian's ribs and wrenching Sebastian's spine. But Sebastian got his arms free and—all this Timmy could see—sledged his big-knuckled fists into Galt's exposed temples. He struck twice. Galt's arms fell. Stunned, half blinded, he reeled away: and then, Sebastian, measuring his man without mercy, stepped forward and crashed one terrific blow against Galt's askew chin. Galt fell as though struck by a slaughter house maul, all his joints giving way. Blood began to lace its way through his yellow hair.

One man seized the lantern and lowered it down against Galt's face. Sebastian rocked slightly on his heels, his coat ripped to pieces, one cheek showing a round blemish. His eyes didn't leave Galt till Galt rolled over and sat upright. He spoke to Galt then. "You're still a yellow dog and the dust is where you belong. Get out of here." He turned and stopped before Matt Strang.

"Ask the girls to come to the car, if they will. Tell the crew to start home." He pushed his way impatiently toward the car. Somebody sighed a word cautiously. "Gun?" Matt Strang, turning toward the schoolhouse, heard that and whipped about. He threw his command at Timmy. "You get the women, Akin." Then he talked through his narrowed lips to Buffalo Galt.

"Got a gun, you?"

Galt had risen. He was still stupid from punishment and there wasn't much venom left in him. He said: "Never mind a gun. I don't need it now. But you tell Sebastian he'll never touch me again with his hands. Tell him that."

Sebastian's voice cut back from the parked car. "I hear it, Galt. Get out of here before I drag you out at the end of a rope."

Galt stared straight ahead. "No, you'll never touch me, again. Next time it'll be a gun."

"Next time?" Sebastian was returning.

"Yes, by God!" said Galt, suddenly waking from his stupor. "I'll break your damned ranch! No Barrier man will ever get mercy from me! Remember that!" He lurched on through the crowd, into the darkness beyond; and presently his pony swept away into the desert at a dead gallop.

Chapter 4

Timmy got down from the wagon box and crossed the yard. He went into the schoolhouse and plowed his path through the people. He said to the three women, "We're going home," with a brusqueness that was not like him, and then this paragon of politeness forgot his manners and preceded them through the doorway. All the Barrier hands were collecting in the yard; Timmy stood aside at the car doors as Lily and Kit passed him. Kit murmured, "What a vile night!" But Charm Michelet, seeing Sebastian sitting behind the steering wheel with his head bowed, at once wheeled. She said nothing, but her hand went in to touch his shoulder. In a moment she turned back. Everybody got in and Sebastian drove the car away.

The glow from the instrument panel illuminated his torn coat, the angry bruise on his cheekbone. His fists were badly scarred. Lily's voice was very gentle.

"I'm sorry to have been the cause of that fight."

It took him a long while to extricate himself from his smoky thoughts. He said finally: "You have nothing to regret. The fight has been on the march a long while. You couldn't help it. Neither could Galt or I."

She spoke with an energetic disbelief. "You were both just blind animals obeying primitive instinct? Oh, Tom, you put yourself in a brutal light."

"Look," he said, and paused a moment. "In your world people change, things change, even the rules change. It isn't so here on the desert, Lily. Barrier is seventy years old and the enemies of my grandfather are my enemies, in the third generation. It's in the cards that Buffalo Galt should fight Barrier. It will always be that way, as long as either of us draws breath. When we're gone two other men will carry it on."

"I despise fatalism," she said, swiftly.

"I'm a fatalist," he countered, "only as to the setup and the eventual ending. I admit the rules of the game can't be changed. But inside those rules I do what I please. It is up to me to survive or die."

"You'd never leave Barrier, would you?" she asked, deeply curious.

"I told you the other day cattlemen don't change. They just die. If I left Barrier I'd be like a piece of tumbleweed blown down the wind."

"I see this then," she mused, almost to herself. "Buffalo Galt will come again."

"And many other men like Buffalo Galt." He pointed the car at the nearing ranch lights. "The days of peace are about over. Barrier's going to fight for its life."

They curled along the driveway and stopped at the front door and got out. There was a new machine parked there and a man stood in the porch shadows, smoking a cigarette. His voice came casually forward.

"Well, Lily, you're quite a traveler."

Kit called instantly back. "Jay! You old pillar of strength!" She went immediately up to the porch. Lily stopped in her tracks. Timmy said: "That guy would come here to cramp our style. I was beginning to enjoy myself, Lily."

Lily went up the steps. She said: "How are you, Jay," quite coolly and passed into the front room, the others following. Lily turned to Sebastian. "This," she explained, "is a very old friend of mine, Jay Stuart from Hollywood. Jay, Tom Sebastian runs Barrier."

Sebastian extended his arm; and for a moment his straight glance explored Jay Stuart. The bruise had spread along Tom's cheek, the unforgiving bitterness was still apparent. Thus hard and lean and quiet he confronted Jay Stuart. Jay was almost as tall, and the superb poise so much a part of his makeup made it possible for him to smile assuredly. He had been once a screen idol, and the stamp would never leave him. He had a strong, broad-featured face. His hair, his greatest vanity, was still thick and black at thirty-eight. And he had a charm that definitely warmed the room. In him, as in Kit Christopher, was the skeptic humor of one who had seen too much of life to trust any of it. His voice struck the exact note.

"I know I'm intruding, Sebastian. But when I reached Reno and found Lily had come here I took a chance on your good nature."

Lily thought Sebastian actually listened to the tone more closely than to the words. Then he spoke with a fine cordiality. "This is your home as long as you want to stay."

It oddly surprised Lily that Sebastian should so obviously and sincerely accept this man who was in every facet alien.

Men, she thought, knew men; and Sebastian's judgment was very keen. Silently pondering, she wondered if she had underestimated Jay's real worth.

The introductions continued around and it amused Lily to note how Jay's manner turned more gallant when he was presented to Charm. Kit flashed a surreptitious glance of high humor at Lily. Gath ambled across the floor, very worried.

"Tom, Bill Speel wants you should call Camp Four right away. He's had the wire hot for an hour."

Sebastian excused himself and walked to a wall phone near the fireplace. Matt Strang turned instantly out of the house; Charm went toward the kitchen. Lily bent her head to watch Sebastian grind the phone crank; his face was thoughtful. His lips moved as he spoke into the phone, and then he stopped talking and his mouth flattened.

"The reward for devotion," murmured Jay Stuart in her ear, "seems to be indifference. Am I not to be complimented at all for making a wild Sheridan's ride across the Nevada wilderness?"

She turned. "Why did you come?"

"To be near you, my dear," he protested. "Hollywood's a damned lonesome spot these days."

Lily's voice curtly checked him. "I won't be hurried, Jay. I'm sorry you came."

He was infinitely expressive with his hands and shoulders. "I shan't speak a word to urge you away. That's farthest from my heart. I came only because I wanted to see you."

"You're the smoothest liar west of the Rockies," said Lily, relaxing her vigilance.

Jay grinned openly. "Don't be mean to me tonight. That ride from Reno! My God, what a country!"

The click of the phone hook bit through the quiet. Tom Sebastian went into his office, which opened into the living room, and presently returned. He had a gun and a worn black belt in his hands. Matt Strang appeared from the porch.

"Matt," said Tom, "it's Camp Four. Throw a couple saddles in the car and we'll be going."

Matt Strang vanished. Sebastian turned to his guests. "I hope to see you at breakfast. Meanwhile, the place is yours." Charm came hurriedly from the kitchen and almost ran after Sebastian who had reached the porch. Lily saw Charm's hand reach to Sebastian's coat lapel and pull him about. Some soft word was said and then Sebastian was out of sight. The car roared away. Charm returned. She said, emotionlessly:

"I shall show you your room, Mr. Stuart."

It was some indefinable feeling that caused Lily to turn and put her arm on Charm's straight shoulder. But the girl's answering glance wasn't friendly. Lily dropped her hand.

They were all gathered in the girl's room—Timmy and Jay and Kit and Lily. Timmy said: "It was a terrible thing to see—and it wasn't just a fight. They were like a couple of tigers. I'm telling you they were trying to kill each other. It was the worst—" And Timmy stopped for want of a definite word. He tried again: "No ordinary sort of quarrel could do that to them. It was something more—something in the blood. I'd bet a thousand dollars there's something behind this."

Jay said, "This is the West primeval," and got up. "I'm going to bed."

He turned out of the room, going along the balcony. Kit Christopher followed him and when they were beyond the door she murmured, "You'll have to handle Lily. I can't."

"You've been high-pressuring her. It won't work."

"We've got to get her out of here. There's something uncanny about this ranch."

"I like that Sebastian egg."

"There you have it!" she exclaimed with strange intensity. "I hate the man. He's so brutally compelling. You can actually feel his will hypnotize you. Don't let Lily make that mistake, Jay."

"Softly does it," he said. He stood at the door of his own room, one hand on the knob, looking negligently down.

"Softness is your way," she said. "It has always worked for you. I know that. But I can tell you one thing. You'll get little reward from Lily."

Sleepiness made him indolent. "I'll get what I can. I always do, don't I, Kit? Funny thing is, though, I'm for Lily and it doesn't really matter if I get nothing."

"Magnanimity," murmured Kit, unbelievingly.

He went sober. "I guess I must be getting feebleminded. But I want to see her get ahead, Kit. And so do you—and that's why we're here. Well, softly does it—and we shall pull her away from that hard-boiled, handsome, tough guy."

She looked helpless and puzzled, this woman always so self-certain. She said: "I'm only thinking of Lily's future and I'd hate to be wrong about this. But maybe we are wrong, Jay. Lily believes in romance. You and I don't. Once we did, but that was long ago."

His smile was sleepy and faintly sad. "We did once, didn't we? What happened to us, Kit?"

She didn't answer. She met his eyes and colored perceptibly as she gently pushed him into his room. "Good night, my dear," she said, and watched the door close. She stood indecisively there, staring at the wall. But presently she murmured to herself, "No, this is being silly—we have to get her out of this place." Her shoulders lifted vigorously; she turned back along the balcony.

Racing northward through a pit-black night, Tom explained his haste to Strang.

"Bill Speel and his party were scouting around the Moonstones about dusk when he ran into a bunch driving a couple hundred Barrier cattle straight for the Oregon line. Hell of a brawl there in the dark, he said; but the bunch was six strong and he only had three. So they drove him to cover. Gib McChesney got a bullet in the leg."

"Recognize anybody?"

"Said he heard Duke DePard's voice once."

Matt Strang twisted his long legs uncomfortably under the instrument board. "So the DePards timed it while we were at the dance, knowin' we couldn't get help up to Camp Four in a hurry. I heard a whisper of that tonight in the schoolhouse. Which was what I wanted to tell you before you tangled with Buffalo."

"The DePards didn't think up this mischief. It was Buffalo, of course."

Matt Strang waggled his head. "We're going to have a whole hell of a lot of grief up here in this broken country. I feel it. Bill Speel's not the man you want to handle the Camp Four district. He could've made his three men do against six if he'd had nerve enough. He reads too much."

"Shouldn't be a handicap."

"You can't scrap with your fingers in a book," grumbled Matt. "Bill don't like the sight of a man kickin' around the ground with a bullet in his liver."

"Nobody does," countered Tom, rather sharply.

Matt turned on his boss. "You got to grind those scruples out of your system. Galt means to kill you. Don't give any man a second shot at you. Send me to handle Camp Four."

"I need you at headquarters."

"I'd rather be away from headquarters a while," said Strang, sullenly. Then his latent anger burst out. "One of these days I'll stop Buffalo's dirty mouth."

Silence fell between them, a silence uneasy with strain. Tom knew what lay on his foreman's mind. Buffalo Galt's reference to the unknown father of Charm's baby would be eating into Matt Strang like acid. For though Matt Strang had never opened his lips on the subject, it was clear to Tom that this man loved Charm Michelet. It had been evident to Tom Sebastian for more than five years, or since that day when Charm had turned overnight from girl to woman. And when, three years back, a doctor had rushed from Reno to Barrier to squire her baby into the world, Matt Strang had stormed away from the ranch with madness in his hot blood. He had returned a week later, but with something in his eyes Tom sorrowed to see.

All laughter and gayety had died in Matt Strang during those seven days; and one other thing had died too—that thorough, voiceless understanding which had bound the red-headed foreman and himself together. Nothing remained in Matt now but an unflinching loyalty to Barrier; not even the overwhelming question of the baby's parenthood had yet shaken that. But one day, Tom knew, the cancer of doubt would eat its way through the last tissue of Matt's mind. When that day came Matt would turn on him as savagely as any DePard gunman.

They ground up Piute grade in second gear, with Tom's thoughts bitterly on this problem. Nevada was a tolerant state and Barrier, also tolerant, had accepted Charm's baby without question. It was, to the crew, just one of those things that sometimes happen. But he knew all people believed him to be the father of that robust and chuckling youngster. And he knew they believed he hadn't married Charm because marriage would mean admission of a mistake he did not wish to admit. Neither he nor Charm had ever refuted the covert accusation. The secret lay between himself and the proud, still-eyed girl who was chatelaine of Barrier.

Prisoned thus in his black thoughts, he worried over Matt Strang for whom he had an abiding affection still. He tried, indirectly to take some of the sting from Buffalo Galt's malign words. "Never mind the man. He'll use whatever weapons he can to hurt us. But don't be a sucker enough to let his talk hit home."

His words rang against a stony reserve; Matt's raw-colored cheeks were tipped downward, dangerously cast. Viewing the future with tragic realism, Tom saw the day and the hour when this man who had been his closest companion would turn violently against him.

The thought made him inexpressibly lonely. One by one his sources of friendship were being cut off. At times like these he could understand the reserve and the strictness that had been in his father's eyes.

At the top of the canyon grade the car resumed its forward run for half a mile, or until its headlights flushed four shanties out of the night. Two haltered ponies and two saddled horses waited by the road. Bill Speel came from the nearest shanty, obviously in a bad frame of mind.

"I couldn't do anything, Tom. We ran plumb into 'em and tried to bust up the procession. But they drove us into the rocks and we're lucky not to have lost more blood. I got the boys out there in the rocks yet. Somebody's sniping at us. I don't know if the main gang went off with the beef or what."

"What the hell's the matter with your nerve?" rapped out Matt. Sebastian walked into the nearest cabin, throwing his order behind him. "Saddle the extra ponies, Matt." Gib McChesney, who was no more than a kid, sat with his foot propped on a chair. His trouser leg was cut away and a bandage, soaked red, swatched his thigh. He was dead white, but he grinned at his boss.

"Sure sorry about this," he apologized.

Sebastian pulled a flask from his hip pocket. "Here's the hair of the dog that bit you. Take a long drag on it. We'll have Bill Speel drive you into Reno."

"Hell with that," objected the youth. "I'm not goin' to bust up the weddin' party. I can tough 'er out till you fellows see what the shootin's all about."

Sebastian appraised the boy carefully and then he said in a gentle voice, "That's fine, Gib," and turned back into the night. Matt had slapped on the saddles. Sebastian swung up beside his foreman and Bill Speel and galloped northward.

"I don't know if it's one man or six bangin' away at us," complained Bill Speel. "Somebody's dug in at the pass and we can't seem to flank the spot." Then he added nervously, "It's darker than the belly of Jonah's whale."

A solitary gunshot echo threaded the night. Matt said in cold anger: "You're a fool, Bill! You let the DePards walk through here like a Fourth of July parade."

"Listen—I won't run the boys into a bunch of lead like that."

"If you're afraid," said Matt bitterly, "you better take a high lope out of this country."

"That's enough, Matt," interposed Tom. They galloped

around a descending bend; one more shot burst flat and hard across the night. Sebastian slowed to a walk.

"The boys are in those rocks to your right," said Speel.

"Wait," ordered Sebastian, reining in. From this point the land rolled downward into a small meadow and rose beyond the meadow to meet the dimmest shadow of rocky hills. The trail crossed the meadow and entered the yonder broken area by a gap not much wider than a wagon road. Around that gap were mounds of decomposed rock. All this he recalled from memory; it was too dark to see.

A gun spoke again from that location. Tom listened carefully to the echo rolling over the meadow.

"A bluff," said Matt Strang. "One or two of DePard's gang covering the rest of that bunch as they drag our beef away."

"When did you run afoul of the DePards, Bill?" asked Tom.

"Hour and a half ago."

"If they're still on the run they can't be more than six miles away. We'll go and see who's holding us up. Bill, you stick with the boys. Tell 'em not to fire. If you hear shooting over yonder in a little bit, come ahead. Let's try it, Matt."

"But—" said Bill Speel and was left alone. Tom and Matt Strang cantered down the incline. They reached the ascending slope and went up quietly, flanking a tall rock pile which, as Sebastian remembered, would allow them to pass into the hill trail without entering the main doorway now guarded by the DePard men. Sebastian dropped his arm, fingers seating themselves around the cold butt of his gun; and at that moment the front feet of his horse hit the loose shale rock and burst quick echoes through the suspended silence.

There was an instant answer from the DePard men. But the tall pile of rock momentarily sheltered Sebastian and Strang as they spurred up and over the incline and went clattering down the shale rock into the trail, to the rear of the DePard men. The DePard men faced about, that fact evidenced by the pale light of their gun muzzles licking the blackness at each shot. There were two of them, Sebastian thought coldly, and charged at them. He fired at the nearest flash, and fired again, the sudden impact of Matt's horse throwing off his aim. Matt was a head-long, unsparing fighter in such moments as these. He deliberately jammed Sebastian to one side of the narrow trail and drove by, his gun beating up steady echoes.

But there was, suddenly, nothing on which to pin a shot. The two DePard men faded out of the rocky defile, into the meadow and its surrounding rough sides, the sound of their flight at once drowned out by the Camp Four crew pounding down from the opposite slope. Matt Strang said in his rash, angered voice: "Spread out, you damned idiots, and comb this clearing!"

Tom Sebastian's call overrode the orders of his foreman. "Never mind—follow me. Up the trail!" He whipped back into the passageway. Matt hotly protested but his voice fell farther and farther behind. The rest of the Barrier outfit spurred in single file, hard on the heels of Sebastian who followed the trail into the felted gloom of the pines.

All along that route in the hills he had no sight of anything except an occasional patch of starlit sky appearing through the pine tops. They covered, he judged, three miles through the hills. When they reached the flat ground he veered due north. Matt Strang forged abreast.

"We had those two fellows trapped," he complained.

"Red herring dragged across the trail. We're not after red herring, Matt."

"They're behind us and they'll give us grief."

"Going back," said Tom, "we'll have time to spend on that sort of grief. I'm after my cattle."

"I'm after men, not cattle," was Matt's retort.

"That's the difference between you and me," Sebastian observed. He reined in his horse then, and Barrier riders collected around them. His eyes swept the forward distance and caught vague shadows swaying against the night's paler backdrop. This, he judged, was no more than a quarter mile ahead; the DePards hadn't gotten far with the beef.

"They're just in front of us," he murmured.

Matt said: "They ain't heard us yet, because of the noise of the beef."

"We'll come up to one side of the beef, drive into it and scatter it. It'll discourage the DePards. They'll run. The less shooting the better. I don't want to read burial service over another man this week."

He cantered away, the crew coming behind. He struck off at an angle with the intention of paralleling and drawing abreast of the beef. By degrees the outline of the herd became clearer over on the left and he now and then saw a horseman break from the line and gallop backward, keeping the stock in formation, Presently, broadside to the herd and not more than three hundred yards from it, he stopped.

"We hit the beef hard as we can. We fire a round. They'll stampede. Ready?"

The breathing of the man on his nearest left quickened. Looking to either hand, he saw all the Barrier hands moving into line. Thereupon he gathered his horse under him. Matt had already started to go. The rest of the line was swaying forward. He pulled back sharply then. He said, "Wait!"

Matt Strang turned. "What the hell—"

"Wait!"

The cattle had ceased moving forward. They were spreading out from the column, bawling through the dark. There was a rider sliding along that mass, detaching himself from it without haste. He stopped. His voice cut across the distance.

"Take your damned cattle, Sebastian. Come and take 'em!"

Matt Strang's arm dropped and rose. He made a snap shot through the shadows. The rider was wheeling back around the edge of the beef. He yelled: "Next time, you'll need more help!" And he raced on, into the west. There was a flurry of other riders beating away from the herd.

"It was Duke DePard," said Sebastian.

"God damn you!" cried Strang. "Come on!"

"Wait," said Sebastian. "It was a trap—and it didn't work. We ram the herd and scatter it. That's all. We don't follow DePard. Do you understand? Come on."

He spurred his pony forward, meanwhile catching sight of Matt Strang's queer actions. The foreman made a wide circle away from the group—and stopped. The Barrier men left him behind, spreading as they galloped. Sebastian pulled his gun, alert to trickery on the dark side of the herd; but he saw nothing over there and his quick shot was aimed into the air, meant only to stampede the stock. He fired twice again, the men around him following suit. The beef, bawling and nervous, broke instantly out of that lumpy formation. Dust shot up; he could see the shapes of his cattle spreading in all directions. Bill Speel had come up.

"They're through for one night," said Sebastian. "The beef'll scatter over five miles of country and they'll never try to collect it now. Duke DePard won't try two bluffs in the same game. He'll go home. So will we."

"The beef?" said Bill Speel.

"The beef will drift back to the hills," stated Sebastian. "We ride."

He turned homeward. At the beginning of the hill trail he joined Strang in the rear. "Take this bunch back to Camp Four. Then drive Gib McChesney into Reno to a doctor. On your way, stop at the ranch and start Jim Kern and five of the boys up this way to reinforce Bill Speel. We're going to lay a heavy guard on these hills."

"You lost your great chance," Matt said gruffly.

"I'm not a killer, Matt."

"Then," said Matt Strang, not mincing his words, "Barrier's going to be nothing but a ruin ninety days from now and you'll be dead."

"Barrier can bide its time."

"I don't like that soft streak in you," said Matt. "You're a marked man in this corner of Nevada. Get this straight. When men like Galt set out to kill, they do the job. There's only one way to survive, which is to rub out Galt and the DePards and that whole damned tribe. You've refused your best opportunity of doing that tonight. One of those very men you were soft-hearted enough to let go probably's got the bullet that's going to blow your lights eternally out."

"It was a trap. I don't bite that easy."

They were at the summit of the hills, passing through a park-like opening. Faint wind rustled the nearby pine tops as Tom Sebastian pulled out of the line. "After you've done that chore, bring the car back to Camp Four. I'll meet you there sometime beyond sun-up."

Matt called sharply: "Where you going?"

Sebastian rode silently into the pines. A quarter mile from the trail, on a butte rising above the general level of the broken country, he staked his horse, rolled himself in a saddle blanket and fell lightly asleep.

Chapter 5

Just before dawn an echo in the trees below the butte wakened him as effectively as an alarm clock. Crouched quietly on the rim of the butte, he watched day's color sweep across the land. There was always that rush and vigor to these morning changes. One moment it was quite dark and all the stars were clear in the sky. Then the black eastern horizon cracked apart, a pale violet fissure divided earth and sky, and long waves of light rolled out of the east. In the foreground tree and gulch and promontory broke through the sea of night, shadows cascading down-slope in the manner of water.

Visibility raced southward toward Barrier headquarters; the far desert lay beneath a cloudless, stainless morning atmosphere. Camp Four was hidden in the trees two miles on, but the hollowed-out meadow in which the two DePard men had tried to make a fight was directly below. A few Barrier cows grazed there.

Sebastian turned across the butte to sweep the open forest below; and his eyes attentively and patiently rummaged all the corridors there and weighed the obscure timber barricades. Seeing nothing, he cast a farther glance to that northern desert where the night before, he had broken up the rustled herd. He could not get a clear view. Leading his horse down the side of the butte, he mounted and rode that way.

His purpose in remaining here overnight was to catch by first daylight any subsequent maneuver of the DePards. He had no assurance they would remain in the hills, but he did know that somewhere in this rugged terrain they maintained a hide-out. He wished to find it, for he was certain the DePards would again, as so often in the past, spill down from the broken land to drive away his beef. Buffalo Galt was not a poor man. His money had not come from the mines he owned around Tumpah. Buffalo's prosperity was founded on Barrier beef.

All big ranches suffered from the rustler. It was now, as surely as in 1870, the cattleman's greatest source of loss. It was old knowledge to Sebastian that many a family in this country lived solely from the proceeds of stolen Barrier steers, and had thus lived for three generations. With some it had come to be a natural habit, so openly condoned by the outlying settler that the factor of guilt had really disappeared from the business.

Towards the small thief Sebastian really held no great resentment, realizing that the disappearance of a steer now and then was part of the tax Barrier paid for being great. More than once, when night found him at a remote corner of the domain, he had unexpectedly dropped in on some little settler and had been served steaks which he knew came from his own herds. He could grin at that. It was a rule of the game they all played.

But it was another matter when Buffalo Galt sent the DePards out to despoil Barrier. Galt was a deliberate brigand who if not stopped, would ruin Barrier.

So thinking, his glance continually roving the floor of the forest, Sebastian came to a ravine cutting east and west through the hills. A small trail descended to the ravine's bottom, crossed it and climbed the farther bank, passing into a stand of brush. Sebastian's attention riveted on that brush and its possibilities, and presently he turned left to avoid the crossing and pushed his way a good five hundred feet westward. At that point he scanned the ravine again and urged his horse into it. The pony picked its way through the depression's rock bed, and lunged up the farther bank.

Not quite arrived on the top, Sebastian heard a swift rush through the bushes farther down the ravine; and when he heard it all his nerves warned him and he raked his spurs across the pony's hide and swung low in the saddle. Next moment the deep dreaming peace of the forest was shattered by a gunshot, echoes crashing all along the slopes and swirling around the red pine buttes.

The bullet struck a rock in the ravine bottom with a flat small report. Sebastian smashed through the marginal brush and wheeled on into the pines, his own gun jerked up. The sorrel rump of a horse was just sliding into that brush a hundred feet to the eastward, the sound of its hoofs rattling across the ravine, crashing into the farther thicket. The ambusher was in retreat; but Sebastian, intently listening, heard the echoes die too suddenly, as though the man had come to a halt in the near distance. He swung to the right, made his way to a higher roll of ground and stopped to look into the ravine. He had a good view of the brush from this elevation, but the unknown marksman had meanwhile dropped quietly into some other hidden pocket. The game, Sebastian realized, had begun. Retreating to heavier timber, he pointed eastward, labored up the side of a hill and in a few minutes came to the edge of a narrow, deep-slashed canyon.

"Crossing over to flank me," he thought, and studied the land beyond the canyon. Over there a rugged, irregular area marked by timber and dry creek beds marched on a quarter mile or so until it bumped into a sharp-rising butte on which timber thickly stood. "He wants to get up there to keep me in sight," considered Sebastian, and immediately pushed the pony into a narrow trail that dropped to the canyon's bottom.

Dust whirled up from the pony's stiff legs; first sunlight turned the day instantly warm. It was seventy feet to the bottom of the canyon, a dozen paces across it, and seventy feet to the top of the farther rim. Half expecting a long range shot, Sebastian moved faster and sweat started under the brim of his hat. "He's seen me," he grumbled, "but he's holding his fire to keep me on the defensive." That suspicion drove him rapidly across the broken area, once he had gotten out of the canyon. A windfall barred his direct advance; as he circled it, the dry brush rattled. An antelope, quietly hidden, sprang to life at his very feet and boomed away across the uneven ground.

Sebastian said, "Damnation," and knocked the sweat from his forehead. He rode his horse into one of the dry creek beds, got down and went ducking forward around the pine trunks. A little ahead of him the timber quit and there was a wide, rocky strip along the foot of the butte—a hazard he had to cross before reaching the protecting forest again. Reaching this open spot, he crouched behind a rock slab and scanned the scattered boulders ahead of him.

It was a tricky piece of country. But across this open stretch he had to go. He mentally calculated the distance from the point he had last seen the opposing marksman to this strip and wondered if the fellow had crossed it and reached the butte's side. Or the man might have stood pat at the edge of the canyon, or he might now be coming up from the rear. At that thought he turned to have a look at his back trail, and then squared himself to the front once more—and caught the tag end of surreptitious movement out in the tangle of rocks. Something had risen from a dry creek bed and had dropped instantly behind a mess of heavy boulders. The spot was two hundred feet to his left.

Sebastian grunted his relief. He backed into the pines and worked his way leftward on hands and knees, paralleling the open stretch. But he didn't get far. A big arm lifted above those rocks on which he so steadily kept his eyes and a heavy shout sailed across the interval.

"I see you, Sebastian. Let's call this off."

It was the voice of one particular individual—to be recognized anywhere. Sebastian saw the huge head and shoulders of Star Humboldt rise above the rocks like a grizzly rearing on its hind legs. His torso spread ponderously against the fresh sunlight. Sebastian even made out the swart, sullen cheeks. The man was coatless; his shirt lay rolled back from his great hair-felted chest. He said again: "Don't fire, Tom." It was beyond accurate revolver range. Sebastian went on a dozen paces and stopped.

"Step out from the rocks," he ordered.

Humboldt took three paces to his left and stood fully exposed. His arms hung straight down. He tipped his head, hatbrim cutting some of the sunlight from his eyes.

"Reach over with your left hand and draw and drop your gun."

Humboldt's heavy arm crossed his stomach, obeying; the gun fell. Sebastian walked on a half dozen feet before a clear warning slapped him deliberately across the face. His quick glance went to his exposed rear. He said sharply: "Come over here."

Humboldt twisted his shoulders and for a long moment held them rigid. Then his heavy voice lifted to a violent yell and he whirled and dropped behind the rock barricade again. Sebastian started his forward run—for he knew how schemingly Humboldt had drawn him into this trap. Humboldt's revolver lay useless on the rocks, but that meant nothing, as he was instantly to discover. Wrenching himself over the tricky rocky footing, Sebastian had gained perhaps ten yards when Humboldt raised his head and laid the black snout of a rifle across the rock parapet, his heavy head against its stock. The distance was too great for accurate revolver play, which Humboldt had shrewdly figured. But the rifle balanced there was a deadly possibility.

Never stopping, never trying to dodge, Sebastian realized he had but a single chance, which was to cause the half-breed to flinch his first shots. And so, already having lifted his revolver, he laid a rapid shot against the rocks. The explosion of his gun beat Humboldt's fire by a thin margin, both echoes running down the slope together. The muzzle of Humboldt's rifle yawed a little, throwing off the bullet. Instantly later that wicked muzzle came relentlessly back to its target. Sebastian fired a second time and saw rock flakes fly against Humboldt's face.

All this while his headlong charge carried him on. Humboldt was holding his shots, waiting for one utterly certain opportunity. Sebastian's third shot struck nothing but thin air, and that was the lull Humboldt waited for. Nothing but guesswork caused Sebastian to leap aside. Humboldt's rifle cracked; somewhere behind Sebastian the slow-traveling lead ticked a rock and went whining on.

There was this moment, and this moment only. Sebastian checked his run; he stood dead still, taking a last aim. It was then that Humboldt, pumping a fresh load into the Winchester, did an odd thing. Some impulse caused him to abandon the security of his barricade and pulled him up to his feet. Sebastian's glance centered on the blackened, hairy triangle of skin showing between the open edges of Humboldt's shirt. When he fired, he fired at that.

If there was a reply from Humboldt's gun, he didn't hear it. If Humboldt's bullet had hit him, he didn't feel it. Frozen in his tracks, without an atom of regret, he crashed another bullet at that triangle patch of bare flesh.

Sebastian returned to Camp Four around nine o'clock of the morning and found Matt Strang waiting with the car. Bill Speel was there; the rest of the crew was out on scout.

Matt said: "Did I hear firing over toward Hermione ridge?"

Sebastian crossed to Bill Speel. He spoke briefly to the man and went to the car. Matt moved over in the seat. They bounced across the bumpy road and swung around for Barrier headquarters.

When Tom drove into the Barrier plaza Lily Tennant was on the point of riding away from it. She wheeled her horse over to the car.

"Could I interest you in a ride, or are you very weary?"

Sebastian called to Gath, crossing the plaza. "Gath, saddle up for me, please," and lifted his plainly approving glance to her. She was in breeches and boots, with a tan shirt covering her small, square shoulders. A borrowed sombrero, tilted slightly, strengthened the liveliness of her features, and he thought instantly that his first impression of her had been right. She wasn't something fragile from a picture book. Buoyant, robust emotion was very strong in her. He showed his reaction, for Lily's color deepened and she turned her horse away. Sebastian swung up to the pony Gath had brought him. They cantered together across the plaza into the rising blaze of sunlight.

"You do look tired, Tom."

It brought out his grin. "Sebastians are like St. Bernards. They look old and weary from birth. How have you made out? Been bored?"

"Not for a moment. I don't think it would be possible to be bored here."

He turned the course slightly, pointing toward a lone tree in the distance. "Wait till the strangeness wears off. The monotony will weigh on you then."

"Trying to get rid of me?"

"No—I hate to think of your leaving."

Her glance touched him quickly. "Then let's not think of it until it happens."

"That's right."

"But you're wrong about the monotony. I feel just two things. Violence and security. The violence seemed to be all around, but inside the ranch house none of that penetrates. I sit there in front of the fireplace and nothing in the outside world is very important. I'm supposed to be worrying about my job. But I'm not. I eat, I let the sensations of day float me along and then I sleep. It's a very insidious and comfortable place. Whirlwinds beat against it and storms strike out of nowhere; but all these things pass by, and there it sits, as though it were ageless. Am I being romantic?"

"No," he said. "The ranch has survived a lot of trouble and a lot of people have lived out their whole lives on it. That feeling is soaked into the house."

"And soaking into me."

"You're getting a rest. I'm mighty glad of that."

"You're reminding me again that I'll soon be gone."

He said nothing more for a while. Their steady canter carried them across the undulating range, out into pure space that, save for the nearing tree, would have had little to define it. The tree, when they reached it, turned out to be a massive-branched oak casting a solid patch of shade. They dismounted here. Lily sat down and hugged her arms around her knees. Sebastian built himself a smoke, still standing.

"Well," he said, "we can't escape the fact that one day you'll have to say good-by to us."

"I suppose," she murmured. "Back to the schemings and contrivings that end up in heartache or a little bit of luck."

"You fought for that," he pointed out. "So you can't let it go."

She turned more directly toward him. "What's happened to my sureness? I don't possess it any more."

He sat on his heels and drew patterns in the loose soil. The scars of the schoolhouse fight were still cut across his broad, heavy fists.

She said: "You had trouble up in the hills last night."

"Why?"

"You're still remembering. In anger your eyes turn smoky."

"A little trouble," he admitted reluctantly. "Where's the rest of your party?"

She was smiling again. "Jay's tired, Kit's afraid of the sun and Timmy is probably out following your men around like a beagle."

He dropped back to one elbow so that he might watch her slow gestures. To him the curve of her lips was something as anciently feminine as Eve. It hit him hard. It cut recklessly across his ordered thoughts and caused him to speak his abrupt convictions, as he had done in Reno.

"You're a damned beautiful woman, Lily."

She said in a half-breath: "Are you always so frank?"

He punched his cigarette into the soft ground; he kept his head bent down. After a while she went on. "I've never met anyone like you. I don't think you know the effect you produce in me."

He said: "I told you the other night you and I were the sort that could never be mild. We go to extreme ends."

She didn't answer until he lifted his eyes to her. Then she said, just above a whisper, "Yes," and suddenly they were magnetic poles between which an exciting current raced. He broke the tension by brusquely pulling his eyes away. Lily's words were limpidly cool.

"It might be wonderful or it might be tragic, or it might be—" Her voice trailed off and then rose with a touch of skepticism. "—a summer night's dream, soon lost."

"People never know a drenching until they go over the falls, Lily. Love's a hard, compelling thing."

"I'm not sure I want to go over the falls, Tom."

"Not if you want fame."

"Not if I want fame," she echoed softly.

He got up and said, "Shall we ride back?"

Lily rose, still watching him. "I haven't made myself clear," she said. "Time without end women have abandoned everything for love. Some of them have been supremely happy. Some of them have been supremely miserable. There's a lot of sloppy sentimentality, a lot of illusion around love. I don't want to do the sloppy thing. I want to be realistic about this. It isn't fame, Tom. It's being useful and happy. If I make mistakes, if I have to surrender some dreams—that's all right. It's all right if in the end I find the job I'm best fitted to do."

"Yes," he said, and gave her a hand-up to her saddle.

"Above all," she told him soberly, "I don't want to be a person drifting aimlessly through life. I have to mean something to myself."

He was a man who covered his feelings when they were strongest. "You'll do what you have to do," he said. "That's the long and short of it."

"Bargains and compromises? Of course. Men do a lot of surrendering to reach the top of the ladder. Do you suppose women are any different? I know that men would like to believe that women are different. But that's idealization. Women are human, too, Tom."

They struck out from the little patch of shade, into a light burning more intensely down; all the air was dry and scorched. Lily's voice broke a long riding silence. "Does that philosophy hurt you?"

"You're an honest woman, Lily. You're not fooling yourself. That's the important item."

They paced the rest of the distance in silence and entered Barrier's plaza, dismounting and going into the grateful cool of the living room. Timmy and Kit and Jay Stuart loafed there. Stuart waggled a highball skeptically at Lily.

"Moderation is the essence of all things, including fresh air and exercise."

Kit's alert eyes ran from Lily to Sebastian. Charm came quietly in. "Judge Sillavan phoned from Reno, Tom. He wants you to call him."

Sebastian walked to the phone and lifted the receiver. He said, "Judge Sillavan at Reno, please," and waited. The dining room door swung open then and Charm's boy came forward on his uncertain legs and stood looking at the group. He was a plump, extraordinarily grave youngster with black hair faintly curly.

Charm said, "Tommy—" But Tommy saw Sebastian and crossed the room, hitching his shoulders to help balance himself. He got hold of one of Sebastian's legs and hung to it, tipping his head to watch the tall man. Sebastian put an arm down to Tommy and spoke into the phone.

"This is Sebastian, Judge," he said and then listened. He winked at Tommy. He said to Sillavan at the other end of the line: "What are you so mysterious about? When? Now? . . . All right." He hung up, and he pulled Tommy up to his chest. "I'm driving into Reno. Anybody care for the trip?"

Both Kit and Jay Stuart looked at Lily. Kit said: "We've got to end this vacation sometime. Shall we pack up and go now?"

But Lily was seeing something which, visible to her before, had never been quite so clear. Sebastian's affection for that child of Charm's was plain and deep on his face. She turned her eyes to Charm and observed the faint aggressiveness of that dark girl's manner. Charm was looking directly at her, at Lily, and something in her eyes said to Lily: "Look and see for yourself."

"Shall we go?" urged Kit.

Doubt crept reluctantly across Lily's mind and made the room less pleasant. "Yes," she said, and noticed the faint flare of satisfaction in Charm Michelet. Her doubt and her curiosity made her a little bit cruel, for she instantly added: "But not for good. Let's run into Reno, have a party for Jay, and come back."

"Will you never make up your mind?" exclaimed Kit in despair. She turned to Jay Stuart for support.

Jay grinned. "If she's having fun," he said negligently, "let her have it. Providing the hospitality of our host isn't wearing out."

"I'd be happy to have more guests like you," replied Sebastian and made a wicked face at Tommy. "Kid, you go shoot a couple Indians for supper." He laid the youngster flat on the floor.

"Tommy," said Charm.

Lily knew the girl was disappointed in not being rid of her guests. It was something she could not quite hide. She was in love with Sebastian. That realization kicked a queer, cold feeling through Lily. She spoke to Charm.

"Why don't you come with us?"

"Thank you—no," said Charm, and got Tommy and walked back into the dining room.

"So it's a party?" said Jay.

"A party in Reno, for you," agreed Lily.

"Sounds like something good," reflected Sebastian. "I'll bring the car around." He started for the porch, and then turned and went into the dining room, carefully closing the door behind him. Tommy was flat on his stomach, under the table. Charm stood in the center of the room, looking strangely at the floor, her small hands clenched. When she heard Sebastian she turned to him. There had been a strong expression on her face, but it vanished instantly.

"Why not come with us?" he said. "It will do you good to get away from here."

"No."

"No reason to tie yourself down to this ranch, Charm."

Her black eyes showed a sudden proud resentment. "They are not my kind of people. I wouldn't fit in."

"You're good enough for anybody," he told her sharply.

"It isn't that," she said, and went on to the kitchen.

Puzzled, Sebastian watched her go. A car came off the desert and coughed consumptively in the yard. Sebastian shrugged and went back through the living room to the plaza. Sheriff Lot McGinnis stood in front of his flivver's boiling radiator and rolled a cigarette with a mild disgust. He said:

"It's scandalous the way I have to wrestle this dumb hunk of balin' wire around. And it only twelve years old. I bet I scare hell out of every jack rabbit inside of ten miles—she's that noisy. Machinery just ain't natural to this country anyhow."

He sat on the running board and cocked his hat. His eyes ran idly around the Barrier yard, and came back to Sebastian with a gentle interest. His body went slack; he seemed only a harmless, disinterested old man.

"You had trouble the other night. I hear it was the DePard boys that did the shootin'."

"I didn't identify anybody. They were out in the dark."

"Buffalo called out a name. It was the DePard name, I understand."

"It escapes my mind," said Sebastian.

"Funny thing about this country," observed Lot McGinnis. "Practically nobody can remember names of folks a sheriff's after." He chuckled faintly; then turned sober. "Nevertheless, my boy, it was murder."

"I can't help you, Lot."

"I ain't expectin' you to."

Sebastian said: "It would do no good for me to complain. You might arrest the DePard boys—if it was them—but you couldn't pin anything on them."

"That's right. But watch your step. You've got some mighty clever enemies, Tom. Don't let 'em pin anything on you."

"Is that the plan?"

The sheriff got up. He said enigmatically: "I don't know as it was anything I heard. Maybe it's just a guess. It's your business if you got to fight fire with fire—but don't let anybody catch you with the matches in your pocket. I don't want to come out here with a warrant somebody's swore against you."

Sebastian grinned. "You'd have to catch me first, Lot."

"That's a point, too," admitted McGinnis. He crawled into his car. He said shrewdly: "You can hear me comin' five miles away. So if your conscience bothers you and you make out this coffee mill clunkin' toward Barrier, use your own judgment."

The engine caught on with an alarming racket. Lot McGinnis made a gesture of resignation and drove the machine around the plaza and struck out for Tumpah. Sebastian went to the front of the house and found the Reno crowd waiting. He got in and sent the car southward under the full, blistering blaze of the sun.

Matt Strang stood at the corner of the house, smoking a cigarette under the sultry sunlight, and watched the machine die behind the dust it ripped up. Presently he threw the cigarette away and went into the living room. Charm was on her knees, violently scrubbing the fireplace stones.

"That's no work for you to do," grumbled Matt. "What's Gath for? Quit it, Charm."

"Let me alone."

He touched her shoulder. "I won't have it. You weren't made to scrub up other people's boot tracks."

The force of his arm stopped her. She rose and showed him a flushed, disturbed face. "Let me alone, Matt. What are you doing in the house in the middle of the morning when there's plenty to keep you busy outside?"

"How can I work," he muttered, "with all this going on?"

"Whatever goes on is none of your concern."

"Isn't it?" he said dully.

"Why should you care what the California people do, or where they go? They're Tom's guests. Tom loves company. If you don't like it, stay away."

She stepped back, hand touching the house keys at her waist. "What are you thinking of then?"

"You. You and Tom."

Her voice cut at him. "What is in your mind, Matt?"

He said, "Well," and then the turmoil of his soul spilled out. "Good God, Charm! I can't stand it! You and Tom in the same house—nothing but a wall between your bedroom and his! All the country thinks that boy belongs to Tom. But you still live here! You fool girl—don't you want to spike that dirty lie?"

"That's my affair—and Tom's. It isn't yours."

His raw, tough face was indescribably bitter. "Well, then," he snapped, "maybe it ain't a lie."

Even that failed to break her aloof reserve. The same impenetrable mystery covered her oval face. "I made one mistake in my life, and so you're calling me a common woman. Maybe I am. You've thrown that at me before. If I told Tom he'd cut your tongue out for it. You don't know what's in my heart. Nobody does and nobody ever will. Tom is the greatest man in the world—and you have troubled me enough."

"It's driving me crazy!" he ground out.

Her voice punished him. "It was my mistake and I have to live with it. It is none of your business and never will be. You have made me miserable with your mad mind, with your scenes, with your foolish tongue. I do not belong to you. I am not related to you. I don't owe you sympathy or explanation—I don't owe you anything. When will you see that? When will you let me alone? I think you had better leave Barrier and never come back."

"I'll never leave Barrier while you're here."

"Then you will keep out of my way! I am tired of listening to you!"

He sat down in a chair and bent his head. "Charm," he muttered, "it hurts me like hell. If I could ride away and forget I would. But I can't ever forget you. That's what sets me crazy."

Her voice was kinder, it was sadder. "If you think you love me, you shouldn't make me unhappy. You ought to be patient. You ought to understand."

He had control of himself. He spoke more quietly. "My name don't mean anything, Charm, but you can have it and the boy can have it any time you say. That's been my offer for three years. It will always be my offer. I know you want Tom and I know you're waiting for him. But I don't think you'll ever get him. Well, you'll break your heart and Tommy's growing up under a shadow, and meanwhile here I am, wanting you and seeing you get hurt."

She came over to him and the light touch of her hand brought him to his feet. She said, quietly: "You're a good man, Matt. I know that."

"Charm," he said gutturally, "is there any chance for me?"

Her small, obscure smile softened her answer: "You can't stop women from hoping, Matt. Now go away."

Matt Strang started to speak, but changed his mind and wheeled away. Out on the porch he stopped to roll a smoke with fingers unsteady enough to spill tobacco out of the cigarette paper.

Chapter 6

Tom dropped his passengers at the bungalow and listened to Lily's command. "Don't," she said, "forget the party. And if you see the judge, bring him along."

He turned the block and drove back to the center of town and left his car at a garage for a grease and oil job; and went straight to Sillavan's office. The old man was in a characteristic attitude, feet on the desk and frail body sunk deeply into the swivel chair. Cigar ashes lay generously on his vest; the room was blue with smoke.

"What's the mystery you couldn't tell me over the phone?" inquired Tom.

"Hell of a hot day, ain't it?"

"I drove through it to hark to your pearls of wisdom, so I ought to know. You'll kill yourself smoking those stogies."

"So my father said, forty years ago. I'm afraid I won't."

"A fake statement," grunted Sebastian. "You're too interested in the contemporary scene to want to die short of a hundred."

Sillavan rolled his white head around the chair's rim and grinned wistfully. "Growing old's not so simple, Tom. The contemporary scene is for the young. It's your world, not mine. Men like me live in the bright past. When we cut a high, wide, and proud trail. But we're just spectators now, pushed aside by fellows like you. Pretty lonesome business to see the old things go. I regret seeing even my bitterest enemies die. They were part of the past, too. I guess a little bit of me gets burned out with every old-timer. When one of them does pass on it pushes my world farther back into the mist."

"You're gloomy as hell."

"Comes from sittin' here and watchin' old faces look down from the wall. The men and women of my time were big-hearted, wide-handed people. We had a lot of fun out of living. More, I think, than your generation does. We weren't afraid of our emotions."

Sebastian curled himself a smoke, sly wrinkles of humor creeping about his eyes. Sillavan was being indirect. But Sillavan would get to the point in proper time. Realizing that, Sebastian made no attempt to force the talk around. He said: "Lily Tennant is staging a party tonight. Herewith is your invitation."

"I'll be there, to watch the antics of a generation that would like to be tough and can't quite cut the mustard," chuckled Sillavan.

Sebastian strolled out. Down the stairs he stepped aside to keep from been struck by a woman swinging out of the street like a grenadier. Her old cheeks were robust vermilion and her hat was a caricature. Seeing Sebastian she halted decisively and threw back her big shoulders.

"Sebastian," she said in a big voice, "you're a hard man with your fists. You like to killed Buffalo."

"The time of the day to you, Madame, and how's Tumpah?"

"Dead, of course," boomed Madame Belle Gilson. "Usually you're clever, Tom. When you knocked Buffalo all over the lot you were not clever. Don't you know he's an Indian for remembering injuries? That boy is your mortal enemy."

"Always was."

Madame waved her be-ringed fingers. "You watch out for him," she adjured, and went on up the stairs. She walked into Sillavan's office as a battleship floats into harbor, majestically and irresistibly.

The judge rose out of his chair with more than ordinary alacrity. He said, "Why, Madame," and made a distinct bow.

Madame keened the smoke-fogged air and simply said, "Good God," and fell into the nearest chair.

"I know the answer to that," countered Sillavan. "Stop me if it isn't the right one." He went to a wall cupboard and found therein a decanter and two glasses which he brought to the desk. He poured both glasses full; and gallantry came to his manner as he handed the drink to her and lifted his own.

"John," said Madame, "you're a benevolent old pirate and the milk of kindness never went sour in you. But in your salad days you were a fire-eating dandy everybody was a little scared of."

They drank on that, Madame imbibing with an audible relish. She coughed. Sillavan went back to his swivel chair. "I was a skinny little man in a country of bruisers," he mused. "So I had to swagger. I was, I'm afraid, very vain."

"And you slapped the face of George Ryan in the Crystal Room at Virginia City because he made some remarks about the size of my slippers."

The judge's voice was quite low. "Many echoes come out of the long past—all of them soft and gentle."

"God rest George Ryan," said Madame, "and all those we knew. We made some big mistakes in those days, John, but I regret nothing."

"Old people," said Sillavan, "don't think of mistakes or victories. When you live in memory there is little distinction between black and white."

Silence came to the hot room. These two sat quietly lost in the past. "Well," Sillavan said at last, "I was a rash one and bowed my neck to but one man in Nevada."

"King Henry the Great—Henry Sebastian," said the Madame and was smiling.

"I think we'd better drink on that," suggested the judge, and started to rise.

Madame waved him back. "If I took another I'd fall down your confounded stairs. I want to talk to you. Tom Sebastian's in trouble and he made it no better by smashing in Buffalo's face. Buffalo's my own, but I know him terribly well. He's the killing kind, John."

"Madame," said Sillavan bluntly, "you'll live to grieve over that boy's grave."

"I'd grieve less if I knew he couldn't hurt Tom Sebastian. Look here, John. Buffalo was a cheap thief till very lately. But he's got himself some political power and some heavy backing. You know and I know who's behind that."

"Yes, Madame. We're old enough to remember past history and we know who would be wanting to destroy Barrier now."

Madame said, belligerently, "I'll not have it. The gentleman in question is a big name and he's powerful and a solid citizen. But I knew him in less discreet days. If I went to him and shook a few skeletons in his fat face—"

"Madame," interrupted the judge. "Don't do that."

"Why?"

The judge got up and he said, more earnestly, "Don't do that. It may help later, but it would not help now. You are thinking dangerous things. The man can hit you so swiftly you'd never know it. No. You go back to Tumpah and be still. If it were otherwise I'd tell you."

Madame rose and sighed gustily. She wasn't satisfied. "You're a clever man, John, and I'll mind you. But in the last resort I'll break a scandal over him he'll not live down."

Sillavan held the door for her and bowed as she went out.

There were no telegrams from Rex Gilman, which was strange—considering that young man's competent nature. Lily turned an analytical glance on Jay who sat as usual in comfortable repose. Jay saw the quality of curiosity strengthen against him and grinned and threw up a protective arm.

"I'm going to get the devil for something. I see it coming."

"By any chance did Rex Gilman send you down here to do missionary work on me?"

"Let the skeptic, ignoble thought die its own miserable death," murmured Jay.

"You're like Kit," retorted Lily. "You can be so aggravatingly indirect. I want a straight answer."

"Honey," protested Jay, "I told you my only purpose in coming was to be near you."

It was still unsatisfactory but Lily dropped her questioning and walked restlessly around the room, hands briefly touching the furniture. Kit was at the phone, broadcasting invitations for the party. She made an impatient appeal for silence. But the little devils of discontent would not let Lily alone. What was she to do? What was she to be? Stopped in front of a wall picture, looking at it and yet not seeing it, she realized how unobtrusively Barrier had soothed her—how quietly it had carried her for a while beyond her troubles.

She wheeled. "I'm going for a walk."

"In this heat?" exclaimed Kit, and then spoke into the phone. "No, I was talking to Lily." Jay made a weary gesture, but he got up.

"You don't need to go along," Lily told him.

"Why did I come from Hollywood, if not to be with you?"

They went into the street and turned toward town, with the trees along the curb shading them for a few blocks. Afterwards they passed into the hard sunlight, two bare-headed, striking people, walking indifferently and silently beneath it. On the bridge across the Truckee they stopped to lean over the railing and watch a man, hip deep in the center of the river, cast his fish line across a patch of shallow riffles.

"Can't see much purpose in fishing where there's not apt to be fish," reflected Jay Stuart.

"Maybe he hasn't any purpose. Maybe he's just fishing."

"What?"

"Sometimes it is a comfort not to have a purpose."

"That's the way vegetables are."

"Struggle and triumph and glory isn't the only philosophy, Jay."

"True enough. There are a lot of unambitious souls who don't want victory. Comparatively few people are built to take the blows of battle. But those few always answer when the bugle blows. They may think they can sit by the side of the road and let the world go by, but they can't. They only kid themselves when they think they can step out of the parade."

"Pointing the finger at me, Jay?"

"I know you very well," said the man quietly. "The pastoral scene looks very attractive right now when the thought of the Hollywood treadmill oppresses you. You want to break free. But idleness would irritate you. Not being in the full current would sooner or later make you supremely unhappy."

"Now and then your words make me uncomfortable."

"Because they ring true to your conscience, my dear. There are strivers and drifters in this world. Give me credit for knowing a striver when I see one."

She turned and found his broad lips holding quiet humor. In his way he was a full man. Meticulous as he kept himself, tailored and groomed and handsome as he was, the weakness of the matinee idol type was not in Jay Stuart. The touch of ruggedness about shoulders and chin and mouth saved him from that; and there was always in his manner an infinite comprehension. She never had known a man more removed from the extreme of masculine aggressiveness or dramatic sentimentality. He was simply himself.

She shrugged her shoulders and walked on, across the bridge into the town's center. Jay said casually: "Fay Marlowe's last picture has turned out to be a flop and so Fay's on the way out. That puts the Leland outfit in a bad hole for a star. We'll see a scramble over there for the number one dressing room."

"I liked her, Jay."

"She was a publicity build-up that couldn't deliver. New times, new faces, new techniques. I hear Goldman's going to do a costume thing—Victor Herbert style. If that stuff comes in you'll hit the top of the class, Lily. You'd make the loveliest Gibson girl ever put on celluloid."

Suddenly Jay's quiet, unstressed words opened a door to familiar scenes. There was something in his talk, painting as it did the picture of Hollywood life, that warmed the memories of her own four-year struggle there and made them pleasant. In that little interval the clatter and confusion of rehearsal, the tense moments of action, the jargon, the smell of coffee late at night, the explosion of temperament, the intrigue and all the recollections of a swift touch-and-go life came through the door Jay had opened to stir and pull her. It was like the rousing of dormant hope.

He couldn't have known what was in her mind but he turned and said something that struck a full chord. "Picture people are a queer lot. Once Klieg lights baptize them, they never live for anything else. Look at me. I'm through with pictures but do you suppose I'm happy about it? If I were ten thousand miles away I'd drop everything and rush back at the casting director's call. You'd think the old-timers who have made their money and are out of the game would leave Hollywood. They never do, and they never will. It's the greatest game in all the world."

They were passing the Riverside. Looking idly across the street, Lily had her attention momentarily diverted. Tom Sebastian stood at the curb, talking with three other men, now and then making a lazy gesture with his hands. His hat was shoved back from his face and he was wholeheartedly laughing—almost the first time Lily had seen him thus shaken out of his gravity. Unconsciously she stopped, touching Jay's arm.

"I wish you knew him better. If you did, I think you'd swear loyalty to him forever. It's a queer feeling. He's the most exciting man I've ever met."

"You met him two or three days ago. How can you know him so well?"

She shook her head. "It isn't a matter of time." She looked at Stuart. "He lives a long way from anywhere and he's rooted to his ranch. Would you say he lacked purpose?"

"The ranch is his purpose. That's his battle." Stuart paused, then added quietly: "But is there a place on Barrier for two fighters? Sebastian does the leading. Everybody else follows. Do you want to play the part of a follower?"

They swung back toward the bungalow; and not until they were within a block of it did either speak. Lily said then:

"I wish I could implicitly believe you. You're so easy to believe."

She noticed how much of his indolent manner was gone. He was deeply in earnest. "Of course you suspect me of coming here to take you back. I don't blame you. Well, I did come to tell you one thing. Doesn't matter what you think of my sincerity. I've got to say it because all Lily Tennants need to hear it. This is it. Love is a universal thing, but talent is very rare in the world. Love dies. Talent grows always richer. The great story in life is the story of somebody, with the precious ounce of genius in him, smashing through all the rules and the barriers and going to the top. I don't want to jar you too hard, Lily. I don't want to be cynical. But to me it is supreme tragedy to see a great spirit get caught in the bedtime stories of a mediocre world. Everything's against you. All the rules, all the ordinary beliefs, all the sentiment of the common run. You are even against yourself. And so, if with all this nonsense handicapping you, you do rise—God bless you, my girl, and the stars are yours."

He quit on that; he quit abruptly. And his fine, quiet smile took all the sting from his words.

Held up by an impromptu gathering of cattlemen, Sebastian didn't get to Lily's party until well after nine. A great deal of aimless noise met him when he entered. Lily came out of the crowd with a mildly reproachful glance.

"I thought you'd forgotten. Is there anybody here you don't know?"

He surveyed the twenty or more people gathered in the room and shook his head. Most of them were of Reno's younger crowd, though Judge Sillavan and a retired army officer by the name of Arthur and one of Reno's older divorce lawyers added a touch of salt to so much obvious youth. And there was a heavy man in a cream-colored suit standing at Kit Christopher's elbow, alternately listening to her and sipping at his highball. Sebastian looked at him with a close interest.

"How did Kit happen to pick up Ed Brean?"

Lily said: "She doesn't quite know. She was introduced to him this afternoon. And here he is. We think there was a touch of maneuvering about it."

"If he wanted to meet her, he'd manage to arrange it," agreed Tom and accepted a drink from the unobtrusive Hannah. Somebody called to him and there was a moment's diversion while he grinned and acknowledged the crowd. Ed Brean turned his head and coolly stared. He was a big, round, formless man with a pear-shaped face and two agate blue eyes which refused to admit emotion. A monumental indifference flowed out of him; a sort of careless authority. He barely nodded to Sebastian, and returned his attention to Kit.

Lily was quite curious. "He seems to have a reputation for being powerful. Is there something particular about him I ought to know?"

He said, "No," and plunged his hands in his pockets. She had changed into a wine-brown evening dress and light flowed along the supple curves of her body and turned them untranscribably graceful. The smooth joining of her neck and shoulders was something vivid to see; the chestnut hair glowed under the room lamps. The love of life was an alive quality in her eyes, in the rose flush of her cheeks. And once again the womanly substance of this girl hit him hard. She stirred his deepest, most reckless emotions. It was something he couldn't help.

Lily turned and pushed slowly through the crowd to the table. Ed Brean, who seemed to be oblivious to all things, jerked up his head and watched her go. He wheeled away from Kit, who was talking to him, with a curt impoliteness and headed for Lily. But he had to shift his course, for Lily came back to Tom with a tray of thin sandwiches. Brean ambled heavily toward them.

"You shouldn't let one man have more than his just amount of time with you," he said to Lily. His voice bore down, insistent as it was indifferent.

"Perhaps I'm paying a debt."

"Pay it and be rid of him. All Sebastians are unforgivable creditors."

Lily said: "What makes you so sure?"

"I know the breed," said Brean. "I'm sixty-five and Henry Sebastian and I fought each other as long as breath lasted in him. Tom here is a polite man but he's hard as his dad. I think this is the first time since 1905 I have spoken to a Sebastian." He looked casually at Tom. "I'm disposed to let old dogs sleep."

"Let them sleep then," said Tom, civilly.

A soundless chuckle erupted from Brean's vast diaphragm. "I was curious to know if a Sebastian ever changed. They do not, I see. Let me wish you luck." He turned definitely away.

Tom Sebastian lifted his glass to drink the last of the amber liquor, glance narrowly striking across the rim toward Ed Brean's rolling back. Lily observed his sudden, concentrated attention.

"You are, as he said, rather unforgiving," she reflected.

"Where would I learn charity or mercy?"

It was almost harshly said. He recognized it and at once smiled the abruptness away and accepted the sandwich she silently offered. The crowd had turned unaccountably noisy and a girl in a far corner laughed in a high, shrill voice, that raked him like a file. These people moved restlessly, pointlessly around. Judge Sillavan sat on a divan, cigar between his fingers; he seemed to be seeing distant images. Talk eddied out toward Tom in disconnected fragments.

"Frankie and Johnny's a dead song now. It was sung to shreds. Nobody's written a good new dirty song for ages."

"Dirty songs aren't written. They grow. They're the folk tales of the waterfront and red light districts. Trouble is, all the nice people have thoroughly raided the sewers—and the sewers can't produce enough to keep the nice people entertained."

"Bill, don't be philosophical. You can't handle it."

"Who's the new blonde in town? The one with the wolfhound?"

"Probably figured she'd better shake the guy if he was going in for dog gifts."

Jay Stuart, over there in the middle of all this, suddenly cut through it and came beside Lily. "So this is the party you put on for me?"

"I'm paying a debt of kindness," Lily said. "These people have been nice to me. In return, I show them what they want to see. Which is Jay Stuart, whom they once applauded on the screen."

"You're spoiling their illusions."

"You cut a fine figure wherever you go, Jay."

Over by the fireplace Kit Christopher was listening to Ed Brean, but her glance kept roving to Lily; and then she served Brean his own formula by suddenly moving away from him, leaving him with his gesturing hand half lifted. She said to Tom: "Your big friend is a very excellent monologist."

Jay Stuart shook his head at Lily. "I didn't come here to cut a figure."

"Why did you come? You haven't told me the truth yet."

Jay put his cocktail glass before his eyes and tapped the rim of it. His bland skeptic smile touched Lily with a personal effect. "Here's to our private fortunes, Lily. Here's to what we now know, and to what we'll know tomorrow. May we continue to be good for each other."

Lily said, instantly, "What does that mean, Jay?"

But he took her arm. "You're neglecting your guests, my dear," he said, and led her across the room. The crowd closed around her.

Sebastian grunted, "Wait," to the passing Hannah, and got a fresh drink from the tray. He wheeled and went out to the porch, mouth pressed into narrow shape. Posted there, with his back to the door, he didn't hear Kit come along till she spoke and drew him half around.

"When you are angry," she said, "your face gets black as night."

He didn't answer. Kit's hand fell on his shoulder and its pressure was definite. She spoke again, quite gently: "You are an individualist. So you should let other people be individualists, too. How do you suppose girls like Lily get ahead in pictures? She worked four years as an extra girl until Jay saw her. It was Jay that gave her the chance to go ahead. That's the bargain between them, and whatever Jay may have meant by his toast is their own affair."

He said: "Kit—" in a grating voice, and was stopped by her impatient interruption.

"Why should men always be so romantically minded about women? Be realistic for one moment at least! Lily is free and she has courage to dare. Why should you show so much moral shock if she has already struck a bargain with her career?" She went back into the house with a quick whirl of her picturesque body. She crossed the room and turned down the hall toward the kitchen and her glance, in passing, touched Jay Stuart. In the kitchen she drew herself a glass of water. Jay came in. He closed the door.

"Jay," she said swiftly, "you are the smoothest creature alive. If there was something between them it is dead now."

"My little speech?"

"It hit home. You knew he was too masculine a creature not to be outraged by what you implied, didn't you?"

"Did he say so?"

"I sank the knife a little deeper. We shall have Lily out of here soon."

He grinned and went from the kitchen, Kit following. Lily's glance crossed to her, openly curious, but Kit's manner was superbly unrevealing. The phone rang and Judge Sillavan rose from the divan. He went to the phone and bent his head soberly down. The talk fell off as he said, "Yes?"

On the porch, Sebastian drank his highball in one breath and carefully set the glass on the porch rail. He murmured, "I suppose that's it," and turned into the room. The crowd had quit talking. Judge Sillavan was uncomfortably bent over the phone, listening carefully. After a long interval he spoke a few brief, meticulously exact words. "I'm sorry, George, but it was only a thin chance anyhow. Yes, I'll take care of it. You had better come back by plane." He hung up. He swung about, running his fingers through his unruly white hair. He saw Sebastian in the doorway and made a small, tired gesture.

"I didn't want to say anything till I knew the worst. You've just taken another bad fall, my boy. Along with a lot of the rest of us. Your bank won't open in the morning."

Sebastian said, evenly: "Was that George Grannatt talking?"

The impressionable crowd wasn't making a sound. Lily stood against a wall and showed a deep concern. But it was strange that he should also see concern just now in Kit Christopher's dark eyes. It puzzled him unaccountably.

He said: "That's all right, I guess, John. I felt it coming."

Sillavan said, gruffly, "You knew your money was going down the spout, so why did you stick by the bank?" He stared at Sebastian and then added: "It's something almost dead in the world—loyalty."

Ed Brean moved away from the fireplace. He said: "Sebastians are like that. I wish you luck, Tom." He bowed briefly at the crowd and left the room.

Chapter 7

Sillavan's announcement killed the party. After the guests had gone Sebastian went to the porch and waited for the Hollywood people to collect themselves for the return to Barrier. When Sillavan, last to pay his respects to his hosts, came from the bungalow Sebastian stopped him.

"Something's been on my mind all day," he said. "According to rumor Dad was killed by a man who surrendered his gun and then jumped back into the brush to get a rifle. I had the same trick pulled on me this morning. Was it Humboldt who shot Dad?"

"No."

"Well, Humboldt got the idea from somebody. It ties in."

"Where's Humboldt now?"

Sebastian said quietly: "Don't worry about the bank business. I'll squeeze through. We can live off Barrier's surplus fat for a little while."

Sillavan struck a match ostensibly for his cigar, but he lifted the light so that his sharp old eyes might read Sebastian's face. The glow died; a moment afterward he said: "The game always was rough. It's getting rougher. Nowadays the crooks use the law against honest people."

"As for the bank," repeated Sebastian, "I'll make out."

"You're broke. A big outfit can't run without ready cash."

"I'll sell off some beef for pocket expenses."

"Providing you can collect the beef," pointed out Sillavan. "You may suddenly find that difficult to do."

"I know. But why do you suppose I've been keeping thirty-two tough hands on the place."

Sallavan said: "You have no legally recognized heirs. If you die you leave a crippled outfit that will sell for a song under the hammer to the highest bidder. It is exactly the sort of a situation one certain man wishes to bring about."

"Buffalo? No, he's not big enough to swing it himself. His breeches are paid for by somebody. Who?"

It was Sillavan's turn to be evasive. "To my knowledge you have made no will. It is high time you did so, naming the proper person to inherit Barrier."

"Who would that be?" grunted Sebastian.

Sillavan said bluntly: "Your natural son, Tommy," and went down the street without waiting for an answer.

Kit, coming out of the doorway, found Sebastian rooted stiffly in his tracks. His lips were turned down at the corners as though he had been physically hurt.

The aloof and utter sureness of this woman broke. Her words were uncharacteristically hurried. "I don't believe in anything you stand for. I hate the philosophy that draws a line between men and women. I hate man's strength and man's obtuseness. I hate the whole bizarre nonsense of hair-shirt fortitude."

"Why waste your energy? You'll soon be gone from here, back to a world that suits you better."

She caught her breath. She was roused, she was oddly angry. "I tell you I hate it! Yet I admire you more right now than I have admired any man."

"Be consistent," he said irritably.

Her voice slid from its high tone down to a strange, humble gentleness. "Women can never be consistent, Tom."

"All of you seem to know pretty well what you want."

"Do we?" she said. "Perhaps. And perhaps we get what we want, too. But it never seems to be what we hoped for."

"You expect too much."

She said dimly: "That's why I admire you. You're not always a pleasant man. But you don't dream of impossible things and you don't cry over spilled milk. If I have hurt you tonight I'm so deeply sorry."

"Let it ride," he said and turned down the steps. The rest of the party came out and got into the car, Lily taking her accustomed place beside him. They rolled through Reno and struck rapidly across the dark desert.

Ed Brean, after leaving the party, drove his car around Reno and fell into the highway leading east and later turned down a plain dirt road about three miles from town. He stopped and snapped off the lights and eased his heavy body back in the seat, slowly pulling on his cigar; and to amuse himself he tuned in the radio set on a Los Angeles program. It was perhaps ten minutes afterward when a car swept out of the east at a roaring speed and slowed for the side road. Brean bent and snapped his headlights on and off in signal. The second car drove directly beside Brean's.

"You're late," said Brean, "and I'm no hand to wait on people."

Buffalo Galt leaned out of the car door. "It's a long drive from Tumpah."

"You talk a lot but you don't do much. If you can't handle it I'll get somebody that can."

"Well, this thing is tough," said Galt, openly irritated. "Sebastian's a hard nut. We had a jag of his beef on the way north last night. He got up there in a hell of a hurry and Duke DePard didn't feel like making a fight about it and pulled away in a hurry. Star Humboldt's missing—we heard some shooting in the hills."

Brean said quickly: "Sebastian and Humboldt?"

"I think so. But what of it? You can't lay anything on Sebastian and make it stick before judge or jury. Not up there."

"So it's getting rough and you're squawking?"

"Cut it out, Ed. You're safe in Reno, havin' a high old time. I guess you've forgotten what sort of country that is up yonder. The boys play marbles for keeps."

"They always did," reflected Brean. "Hell, the only fun I ever had was when I was a kid ridin' the desert. I was there when King Henry ruled the roost. You had to have a passport when you got within forty miles of the Moonstones. If you managed to get across Barrier into Oregon you were lucky. I crawled across that ranch one year on my belly, horse shot and water gone, all the way from Hermione Peak to Tumpah with King Henry and fifty men looking for me. When Henry Sebastian personally went after a man, Buffalo, it was something to tell the relatives about afterwards. Don't squawk to me about that country."

"Well," said Galt sullenly, "it ain't changed any."

"You go back there and get busy. Sebastian's broke. I want the screws put on. Don't bring me any more stories of bad luck."

"Sebastian ain't going to sit still," said Galt.

"Use your own judgment," stated Brean, and laid his heavy eyes on Galt. "The sky's the limit."

"Maybe," said Galt. "And maybe not. I'm not bothered about Lot McGinnis. But what happens if the governor gets interested and sends some special officers up there?"

"Who's going to ask for state help? Sebastian won't and McGinnis won't. Don't worry about it. If somebody finally does yell for protection it will be after we've put in our licks anyhow."

"You're a damned cold man, Ed."

"I learned my trade in a tough school. God hates a piker, and I know what I want. Get goin'."

A long, low machine roared down the near-by highway, its tail lights soon vanishing in the distance. Galt said: "That's Sebastian, travelin' like a bat out of hell, as usual."

"Get goin'," repeated Brean and slumped back in his seat. Galt drove away. Brean tuned in on a radio program again and listened for a while, then swung his machine toward Reno.

Past midnight Sebastian and the Hollywood people walked into the Barrier living room. Charm, obviously troubled, rose from the divan and walked to Sebastian.

"Matt started for Tumpah after dinner."

She had her hands behind her back. But when Sebastian said, "What for?" she brought them forward, offering him a newspaper. It was the Tumpah weekly—Blagg's paper—and Sebastian guessed the trouble before his eyes struck the heavily leaded editorial centered on the front page.

It is high time the people of this section take issue with the blood-sucking creature that has been feeding on the prosperity of all of us for better than seventy years. Maybe others are afraid to speak out. We are not. We mean Barrier ranch.

There it lies, grasping the best lands of the district, spreading out year by year without mercy for the little fellows. Oh, yes, we are aware that Barrier buys its lands nowadays instead of stealing them from the government as in olden times. The transactions are all properly recorded. Barrier pays a grateful Sam Jones for Sam's range and Sam humbly takes his pittance and moves away from the soil he lived on thirty years or so.

You say Sam sold of his own free will? You know better. Sam sold because Barrier forced him to. Sam, and a lot of Sams, sold because Barrier beef kept getting on his grass and stripping it. Sam sold because the fear of God was put into him. He never knew when a bunch of Barrier hands might drive him off his own place and rip up his fences. Sure Sam sold. You'd sell too if you had a gun muzzle stuck at your face day and night till it broke your spirit.

We hear Mr. Sebastian is not happy over the fact that some of his cattle are being rustled by big, bold bandits. Now isn't that too bad? Why doesn't our magnificent baron call out the militia, move all the little fellows into Oregon so they won't bother him? Why not convert Tumpah into one of Barrier's minor line camps?

The trouble with this section is that it has lost its grip. The name Sebastian has ground fear and hatred into it. This country might be fair and prosperous, full of independent ranches. Tumpah might be the paved and extensive metropolis it was meant to be. Why isn't it? Because Barrier has absorbed every penny of profit from the land and gone its own high-handed way.

Mr Sebastian sits in his palatial mansion, in his polished boots, entertaining California guests and putting on his domineering airs while the little fellows eat dirt. It's a very swell place, that mansion, with an extremely good-looking housekeeper who doesn't happen to be married to Mr. Sebastian. We hear the child is three years old now. Its name is Tommy. Mr. Sebastian's name is also Tom. Now isn't that a coincidence?

How long are people going to endure this octopus? By the way, isn't it queer how some men not in Barrier's good graces disappear? What, incidentally, has become of Star Humboldt?

Sebastian slowly folded the paper together and looked down into Charm's pale face. "I'm sorry, Charm. I know it hurts you."

"Not the part about me," she answered. "But what he said about you—it's nothing but a lie!"

"Blagg has asked for a whipping," he said, heavily, "and he'll get one."

"That's what Matt said when he left. That's why he left."

"I told him to stay out of Tumpah." He jerked up his head, and saw Gath standing unobtrusively in the background. Gath said:

"He didn't go straight for Tumpah. He took the schoolhouse road."

Sebastian thought about that, mouth hardening. He said, more to himself than to the others, "I don't see what's over there to interest him." The Hollywood people made a loose group in the middle of the room. They were all watching Sebastian intently.

"I'll have to find him before he gets into trouble," decided Tom, and Lily unexpectedly went to him.

"Take me along—please."

"Lily," protested Kit Christopher. "No."

"Please," said Lily. "I won't be in your way."

He said, "Come along," briefly, and walked out. They crossed the porch and got into the car. A man ran out of a bunkhouse at the sound of the starting motor, but Sebastian turned the car around the house into the schoolhouse road running away to a flat, shadowy southwest. Sebastian settled back against the seat. He glanced at Lily.

"Why?" he said.

"Do you always need exact answers?"

They ran along silently through the sharp blackness gripping the desert. Heat was out of the earth; the pungent night air contained a biting chill. To the left Lily saw a lone far light move gently like the riding light of a ship. Except for that they were lost in space and there was again for her that powerful feeling of lonely mystery. Those stars glinting down through a time that had neither beginning nor end. What was pride and ambition? The glow of these little personal fires was as nothing against that immovable light which had shone upon the earth's first boiling lava; her life was one short beat in the long pulse of the universe; and if that were true then nothing mattered in this brief flicker people called living but a moment of happiness grasped before breath stopped. Ambition died and glory and fame vanished. One thing alone remained, as constant as the stars—the love of a man and a woman.

They stopped at the schoolhouse, Sebastian searching the yard with his spotlight. They went on, deeper into the southeasterly dark. Over there the vague shadow of hills began to swell against the thinner black of the desert. Sebastian spoke.

"You're far away from me right now."

"Thinking."

Sometimes the mood of this man was a force that pushed her away. Sometimes, as suddenly now, it reached out and held her as definitely as though his arms were around her. His voice was extraordinarily gentle. "Lily, don't always be logical. Thinking will do for a while, and then thinking ceases to be any good and only makes you suffer."

"What's left then?"

"Answer your heart. That's enough."

"Tom, where did you learn that?"

He said: "I have had to live with my thoughts a good deal. So I know how useless thinking can be. One honest emotion is worth a year of being sensible."

"You can be badly hurt by following your heart, Tom."

"You're going to get hurt either way. What of it?"

There was, directly afterwards, a faltering of the car's rapid run. The engine spat irregularly beneath the hood, resumed rhythm, and faltered again. Sebastian cut the ignition switch instantly, letting momentum carry them the last possible foot.

"Gas," he said, and got out. "That panel gauge must be stuck."

He went to the rear and she heard him knocking around the tank. He came back and turned on the spotlight, tilting it toward the running board. He unscrewed a red container from a rack and held its mouth into the light and then went back to the rear. In a little while he replaced the container and got in the car, sitting there with his hands idly on the wheel.

"What, Tom?"

"Wasn't more than two quarts in the container. Top wasn't screwed tight and it evaporated. The Winnemucca-Tumpah road's about five miles ahead, but we won't make it. No travel on it this time of night anyhow. So—"

He had to hold the starter down a considerable time to pump gas into the carburetor. When the engine caught on he went forward in low gear for a little while. Presently she felt the car swing from the road into another one, less smooth. The thick shadows ahead at once marched up from the foreground and closed around them; they were climbing through a ravine with stiff walls to either side.

"This hill sticks up like a sore thumb. Schoolhouse road circles it to hit the Winnemucca highway. We're shortcutting over the hill."

The hill wasn't very high but the road went twisting from point to point quite steeply. Somewhere short of the summit, in a moderately level area, Sebastian pulled aside and turned the headlights on a board shanty sitting beneath a solitary pine. "Might make the top and coast down to the main road," he said. "But it's too late at night to catch anybody traveling through, and this car's no good for sleeping." Sitting there he raised his voice. "Hey, Bill! Wake up." Then, waiting for an answer he added a quieter explanation for Lily's benefit.

"Bill Fell's an old prospector. Came into this country after the San Francisco fire with one truck and a broken heart. He lost his family in the fire. Made him queer. But he's all right. He's not home, or he'd be out here by now. Let's go in."

They left the machine. Sebastian opened the shanty door and went ahead, and in a moment he had found and lighted a lamp. There wasn't much to the place. A built-in bunk held one side of the room, a sheetiron stove and small table occupied the other. A chair and a trunk completed the list of furniture. Everything else was arranged on pegs sunk into a wall covered by newspapers; but all articles had an exact place and the room was neat. Sebastian took a dipper and tasted the water standing in a bucket by the stove. "Fresh," he commented. "Bill probably pulled out for the hills this evening. Notice that trunk. In all the years I've known Bill I've never seen it opened or moved. He told me once that when he died he wanted it burned before he was buried."

He went out to cut the car lights. His arm touched the horn button and a hard current of sound poured across the night. Lily sat on the quilted bed and rested her back against the wall. Sebastian came in again. He lighted a cigarette. "You sleep here. I'll roll up outside with a couple of blankets I carry in the car."

Lily said: "How sad to think that most of this man's life lies inside that faded old trunk."

"Well, he had his happiness for a little while. That's more than some of us can say."

"Yes," she murmured. "He had a little. And the memory of that little is enough to carry him along now." She raised her eyes to him. "Like the scent of perfume that remains when the bottle is empty."

"Which is real—the perfume or the scent we remember?"

"Don't be bitter."

"I don't know the answer, Lily," he said, almost humble.

Her voice dropped lower. "You and I are too much alike. We fight against the pressure of life and our feelings make us strike rashly and sometimes foolishly."

"I told you we were not mild people."

Her fingers ran idly along the patch-patterned quilt. She didn't look up. "You wanted to know why I came along tonight. Well, in Reno this afternoon I caught Hollywood again. At five o'clock today a career looked desirable; then you came and I wasn't sure. I wanted to come along with you on this trip to see if the sensation lasted. I'm being frank with you. If you have the power to change my mind like that,

Tom, I can't be sure Lily Tennant will ever be ruthless enough to climb to stardom."

He said, extremely blunt: "I think you made your decision on that in Hollywood some time ago."

Her head came up and her eyes absorbed his face. She said quietly: "Jay?"

He only lifted and lowered his shoulders; there was a ruffled look about him. Lily straightened herself against the wall. "That's another thing I'm curious about. You heard Jay's toast. He suggested certain intimate things. Do you believe them?"

"Lily," said Sebastian, "I told you you'd make whatever bargains that had to be made if you wanted a career badly enough."

She wasn't satisfied. "Would it matter to you if I have made them?"

His answer was barren. "No." Then: "But if you've made them you'd be a fool to turn back now. That makes your bargains useless and leaves you regretting something given for nothing."

Her eyes showed a half-startled expression that he didn't want to see. He turned and dipped himself another drink of water. Lily's words came over his shoulder, soft and wistful.

"Men can never be different than they have always been—about that one thing."

He turned. "I'm trying to keep out of your way. All I could bring you is grief."

The languor of physical fatigue showed itself in her heavy lids, in the higher color of her cheeks. She sat purely relaxed against the wall, her body graceful and careless. Her self-sufficiency had deserted that door which hid the wilder and more vital spirit lying within. He saw it—a bright fire burning in a deep place—and then the sense of it was in the room, unsettling both of them, waking recklessness.

She saw his face clearly express what he felt. She rose at once, quicker breathing unsteadying her talk. "The truth is, Tom, I'm afraid of you. I'm afraid of you because I want to go on with my career. I don't want that interrupted. I wish—I wish we could kill whatever romantic illusion there is between us."

He said, "You don't kill things like that, Lily," with a gusty intonation and took a step forward. Light glowed across the chestnut hair and the scent of perfume lifted its intangible lure. He dropped his cigarette and watched her eyes lift and observe him. The expression in them was something he couldn't read, but the deep fire there still glowed. There was no help for this, no way of stopping it. He put his arm around her shoulders and bent his stubborn head and the full wild sweetness of this girl's lips thundered through him. Her arm steadied itself, without resisting pressure, on his elbow. The room was without a shred of sound.

He pulled himself away, the savage satisfaction in him overriding one small thought of regret. Her lips were faintly apart and her smile went clear through him and seemed to see some strange wonder beyond.

"That's all of it, Tom. You had every bit of me then, but it will never happen again. I'm going back to Hollywood tomorrow. While I have one single sane impulse left I'm going to get away from you."

He said: "I don't understand you, Lily."

Her voice vibrated with feeling. "I do—very clearly. You're a wild man and your kiss hurt me physically. It was something like glory. But glory doesn't last. That hunger which hurts us so much doesn't last. I think we've had the best of it just now. We had better stop there. So that we may have something worth remembering."

"I don't understand," he repeated.

"I'm desperately trying to be realistic about this."

She was still smiling. He turned sharply and left the room, drawing the door behind him.

When she came from the shanty a strong fresh sunlight poured down the slopes of the bare hill. The brief coolness of the night had already gone; day's heat was beating in. Sebastian sat on the running board, smoking a cigarette. He got up immediately.

"I walked down to the Winnemucca road and flagged some gas from a fellow going by. We can get breakfast back on the ranch or rummage some bacon and coffee from Bill's cupboard."

She didn't want to go back into the shanty. She didn't want to be inside those four walls with him after the scene of the night before. What she feared was anticlimax. "Let's not eat here, Tom!" she said, and got into the machine.

He took his place, started the engine and followed the grade to its near-by summit. They tipped over it then and rolled a mile and a half to the Winnemucca highway. Here Sebastian swung north. "We'll hit Tumpah first and have a look. You never saw a town living on nothing but its past. Tumpah's a place like that."

He was quite cheerful. She had feared he wouldn't understand how ridiculous the conversation of the night before could be made to sound if precipitately resumed. But he did understand. He was, in his fashion, ignoring the scene, leading away to surer ground.

They left the solitary hill behind, aiming for a clump of poplars at the base of a higher and more continuous line of hills not far away. "Behold," he said. "There's Tumpah, behind the trees. Nothing keeps it from turning to dust but the preservative effects of sunlight."

They were almost immediately slowing down at a sharp curve that led them into a main street. Sebastian stopped before a garage pump and waited for a man to come laggardly out of the place. The man said, "How are you, Tom," and went to the back of the car. He was, as far as Lily could see, the only citizen abroad at this hour of the day. The garageman filled the gas tank and came forward. Sebastian paid the bill.

"Matt Strang been here?"

"Last night," said the man. Then he said, "But Blagg wasn't around so Matt started home."

"Which is a relief to me."

The garageman lowered his voice. "If I was you, Tom, I'd not dally here this morning."

"That's all right."

"No," said the garageman, "it ain't."

Sebastian nodded and drove on. Beyond the street-end the road curved to skirt a detached, two-story structure that held on its surface a faded sign: "Gilson's House."

"A hotel?" asked Lily.

"Yes," he said.

"I wonder if I might have a glass of water."

He pulled the car abreast of the porch and stopped. Lily started to get out, but Sebastian shook his head. "I'll bring it to you."

"I'm really curious to see what such a place looks like inside."

"Not this place," he said. "It isn't that kind of hotel."

She said calmly: "I've heard that Nevada has its own system of morals. So that's it?"

In stepping from the car his coat skirts swung back and she saw, in quick surprise, the gunbelt at his waist, with its holstered weapon slung below the right hip. It was the first time she had seen him wear a gun. And so, watching him cross the porch of Madame Belle Gilson's place and go through a door that closed behind him, a slow pulse of fear ran along her nerves. It was, she suddenly recalled, a hundred and forty miles from Reno, with the tremendous and empty horizons isolating this lonely corner of the state from the orderly world. Something moved across the extreme corner of her vision; turning, she saw a small slender man walk rapidly from a near-by shed and duck into Gilson's back door.

Inside Madame's big barroom, Sebastian put his back to the door and let his eyes sweep the half-darkness. The front windows were painted green to allow no light in at all; little sunshine got through back windows scummed up with tobacco smoke and spilled liquor. It was this reeking, sour odor that tainted the dead air. In a moment his vision cleared enough to show him a man asleep on the floor in a far corner; the fellow's face was turned away.

He had never trusted the place. Belle Gilson was all right—in fact, he liked the bold, trumpet-voiced, eccentric old lady. Madame's word was her bond, both for honest men and for crooks. She told no tales. She was a law unto herself, a landmark of an older Nevada. The younger generation indignantly convicted her by her own manifest record and to this conviction the older people of the state agreed reluctantly. Yet when these older ones saw her they said, "There's Belle," with a softness that contained no malice, and their memories went tracing backward. To the turn of the century and before, when they had all been young and Nevada was new and the world was fresh and robust.

Still alert, Sebastian studied the room. Somebody moved across the floor above him, ceiling telegraphing the strain on the old boards. The sleeping man hadn't stirred. At the far left corner a stairway ran upward; the bar held the right side of the place, with two doors at either end of it leading to a kitchen in the rear. Behind this once impressive mahogany bar stood a back bar. Stepping forward Sebastian caught his own image darkly in its yellow glass. He called out the name of Madame's handy man.

"Hey—Nick. Come in here."

It disturbed the sleeper on the floor; he turned and kicked his boots against the wall. Sebastian called again, "Nick," and slapped his hand on the mahogany. The erstwhile sleeper got up. He grumbled: "What the hell's the noise for?"

Sebastian cut around on his heels and stared. The man's face livened up; his eyes were at once careful. He was one of Buffalo's men and he didn't like what he saw.

Sebastian said: "How are you, Dode?" imperturbably.

"Yeah," said Dode Cramp and licked his lips.
"Did I trouble you the other night beyond Camp Four?"
"Who—me?"
Sebastian heard the door at the south end of the bar—now back of him—come open. A man walked through and Sebastian said, supposing it was Nick, "Get me a drink of water, please, Nick." He had no desire to let Dode Cramp get beyond his survey. But the feel of the place turned increasingly bad and he noticed Cramp's face swing over to the newcomer and bloom with relief. Sebastian's supposition died right then. He took his elbow off the bar and put his back to it and thus rolled himself gingerly around, to keep Cramp within his vision and embrace the new man as well. It wasn't Nick.

Ben DePard stood there, one hand still on the door knob. His shoulder had been swinging forward and he was about to extend his other hand to the corner of the bar. But he stopped, and was careful not to let his arms drop quickly. It put him in an awkward position. Bad as the light was, Sebastian noticed shrewdness gather in Ben's childish eyes. The man was too simple to tie his own shoes; but he was a wicked fighter.

"Nick ain't here," said Ben. "What do you want?"
"Glass of water. Never mind, I'll get it myself."
The faucet was behind the bar, which was a logical reason for Sebastian to move. Neither Ben not Dode had yet quite made up their minds. They understood the chance they had and their thoughts were working through it slowly. But uncertainty clung to them. Ben's glance kept moving from Sebastian to Cramp. Cramp stared at Sebastian with an unrelaxed vigilance. It would stay like that a very little while longer, Sebastian knew. One of them would turn reckless. Coldly considering it, standing on the outside of the bar, halfway to either end and exposed to both men, he made his choice. He could move toward Ben DePard and thus put his back to Cramp for an instant, or he could retreat and gain the far end of the bar, keeping both within his vision. But to back up was to indicate weakness—the one thing these men waited for.

He said: "Pass me that glass near your right hand, Ben," and walked toward the man. The order completely filled the narrow channel of Ben's brain. He swung aside dutifully and his fist closed about the glass. It was six good steps to the end of the bar and Sebastian made three of them uncontested. Cramp was over on his right, momentarily out of his vision.

Sweat pricked through the pores of Sebastian's forehead and stung him. And then another voice said coolly:

"Let him get his own drink of water, Ben."

It came from the stairway and it wasn't Cramp's voice. Sebastian felt it slice down his back. He gritted his teeth and took two more steps and turned and put both hands on the bar's edge and pushed himself gently around the corner and halted. He hadn't reached the back side of the bar—Ben DePard blocked his way—but his body rubbed the bar's end and in that position he took his stand, all three men in view. DePard was directly at his right hand, near enough to touch. Cramp stood out in the middle of the room, on his left. The third man was at the far corner of the room, halfway down the stairs.

This one was high-built and thin, with silver hair on a hatless head and a pale dry face like that of a lunger. The man came down the steps quietly and placed his back to the wall. But his body remained straight and his right palm lay flat on his hip.

"I don't know you," said Sebastian.

The silver-haired man made no answer. Sebastian said, more bluntly: "You'd better be sure of this before you get into it."

The other raised and dropped his shoulder quietly; and through the half-gloom, Sebastian made out an odd expression of amusement. Sebastian understood immediately. The man was dying of disease and didn't care what happened.

Motionless, coldly attentive, Sebastian felt the swing of their tempers. They had been uncertain, but they were no longer so; they knew now they would get him. One by one he checked off his chances and discarded them. The street door was too far away. The door leading back to the kitchen was two paces to his right, but as remote as China with Ben DePard at his side. The breast-high bar's end partially protected him against a straight-on shot from the silver-haired stranger. Ben DePard was handicapped by being too near. But over on the left, Dode Cramp waited in calculating stillness for the break. A clear shot was possible from that quarter. It was, Sebastian knew, his weakest angle.

Cramp said: "Ben, what are you doing there? Walk away from him."

Ben started to move down the bar. "Stay in your tracks," snapped Sebastian.

Ben went steel-stiff; he pulled himself around until he was square with Sebastian. His thin face was as thoughtful as the face of a man reading some difficult paragraph in a book; it held that studious, fully centered expression.

Cramp's voice sailed flatly through the room. "Go ahead, Ben."

But Ben DePard's unbalanced mind had tipped once and would not tip again. The ferret gleaming in his eyes grew more pronounced, and for Sebastian the tale was being plainly told. Ben would break first. Thus warned, Sebastian placed the weight of his attention on the little man, crowding Cramp to the extreme corner of his vision; the silver-haired stranger was nothing but a shadow across the length of the room. It was the best he could do.

He rubbed his belly against the bar gently, thus pushing the skirts of his coat farther back from the gun holster. He let both hands remain on the edge of the bar, but all the pressure of his body began to flow into his left arm, with which he presently meant to throw himself around the corner of the bar toward DePard and away from Cramp.

Cramp said: "Look, Sebastian—"

Ben DePard's teeth clicked together; his hand dropped. He was fast but it was the click of his teeth that hit Sebastian's cocked nerves and put him in motion. Ben DePard's forearm swept down and up in a single motion. Sebastian fired from his place at the bar's end and lunged on against the little man. The smell of powder flowed unpleasantly into the dead air. Hard detonating waves of sound expanded through the room, cracking into the walls. Upstairs a woman screamed. Ben DePard's little face lost the coherence of a human being; all expression on it was blurred and mushy. It was a dying man Sebastian's shoulders knocked to the floor. It was a dying man's hands that weakly slapped at Sebastian's legs as he stepped over Ben DePard. His boot heel hit and pinned one of those palms to the boards; he veered and flung a shot at Dode Cramp. It had to be enough, that one shot, for he felt that lead from the silver-haired stranger's gun breathe by him. The glass of the back bar fell with a jangling sound. He saw the stranger standing straight up and down, firing deliberately; he surged forward and pinned his shots on that still target. He had reached the north end of the bar and noticed then that he had wasted his last shot on a blank wall. The stranger was sitting down on the floor with his legs apart, with his head bowed. The man got one arm up and pushed his palm outward in Sebastian's direction, with a gesture of defeat. A lane of light suddenly crossed the floor and touched him, and Sebastian whirled to see Dode Cramp duck through the street door.

Madame Belle Gilson's voice howled down the stairs.

"Stop that—stop that in my place!" Sebastian reached the porch. Cramp was thirty yards away, on a dead run for the shelter of the nearest house. Halted, Sebastian lifted his gun and sighted carefully along it. Cramp threw a backward glance, saw it, and fell flat on his face. Sebastian abruptly pulled his gun down. Sebastian said:

"Stay there, Cramp."

Belle Gilson hurried to the porch, her big washerwoman's arms clutching a violent red silk kimono about her. She said: "Good God, Sebastian! In my place!" But Sebastian saw Lily Tennant standing sick and pale beside the car. He went around and got in the driver's side and waited for her to seat herself. She had forgotten to close the door and he reached over and pulled it shut, and looked back at the prone Cramp. Belle Gilson called out: "Never come to Tumpah alone again, Tom! You fool, Buffalo set that trap!"

"Madame," said Sebastian, "tell Buffalo I'm coming after him," and drove away.

Chapter 8

Two miles from Barrier Sebastian stopped the car beside a water tank and went over to fill a canteen. He came back to Lily.

"Your drink."

She hadn't said a word all the way from Tumpah and though most of the pallor had gone from her cheeks there was still in her eyes a gathered darkness which seemed to imprison the recent scene. Preoccupied with his own violent afterthoughts he hadn't noticed until now the strain compressing her nerves. She had to unlock her small fists to take the canteen.

He came about the car and got in, and for a moment relaxed there. He was weary to the bone. It made his arm move clumsily as he fished for a cigarette. Dragging in a deep breath of smoke, he rested his elbows on the steering wheel and stared directly ahead.

"I'd like a smoke, too," said Lily.

He got out the cigarettes again. "Sorry," he apologized, and noticed her fingers tremble. He lighted a match for her and had trouble keeping it against the tip of her unsteady cigarette. Her eyes watched him, not the match. And then a long, high breath escaped her and she took the cigarette from her mouth and fell against him. He knocked his smoke away, nearly burning her with it. He put his arms around her shoulders. She wasn't crying—not in the way women usually cried. It was worse than that—a silent, tearless upheaval that shook her body. Her hands, creeping behind his neck, were quite cold. There wasn't anything he could do or say, so he kept still while her fear wore off. Looking down he could see the graceful edge of her chestnut hair against a white, smooth temple. Nothing in the world could check that feeling of satisfaction the nearness of this girl stirred in him.

She pushed herself back and straightened. Her eyes searched him with a strange, personal, possessive quality.

She said: "How do you feel?"

"Like hell."

"I can't describe how you looked when you came out of that door."

"I wasn't in a pretty frame of mind."

"Men inside?"

He said reluctantly: "There were."

"You could have killed the one running. You didn't."

"Because he was running. This thing will be dirty enough without that."

"Will be? Isn't it over, Tom?"

"I told you the other night Barrier was fighting for its life."

"It—it doesn't seem possible. Last night we sat around a table in Reno. And now, it's this."

"Reno's a hundred and forty miles away. It's sixty years away. Nothing has come here to change us in all that time. This is cattle country—beef and land and water, and men quarreling over those things.

"People die or move out, nobody new comes in, the distance between ranches gets longer, and the desert has fewer travelers. Nothing changes our ways. Reno's only a spot on the map far off, and the desert and hills shut us in."

She said nothing for a moment. Sebastian lighted another cigarette, feeling better. Sitting with one shoulder touching him, she seemed to feed strength into him. Her presence filled his mind, pushing Tumpah far back into his head.

"Tom," she said, not looking up, "do you want me?"

"Yes."

"Rather badly?"

"You knew that last night in the shanty."

"I have been too long with you to get away. Your fortune is my fortune. I found that out twenty minutes ago in front of that hotel. I can't do anything about it. I'd be a fool to try."

He said slowly: "You want to stay?"

"I noticed the faces of the older women at the dance the other night. They seemed so weathered and patient—so resigned. Will I get that way?"

"Patient, perhaps. The land slows all of us down. We can't go faster than it goes. But I don't think you saw much unhappiness there, Lily."

"I don't ask a guarantee of happiness."

"You'll never be resigned. Life runs too fast in you."

She lifted her head. "I want you, Tom. If you want me, that's all there is to it."

He bent a little and put his broad palm behind her head, pulling her forward. He kissed her, in the manner of a man forcing himself to savor water gently after being starved for it. Then he turned and started the car and drove toward Barrier. He had nothing more to say.

Lily let her arm lie quietly on his shoulder, watching his profile. A puzzled expression clouded her eyes. His kiss had answered for him, yet there was in it a reservation she didn't understand.

They were soon in the Barrier yard. Lily went into the house immediately. Sebastian drove to the end of the plaza and left the machine. He called out, "Gath," and didn't see the little man around. He entered the adjoining stable. Matt Strang turned out of an empty stall with a queer, rash haste. He stopped in front of Sebastian.

"Matt," said Sebastian. "What's wrong with you?"

But he knew what was wrong. The old bitterness was burning through Strang's mind again, turning him wild. He laced his hands behind his back and spoke savagely.

"You saw what Blagg wrote about Charm, didn't you?"

"Yes."

"If I could have found him in Tumpah last night I'd have killed him."

"It's well you didn't find him," grunted Sebastian. Weariness was a heavy thing on his shoulders; all the snap was out of him. The scene he dreaded was here, and he couldn't summon up the will he needed to swing the foreman back to sanity.

"You take it pretty calm," ground out Strang. "By God, Tom, I don't understand you!"

"I can wait."

"Wait!" shouted Strang. "That's all you do is wait! There ain't no time for waiting! Not when a thing like that's been said. This ranch used to take care of its injuries and it used to put the fear of God into the crooks! You've gone soft and the ranch is no good any more."

"Be a little careful, Matt."

"Do I have to stand here and tell you to your face you've turned yellow?"

Sebastian's voice rose upward on a thin still note. "Matt—don't cross the line."

"Well," said Strang with a last, headlong rush of violent passion, "I've crossed it and here I am! You and I been friends a long time, which is all that's kept me from calling you to account. I'm through with you, Tom. You've let Barrier go to the dogs. You let Charm waste her life on you, she thinkin' maybe you'll do the thing you ought to do by her. You let her take all the gossip—you let Blagg print what he does about her. The girl's in love with you because she don't know any better. But you know better. To hell with your friendship! I don't want it!"

"Matt—get off Barrier before we regret what we do."

"I'd not regret it," said Strang and held himself dangerously still.

"I would," sighed Sebastian.

"Soft!" breathed Matt Strang, his scorn cutting indescribably through Sebastian. He was carrying the quarrel relentlessly to Sebastian, the flame of his temper burning out his reason.

Sebastian put a hand against the stable wall and steadied himself. "Matt," he said, "you've always been pretty certain you were right in everything you did. It's been black or white, yes or no. Some day maybe you'll find out there's no exact answer to anything in this world. I can't give you the satisfaction of the fight you want. I haven't got the heart for it. So-long."

Strang stared at him with hot, unbelieving eyes; then without another word he walked past Sebastian, into the plaza. Sebastian watched him rush toward a pony tied near the house, climb into the saddle and ride away. Sebastian scrubbed his hand across his face and turned toward the house. The Hollywood crowd loafed in the cool living room but he went by without speaking, on up to his room.

Charm, following him a moment later, found him sitting in a rocker, his smoky eyes pinned to the floor. She stood a moment inside the door, reading the utter fatigue, the bleak loneliness in the man. Then, crossing the room swiftly, she knelt beside the chair and collected his hands against her breast, intense dark face softened by a smile that was strangely maternal. There was a glow to this girl like actual warmth; a receptive depth in which a weary man might find forgetfulness.

"Charm," he said, "you know what it is to be hurt."

"I know you, Tom."

"Yes," he said, "I think you do. You've got a lot of sympathy in you, Charm—"

Her small voice interrupted him. "Sympathy? Tom—Tom—is that all you see? Is it all you feel?"

His long solid lips set. "What's this life for, Charm? I wish I knew."

"If you don't know, how could I?" But she turned one of his palms against her heart and held it there, mysterious eyes eagerly shining. Somewhere in the Bible one of the singers spoke of a woman like her. He thought of this, and heard her speak rapidly again. "But I do know." She pressed his hand more tightly against her heart. "This is what life is for, Tom. What else is any good?"

Timmy Akin went into the dining room and kept Lily company while she ate breakfast. She hadn't seen a great deal of him the last few days and it occurred to her he was not quite the same Timmy. Timmy's soul contained little iron. He was a man destined always to be squiring women about town, pulling out chairs for them, standing gently in the background while others ignored him. But some of the eager deference was gone now. He didn't talk much.

"Having fun, Lily?"

"Isn't it obvious?"

"Yes," he said. "You don't hold back your feelings like Kit does. You show happiness in your eyes."

"Aren't you having a good time?"

"I could stay here forever."

It brought out her slow smile. Timmy's enthusiasm for the new thing was very real while it lasted.

He knew what she was thinking. "I realize I'm the type that tries to fit in any place. The sort that goes to a dull party and tries to convince the host I've had a perfectly swell evening. But this is different." His soberness was quite genuine; it was touched by real regret. "I wish I'd known there was a place like Barrier twenty years ago. If I had I wouldn't be just an errand boy for this or that gal who couldn't find anybody else to fill in the gap."

"Timmy," she said, surprised, "you're the last person I'd ever expect to speak with such disillusion."

"The boy's growing up," he muttered. He got out a sack of tobacco and creased a paper and made quite a ceremony of rolling himself a smoke. It was, she knew, a trick he had learned from the crew. He'd master this novelty and then he'd throw it aside. That was Timmy.

He said: "What about Hollywood?"

"Let's not think of it right now."

He put his elbows on the table and stared at her. "Don't let Jay or anybody else rush you. You do what you damned please. People have been making up my mind for me since I was a kid—and look at me now. I'm nothing much better than a piece of litmus paper that turns from color to color according to what it's dunked in. Don't let 'em do that to you, Lily. Never mind what's proper or right or sensible. Never mind any of the old hokum people use to pull you the way they want. Everybody's scared stiff of Mrs. Grundy. Don't you be."

She studied him over the rim of her coffee cup. "Something wrong between you and Kit?"

"Nothing was ever right between us. I'm just one of the pieces of luggage she carries around. Yeah. 'Miss Christopher arrived at the Mark Hopkins yesterday, with four trunks, three suitcases and Timmy Akin.' "

It was so ridiculous a picture, and yet so remorselessly accurate that she put down her cup and laughed till tears came to her eyes. "Timmy—Timmy!"

A small grin appeared on his face. "That's right, ain't it?" Then he was utterly sober again. "I hope you get what you want. But don't break your heart over it."

"What's that, Timmy?"

He said: "You love that big, tough Sebastian guy. He's gone for you, too—that's a break for both of you because you're both grand people. But be careful, Lily, about letting yourself go. There's lots of angles to this thing."

"Charm?" she said, and only whispered it.

He got up. "Another swell kid. She thinks Sebastian is

Lord Almighty. You don't see that frame of mind in women any more. I guess it must be the heat. Or something. That's what you're getting into. That and the boy. You find out about that boy. It isn't the moral angle. Both you and Sebastian are big enough to step over past mistakes. It's the boy—if Sebastian happens to be his dad."

"If—" she breathed, and rose.

"I guess I'm old-fashioned. But the boy comes first. If he's Tom's son you have no right to be here at all."

Lily stood motionless, thinking of the scene at the cabin. If Tom were the father of that boy, he never would have kissed her that way. "It isn't Tom's boy," she said.

Timmy shrugged. "Maybe yes, maybe no." He turned to leave. "This will entertain you vastly. Kit's that way about Sebastian, too. Didn't know it? Watch her eyes follow Sebastian when you see them together. What a goofy world." And he passed into the living room.

Lily didn't move. It wouldn't be Tom's boy. Yet she suddenly remembered that when they had stopped at the water tank and she had gladly surrendered to him his silence had contained a reservation.

Tumpah's cemetery didn't have a tree on it, for nothing would grow in that metallic soil. So when Ben DePard was buried and the preacher had murmured his rather noncommittal hope that the mercy of God might cover the sins of that forlorn soul, the few men who had straggled up the hill in the wake of the pallbearers now straggled down it to escape the blistering sunlight. Only Duke DePard, Dode Cramp, and the lunger Whitey remained behind.

Dode stayed because he had something on his conscience; Whitey was there to witness the final ending of that bitter saloon episode in which he had played so important a part. It was Duke DePard who alone possessed more than a casual interest in the dead one. Even in a country where singularity of conduct was regarded as nobody's business, the close tie between the DePard boys had been a strange, discussed thing. Duke had watched over his brother with an affection that contained in it a kind of mothering instinct, and Ben had returned this affection with an absolute and single-minded obedience. Such softness as Duke DePard's life contained had been solely expressed on Ben; and his darkly narrow face showed the depths of his feeling now.

"Buffalo," he said morosely, "didn't come."

"Buffalo's across the desert," explained Cramp. "He won't be back till late."

"He could have come," growled Duke. He lifted a clod of dirt, breaking it between his thumbs. "That damned preacher was anxious to say his piece and get away. He didn't have to hurry. Ben's dead and won't bother anybody any more. But he had a little time and a little speech comin' to him today."

The lunger Whitey sat suddenly down on the baked ground. His left arm hung in a sling; disease had made him a pale, drawn man, but Sebastian's bullet had left him feebler than before. He stared up at Duke DePard, his face an utter chalk white. Against that pallor his eyes were like burned-in recesses.

He said, scarcely above a whisper: "Maybe the skypilot couldn't think of much good to say about Ben."

"He could of said a lot more. Ben wasn't bright, but nobody ever gave him a break. The old man beat hell out of him and me till I got big enough to stop that. All he wanted Ben and me for was to use like work horses. The old woman never cared either. I was damned glad when they died. Ben wasn't so good in the head—what of it? He never asked for anything and he never hurt nobody till they hurt him."

Cramp spoke anxiously. "About the fight. I couldn't help Ben a bit. Sebastian was movin' around fast. Ben got his first shot. I was shootin' and not hittin' anything. Whitey here was shootin' and not hittin' anything. Then Whitey dropped and I tell you it was discouragin'. Three of us firin' and nothin' touchin' the man. When Whitey keeled over I knew nobody was going to get Sebastian. So I got out the door. I'd be under the ground right now if I hadn't run. I ain't proud of that, Duke, but I knew the job was too tough to cut. Well, he had me cold in the dust. Why didn't he let me have it?"

"You're not the man I blame," said DePard stolidly.

"Who?" demanded Cramp.

But DePard said: "Why didn't Sebastian try for you outside?"

"I tell you I don't know. He had the gun lined on me—and let the chance go."

"I don't get it," said DePard, scowling his wonder.

"The man never does what you figure. Why did he light on Whitey instead of me, when I was right in the middle of the floor, bangin' away? Something told him I didn't have the shot that was goin' to knock him over. That's the way it worked out, too. It ain't reasonable—it ain't even human. But he knew. He had it doped. You can't hurt a guy like that. Be careful when you go after him."

"Me?"

Cramp and Whitey both stared carefully at DePard. Cramp said: "Well, he got Ben. So you're goin' after him, ain't you?"

Whitey started to say something. The words got caught in his throat and he began to cough in a long, feeble strangling way. He couldn't support himself then; he dropped his shoulders against the ground, fighting for air. The two other men looked down at him with a narrowed, unsentimental interest. "He could of finished you with another shot, too," puzzled DePard. "Why didn't he? I don't get it. Better for you, Whitey, maybe, if he had. You been dyin' for a year."

Cramp bent over, pulling Whitey up. He steadied the man, and they started down the hill.

DePard's eyes followed them all the way through the town and as far as Madame Belle Gilson's door. He crouched on his heels and stared at the fresh dirt covering Ben. The sun was dropping in the west, kicking its bitter light into his face; he pushed his hat forward and sunk his head between his shoulders and began to grind stray clots of earth between his palms.

It was turning dusk when he pulled himself up and moved to the foot of Ben's grave. He took his hat off and pressed his boot against the soft, fresh-shoveled soil.

"Well," he said, "I was the one that brought you into this business, Ben. So it's me that's got the blame for you sleepin' here. We never made any excuses to anybody, but I guess we knew we were on the wrong track. Only it was too late to change. It's too late to change now. There ain't been any fun in it and maybe this is best for you. What do you suppose is best for me?"

He wheeled down the slope, traveling fast. He got his handkerchief and blew his nose and tipped his hat to shade his eyes, though there was no glare in this last clear soft light. There were a few of Buffalo's outfit in the Madame's drinking, but they left him alone when he came in. He had a glass of whiskey. Then Cramp said: "Whitey stood against the wall by the stairs."

DePard went over and stared at two holes puncturing the walls. Cramp came past him and laid his palm on the wall, covering the holes. "Sebastian was running down the bar, but he put 'em that close together. Whitey wasn't standing up then—Whitey was sitting down. But Sebastian didn't seem to see it right away. He put them shots there just the same, two and a half inches apart. Running."

DePard went back through one of the doors beside the bar into a small dining room. Nick brought him a meal. He ate it and returned to the bar. The rest of the gang had gone. Madame Gilson was standing by a table.

"Duke," she said, "what are you going to do?"

"Madame, I don't know."

"I'm no hand to offer you advice. But just remember the doors of hell are always half open and you don't have to push hard to fall."

He said: "The doors to hell are wide open and I've looked in many times."

Madame's old eyes weighed him carefully. "Only a man with a conscience could say that, Duke. You're not as bad and not as crooked as you think."

He had only been polite before. But he raised his head, interest rippling across his face. "You're a wise woman, Madame."

She said: "I've seen a lot of bad men in my time, Duke. Most of them have lived miserably, full of torment. All of them died regretting the day they turned the wrong way." She checked herself, then added brusquely, "My God, I'm getting moral! Don't let Buffalo make a sucker out of you, Duke."

"What's that?" he said, very attentive.

"He'll push you against Sebastian, as he's pushed the others. He'll do the fiddling while you boys dance. You're all fools. How much money have you got to show for the beef you've rustled these last years with Buffalo?"

"Not much, Madame."

"You're all broke but Buffalo. I know, because I carry you all on the books. That's why you're fools. Now you'll ride back to the Barrier hills because Buffalo intends to ruin Sebastian. Some of you won't come back from there. Maybe you'll get Sebastian. What happens then? You think it will be green grass and clover for the rest of your time?"

She stared at him, remaining silent until he said: "Go on, Madame. What happens then?"

"Somebody else will get the ranch. Somebody, I said. But he won't need Buffalo or you any more. So you're through—and just to make sure you understand it he'll shoot you all out of the country. If you think Sebastian's cruel, wait till you see this other fellow run Barrier."

The veins on DePard's forehead began to stand out. He said, softly: "You know a great deal, Madame."

She looked around the room carefully, at the closed doors, at the stairs behind her. "You're only a bunch of stock Buffalo drives where he wants. Humboldt's missing, your brother's gone. Who started this war—Sebastian or Buffalo? Use your head, Duke." She watched him and gauged his temper and drove her last contemptuous words through his pride. "But you'll go after Sebastian, because you're just a monkey on Buffalo's stick."

She went up the stairs. In her room she lighted a cigarette and stood in front of the mirror, glaring at the formidable and unlovely vision of herself. "My God, Belle, what are you doing? That's your son!" She strangled on a deep gust of smoke and her eyes watered. But it wasn't tears she saw glittering out of the mirror. She had no capacity for tears. All her crying had been finished that long past day when she had seen her girlhood and her girlhood dreams vanish. She was just an old woman, too roughly used by life to feel the full force of the tragedy she saw coming.

Duke DePard went down the street to his horse standing in the stable and followed the trail to Buffalo Galt's place on the hill. Buffalo was there with about half the crowd—the other half being in the hideout back of Camp Four. Buffalo sat in a chair with one leg hooked over its arm. He had on a good suit of clothes and a white shirt and his eyes were almost green against the flush of his cheeks. He had been chuckling at something said by Blagg, but when he saw Duke DePard he quit being amused. He caught something in DePard that caused him to pull his leg from the chair arm and drop it to the floor.

"I'm sorry, Duke. Ben was a good boy."

Duke said, "Yeah," in a dry, uncommunicative manner.

Buffalo went thoughtful. He ducked his head at the rest of the crowd. "I'll meet you in the hills tomorrow sometime. Start riding."

The crowd drifted out. Blagg stayed behind. "About the Michelet girl—"

Duke DePard, not raising his voice, said to Blagg: "You flannel-tongued filth-eater." He drew a deeper breath and called Blagg by three obscene names. He said: "Crawl out of here!"

Blagg stepped back. His complexion turned. Buffalo Galt showed his surprise. "What's wrong with you, Duke?"

"Get away, Blagg, before I knock in your jackass face."

Blagg grumbled, "Who stepped on your corn?" But he went out. Buffalo Galt spoke again.

"Don't ride him like that. He's useful to me."

DePard showed his disgust. "The dog's too yellow to fight back."

Buffalo absorbed what he saw, weighed what he heard. "You're pretty much upset by Ben's dyin'. Well, why take it out on Blagg? He didn't kill Ben. If you're the man I think you are you'll go after Sebastian."

"Yeah?" murmured DePard looking down at Buffalo.

Buffalo said, "Yeah," equally dry. His hands slipped to the arms of his chair and remained there. "What's on your mind?"

"Nothing."

Buffalo moved his shoulders. "I can't make you out, Duke. You don't ever jump the way a man might expect. Sometimes it gets under my skin. I like a man that stays put, that doesn't have a lot of funny ideas in his nut to turn him queer."

"Who's queer?"

Buffalo rapped out his reply. "Don't snap at me like that. Look here, Duke—fish or cut bait."

"Well?" said DePard. His eyes stayed on Buffalo.

"You ought to be on Sebastian's trail," suggested Buffalo.

"Afraid of that job yourself?"

Buffalo's flush grew fuller. He got out of the chair. "Kid, you're not talking to Blagg now. I won't take that."

"No?" growled DePard.

There was a long silence, a creeping tension. Buffalo's green eyes were framed inside the sudden tight triangle of his lids. "Going sour on me, Duke?"

"I watched you build up Humboldt. He went out and he didn't come back. Ben took it the same way. I'm gettin' kind of curious to know what you figure to do in this business."

Buffalo abruptly laughed away his resentment. "That's all right, kid. I know you feel bad."

"What are you going to do?" insisted DePard.

"Mister Sebastian," drawled Buffalo, "has sent his full crew up to the Camp Four. I found that out. He's going to ship a lot of beef. That's where we're going, Duke. The end of his business ain't far off. Sebastian's always said he could wait out the proper time. It's changed now. He's got to get beef out of the hills—and I'm the one that's waited for the proper time. We're just about caught up with that fellow."

"I'll see you in the hills tomorrow," said DePard and turned away.

Buffalo stood still, listening to DePard ride off. He shook his head.

DePard rode down the hill and came into town. There was a light shining through Blagg's shop window when DePard passed it. He went on a hundred feet or so and then something happened in his head and he put his horse about and came back. He crawled from the saddle, crossed the walk and put his hand quietly on the shop door and pushed it before him. Thus for a moment he stood in the small front office, undiscovered, and looked through another door to the back of the place where Blagg stood over the cases with a stick in his hand, setting type. DePard watched the man quite a long while, and then went on through to the rear. The sound of his dragging spurs brought Blagg's attention instantly around.

Finding DePard so darkly and silently coming at him, Blagg backed nervously away from the cases. Alarm licked along his slack face. "What you want here?" he said, breath springing out of him.

DePard walked forward, saying nothing. The blackness on his thin face, and the visible hatred there, made Blagg give ground. He came against a make-up table and could go no farther. When DePard was quite close Blagg struck out with the metal stick in his hand, and missed. DePard hit him in the face, and hit him a second time, as coolly as though he punched a bag. Blagg dropped the stick and tried to cover his head. DePard smashed him in the belly and Blagg grunted and groped blindly for DePard's arms and couldn't catch them. He emitted a queer whinnying protest; and he had one moment of trapped courage that sent him charging against DePard. He carried DePard against the type cases and tried to get his hands around DePard's throat. DePard ducked away and struck Blagg on the temple; thereafter Blagg was nothing more than a chopping block for DePard.

Slowly circling the small space, DePard struck and waited and struck, and waited and struck again. When at last Blagg fell the light had been pounded out of him. He lay on the floor with his battered face turned down.

DePard turned to the cases and capsized them, strewing type across the floor. He upset the make-up table; he picked up a heavy two-column newspaper cut and smashed it down across the keyboard of a near-by typewriter. Then, spending one last disgusted look at the man on the floor, he left the place and got to his horse and cantered out of Tumpah. His course was westward; the thin small beams of the Barrier lights pulled him straight on.

After DePard had gone Buffalo Galt turned into his kitchen. He built himself a fire and pushed the coffee pot across the stove top; he got out a side of bacon and sliced off a half-dozen pieces. Standing there then, he did a strange thing. His hands dropped from the bacon and he remained still a long moment, and afterwards made a swift wheel and plunged toward the living room, toward the table on which his gun lay. Lot McGinnis stood in the front doorway.

When he saw the sheriff Buffalo stopped sharply, and some of the cat-like attention left his eyes.

"Kind of set on a quick trigger, Buffalo," observed McGinnis.

"What are you prowling up this way for?" challenged Galt.

The sheriff said mildly, "Wanted to talk with you," and came through the doorway. He sat down, and his eyes, quietly touching Galt, were remotely sad.

Galt remained alert. He said, with faintly contemptuous tolerance, "You're gettin' pretty old, Lot. Riding this country is a tough job, meant for a young man. Why don't you quit before somebody finds you propped against a rock in the hills with your ticker stopped?"

"Wouldn't be a bad sort of end," reflected Lot McGinnis. "Well, I've carried the star a long time. Been kind of interesting, Buffalo. I've seen 'em come and go—the good ones and the bad ones. The bad ones have towed me all over northern Nevada. They sure showed me the country. Funny thing about that. They're all dead now."

Buffalo said: "So are most of the good ones, Lot. It's fifty-fifty. And the bad ones had the fun."

Lot McGinnis shook his head. "Not much fun dyin' like a cornered coyote, miserably and full of lead. That's the way the bad ones went. We never held much with the idea of bringin' outlaws to jail." He stopped and considered his hands; he looked up again with a quick, amused glance. "Buffalo, you're a bright man—and you're a damn fool."

"If I want a sermon, Lot, I'll go to church."

"Here's two dead men in a week. There'll be more. I know this district. Maybe you're ridin' high. But you can't cut it, son. You can't cut it."

"Never mind," said Buffalo Galt, turning angry.

Lot McGinnis got up, a tall and weary shape throwing a thin shadow against the wall. "You're a smart boy, Buffalo, but you don't get this yet. You're goin' against Sebastian and your chances ain't so good with him. But even if you handle him and his crew, you're still licked. The moment you finish the chore Ed Brean sent you to do, Ed Brean will see you're put beyond talkin'."

Buffalo took a step forward. His mouth went thin. "How the hell you know about Ed Brean?"

"It's a pretty old story. I knew about it a long time ago, because I happen to know the way Ed Brean's mind works—and the ambition he's carried in his head since the days of King Henry. You're nothing but a white chip in a game that's been played since '75. You'll be used and thrown aside, like a lot of other white chips. I recall the very night you were born I hugged a rock in the Moonstones and threw lead at Ed Brean's men."

"A funny thing for you to remember," said Buffalo Galt.

"Don't be a sucker," said Lot McGinnis earnestly. "I may be a pretty old man, but I still know what my job is. It would be a mighty bitter thing, Buffalo, if I had to lay a gun on you."

"On me?" grunted Buffalo. "You never will, Lot."

The sheriff shrugged his shoulders. "I wouldn't be too sure."

He had nothing more to say. He went out and walked slowly down the hill, into Tumpah's darkness. He passed Lee Bond who stood against the corner of his garage arch and smoked a peaceful cigarette; but he turned and went back to the man. He said, "You got a match, Lee?"

"Sure."

Lot McGinnis took the match and lit a cigarette. Light glowed across the ancient smoothness of his cheeks and died. He emitted a long sigh and turned away, walking down the street with his hands braced behind him. There was an immediate problem in his mind and he couldn't quite see the answer. He'd have to arrest Sebastian for Ben DePard's death, as a matter of course. The thing would be a formality, nothing else, for he knew the temper and the realistic morals of his people too well to believe any twelve men would do else than instantly release Sebastian from the charge. The moment Sebastian got up and said, "Ben DePard drew first," he was a free man. In fifty years the ethics of the draw hadn't changed at all in this remote land. The deep desert, the mysterious hills, the fierce individualism of those who rode the open—these were constant things.

So the arrest didn't bother him. It was the time of the arrest that did. He felt the growing tension and he knew there would be a further attack on Barrier. Sebastian could ill afford to be drawn away from the ranch in the next few days, for the moment he turned his back to it, Buffalo would make some sort of a play.

Thinking of this, he turned to his small house behind Tumpah, saddled a fresh horse, and swung out across the desert. He traveled northwest, toward the Moonstones. There was in his head, too, a recollection of what Buffalo had said about his being found dead some day, propped against a rock in the hills.

"That" he murmured, "would be as good a way as any. I have outlived my time—and all my friends are gone. It'd be a pleasant thing to see those old faces again."

Chapter 9

Sebastian got up from his desk and put his head through the office window and called to Gath in the yard. "Bring Joe and come in here a minute." Afterwards he returned to the desk, signed and dated the paper on the table:

I, Thomas W. Sebastian, will the ranch commonly known as Barrier, including all lands, livestock, improvements, chattels, brands and records, and every kind of asset whatever found, in trust to Judge John Sillavan and Charm Michelet, trustees, for the following purpose: that when Thomas Michelet, minor son of Charm Michelet, reaches the age of twenty-one the above property shall pass unconditionally to him for his full possession and use.

Gath and Joe came in. Sebastian indicated the paper and handed a pen to Gath. "I'm making a will. You fellows sign at the bottom—and don't bother to read it."

"You know I can't read," remarked Gath.

When they had witnessed the will and gone, Sebastian addressed an envelope, put the will inside and filed it away in one corner of the desk. He had spent a full day at his desk unraveling his neglected accounts and the will represented the last chore of his house-cleaning mood. Thoroughly weary of the job, he leaned back in the chair and packed and lighted his pipe.

He wasn't a business man. He hated desk work and avoided it as long as he could. In this respect he knew himself very well, and realized he belonged to his father's generation. He had the same strange feeling about the range, its timeless swing, its prodigality and its cruelty. How could a man reduce its magnificent rewards and failures to ledger items? He had never tried. The only thing he had ever cared to know was that Barrier made a living for all those on it and maintained its protective margin against the lean years.

Normally, it did. But none of the past six years had been normal. The closed bank had trapped his last fluid dollar; the recent Frisco shipment was swallowed up in that, too. He had, he supposed, eighteen thousand dollars coming from the roundabout ranches. Pine Brothers owed him six thousand on a purely oral transaction; Herman Schneider owed him four thousand; Malheur Land and Cattle Company, thirty-five hundred. All good money, but not to be had on demand. So he was broke, with the ranch eating its way deeper into store credit, payroll, and taxes each day.

Since his father's time Barrier had been without a mortgage, without even an uncovered debt. It had been a cash ranch, from which had come its great power. It always had money to buy when others needed to sell. Credit was all right for a fixed business; but cattle raising wasn't a fixed business. So he had only one way open, which was to cut into Barrier's abundance, to send beef to market. He had sent his riders north yesterday.

He sat back, quietly smoking, eyes going through the low window to the diminishing shapes of Lily and Timmy Akin bound away for an afternoon's ride. He tried to bring his mind back to that particular problem, but his thoughts wouldn't lift. He felt tremendously tired inside his muscles, with that sort of weariness not absorbed by sleep; and added to this weariness was something shadowy, premonitive. He was riding into trouble, toward a showdown he felt rather than saw. So strong was the feeling that it had prompted him to wind up his day's work by writing a will. It was the first time he had ever experienced that definite a reaction regarding the future. Well, it was something the same as the intuition which once, years before, had impelled his father to rise and move away from a lighted window a few seconds before a bullet crashed through the glass.

Somebody knocked on the office door. Sebastian said,

"Come in," but he didn't look around. He recognized Jay Stuart's footsteps. Jay walked past the desk, facing Sebastian, and sat down. Stuart's face was blandly humorous—indicating some idea behind.

"Aren't you getting tired of company, Tom?"

"Wish you could stay several months."

Stuart said: "I'd always regarded Western hospitality as ballyhoo. I come to see that it's real."

"That's because ranchers are lonely people. You do Barrier a favor by being here."

Stuart said quietly: "You're doing us no favor by letting us stay. We're all playing hookey from Hollywood."

Sebastian didn't answer. Stuart looked across the desk. "When are you going to send Lily back?"

"Is it my decision to make?"

"I'm sorry to say that it is. I happen to know where Lily's heart has turned. I know her very well; I've made it pretty much my business to understand that girl. In fact it's been my only business the last six months."

"I've guessed that you've been interested," said Tom noncommittally.

"Yes, but never mind that. All I want you to credit me with now is a little bit of disinterested anxiety over her career. If you knew my record better I doubt if you'd credit me with any decent intentions. But maybe, for once, I can make a straight appearance."

"I like you," was Sebastian's quiet comment.

Stuart stared. "That's damned decent—and it makes it tough for me. But, look. She can do anything she wants to do in Hollywood. I've seen a lot of girls. But Lily's going to be among the great. It doesn't happen very often, Sebastian. Thousands of them break their hearts and starve and make the wrong guesses, and pass out. It takes a lot of breakage to produce one Lily Tennant. Well, I don't look to you like an emotional man, but this is one thing I can get eloquent over. I don't want to see her waste her life. There are damned few Lily Tennants in the world—and those few don't belong on Nevada ranches."

"You're pretty clear."

"I'm trying to be."

"Think she'd be unhappy here?"

Stuart got out of his chair and went over to the window. "I can't say that much," he admitted candidly. "She's too strong a girl to regret the things she does. Whatever choice she makes she'll stick with, till the last trumpet." A little exasperation crept into his voice. "That's why it's so cursed hard for me to see her do the wrong thing."

"You think it's the wrong thing?" questioned Sebastian, voice riding even.

"Throwing up her career? My God, yes!"

Sebastian scrubbed his hand across his eyes. He said faintly irritable, "I don't like the idea of discussing Lily."

Stuart turned about. He was definitely upset. "Some things I can't mention to you. It isn't my place to mention them. But it's your place to consider them before you pull Lily into your life. Think it over carefully." He walked to the door, and said, "Think it over even more carefully than you usually do," and went out.

A small gust of wrath swirled through Sebastian, and passed. He snapped down the top of his desk and left the office, crossing the living room. Stuart stood by the fireplace. Kit Christopher sat on the leather divan. Sebastian paused in the middle of the room.

"I'm sorry to be so poor a host. I have got to go to the north end of Barrier this afternoon. Make yourselves completely at home. Ask Gath for anything you want. Will you tell Lily I'll be back sometime tomorrow?"

He went out to his machine and got in and called for Gath, who came presently from the bunkhouse. "Gath," he said, "don't leave quarters until I get back. There's only four men left here and that's few enough for trouble if it should come."

Yes," said Gath and watched Kit Christopher come across the yard toward the machine. He turned and strolled back to the bunkhouse. Kit put her hand on the car door.

"You're rather troubled these days, Tom."

"Don't," he cautioned, "let it bother you at all."

She said: "I so seldom offer sympathy that I hate to have it refused."

"Sympathy?"

She looked directly at him, her cool, intelligent features a little disturbed. "Why not? I have feelings, too."

He said, rather puzzled, "You have been on guard against me, Kit. You've been counseling Lily against whatever Barrier might mean to her. Why offer me sympathy now?"

"Some day," she said, gently, "you'll know better than to try to analyze women."

"I'm sorry," he said, and cheerfully grinned.

"That," she murmured, "is the nicest part of you—your really reckless smile." She turned away with an abrupt gesture. Tommy came out of the house and waddled across the yard, crying, "Ride—ride," and rolled himself onto the running board.

"Kid," said Sebastian, "you'll grow up to be a hitch-hiker." He put an arm over the door's sill to hold Tommy and sent the car forward. At the end of the plaza he stopped. Tommy got off, full of laughter, and started back for the house on the dead trot. All this Kit Christopher absorbed with a strong, still-lipped interest. Her breathing was faintly irregular as she watched the car swing out of the plaza, bounce through the ruts and grow small on the north-running road. Tommy came up the steps and she bent and extended her hands. "Tommy," she said.

But Tommy, wild as ranch youngsters sometimes are toward strangers, circled and ran into the house. Kit put her hands behind her and rested against the porch wall; and she kept her eyes on Sebastian's car until it vanished behind its dust. The immaculate self-possession was out of her; she looked at that moment rather defenseless and forlorn.

Quartering across the desert, Lot McGinnis entered the Moonstones under cover of dark, rode ten additional miles through the tangle of canyon and tree and made a cold camp. Sunrise found him squatting on the summit of a crumbling rock pinnacle which thrust its spire considerably above the surrounding terrain. Here he stayed, slowly conning the land through a pair of field glasses with an old man's infinite patience. At ten o'clock he marked a traveling puff of dust in the east, which was a rider coming across the desert from Tumpah; around two the rider had reached the foot of the hills and entered them. A little later McGinnis caught him again, this time cruising along a canyon of the Moonstones, northward bound.

There was something going on up north. For his searching glasses had now and then vagrantly caught individual men sliding through rocky defiles and passing into the pines below, all headed in the same northward direction. Once he picked up a dim stirring of shapes out on the desert at the west side of the Moonstones. This was a brief view, soon clouded by the heat haze boiling off there, but he knew a Barrier crew was operating around Huggins Point and so he dismissed that quarter from his mind.

Later in the afternoon, about five o'clock, he noticed a rider break through timber and canter over to Camp Four; and not long after that a car made its appearance in the south, running up from the Barrier ranch. That would be Sebastian. He kept his attention there until the car stopped at the Camp Four cabins; afterwards he saw two men leave the shanties there and canter into the timber.

It was enough. He put his glasses away, stamped his numb feet, and crawled down the butte through a fast-running twilight. He climbed into the saddle and left the butte behind him, keeping to the high ground as he struck into that north which seemed to be attracting so many men. A touch of rheumatism bothered his legs; for a while he rode with one foot and then the other out of the stirrup.

He was traveling through a country as familiar to him as the palm of his hand. He had begun his career by tracking a man through the Moonstones, just as he now reached the final years of his career by trailing another man through them. Thinking back through the long seasons, he recalled vividly and accurately all the outlaws who had raced for the shelter of these dark and protective alleys. It was a pattern that didn't change. They had been of every sort, laughing and reckless men, merciless men, men with some goodness in them, men with almost none. But they had all led him into the Moonstones, playing the same grim game to the same dismal end. After the first few years he had gotten to know the hills so well that he could guess ahead of them—and be posted beside the trail when they came out.

Most of them had cursed him and lifted their hands; a few had tried a last desperate draw. Once his conscience had permitted a harassed, half-innocent lad to get away into Oregon, a single piece of extra-legal mercy he hadn't regretted. Only one fugitive had ever deliberately outguessed and outmaneuvered him—Ed Brean.

"But that," he said aloud, as though justifying himself, "was King Henry's fault, who couldn't bring himself to trap the man who was his worst enemy. Guess it must of been because Henry enjoyed the game and didn't want to see it end. The world's been different since Henry died."

He understood something then with a sudden vivid distinctness. He had been lonely these last years for the voice and presence of all those who had been young with him and now were beyond the last shadows. Somewhere these great and hearty companions were gathered around another campfire, speaking of familiar things. He had been left behind—that last man who in every outfit must tend the final chores. But the gate ahead was open for him, and when he passed through it he would close the gate behind, because there were no more to follow. And he would see the outline of their fire coming through the shadows—and he would hear their long, welcoming shout.

He went on, thus plunged in his whimsical, wistful, and regretting memories. He went on without hurry, because so many other men rushing away from him through these hills had taught him not to hurry. His attentive ears received the blending murmurs of the night, the faint echoes, the sibilance of creatures abroad in the blackness, the rubbing sigh of a small breeze overhead. These things registered, without disturbing the long run of his thoughts. But there was a moment when the clear smell of the hills was tainted by the drift of woodsmoke; and then he stopped and all his faculties became keen.

He sat quite still, with each indentation and slope of the surrounding area lying plainly on his mind. There was no break in the dark; there was no intrusion of foreign sound. Yet his attention advanced the sightless night and stopped at a definite spot. These hills were that known to him. He said to himself: "They're gathered. When they ride, it will be toward the big trail."

He pulled away and headed down a ravine and climbed out of it, pressing on into the anonymous reaches of the Moonstones, drawn northward by the same magnet which had hurried men through the rough area all during the afternoon. He was lost again in his thoughts. "I have played," he reflected, "a lone hand since the beginnin' and I can't change my style now. Maybe I'm doin' this wrong. What legal right have I got to stop these men before they commit the felony I know they're goin' to commit?" Riding on, he considered that with a descending sadness, with a weary fatalism. "Manhunting and Christian charity are two different things. I'm makin' the mistake of mixin' the two. Well, it is an old man's mistake, and well meant. I will abide the result." He vanished then into the condensed blackness.

Fast traveling brought Sebastian to Camp Four within the half hour. Jim Kern, promoted to Matt Strang's job as foreman, waited there at the shanties with a spare horse. Everybody else had gone on to Huggins Point, which was the northern prow of the Moonstones and the extreme boundary of Barrier in that direction. The beef roundup started there.

"We been workin' like hell all day. Some of those cow creatures come out of the brush in a manner just plain spooky."

"You could have saved yourself the trip back here by leaving me a note tacked on the shack door when you started north. I'd found you."

"People," observed Jim Kern, "can tear notes down. Or write new notes to lead you astray somewhere. This is open season on Barrier riders, Tom."

"Then you should have sent one of the other men back instead of coming yourself."

"I wouldn't ask another man to come through those hills alone," stated Jim Kern, very sober with his words.

Sebastian studied this white-haired, stoop-shouldered man who had been a part of Barrier for more than forty years. The feel of the land was in Jim Kern and the messages coming along the vagrant winds were as real to him as gunshot reports. He was like an old hound dog in which knowledge had long since been sublimated to something like instinct. Jim lived by his reactions; and his reactions were truer than his reason.

"Smell something, Jim?"

Jim Kern smoothed his hand through the air, aiming in the direction of those hills rising beyond the small meadow—that meadow wherein the two DePard men had tried to ambush the Camp Four crew a few nights back. "Coming here," explained Jim Kern, "I stuck to the brush. The trail's a bad place to ride right now. I'm certain the hills are full of Buffalo Galt's men. I caught sight of one lately across a ravine."

The sun had gone and faint purple began to tincture that still, lucid light which lies between sunset and dusk. "We'll start now," said Sebastian.

Jim Kern shook his head. "Not till it's dark."

"We'll stop in the trees as soon as we cross this meadow," explained Tom. "But if we're being watched I want them to see us cross it."

They turned to the horses and rode slowly down the grade into the meadow. Jim Kern twisted his small shoulders. "I don't like any of it," he said.

"When you get spooky, Jim, there's usually a cause."

"I feel bad weather comin'."

"That's right," agreed Tom quietly.

"Well, Barrier's stood against it before," mused Kern. And his thoughts went back. "Ninety-five was the worst of all. I rode with your daddy when he was fighting for his life against some strong men. They were all crooked and they all hated each other. But that time Ed Brean got the whole pack of tough ones organized against your dad."

"Brean? I never heard that story completely."

"Henry Sebastian was no hand to tell his troubles. He was a great one. He and Ed Brean were enemies to the last breath. Well, Ed Brean never was no hand to give ground and neither was Henry. They were both prime men then, with Nevada too small to hold both. Brean got the crooks together and moved onto Barrier." His voice was singsong. "They hit Barrier hard. Men simply didn't give a damn in those days, Tom. The world's gettin' older and folks are afraid to die now. They wasn't then. It wasn't safe for a man to trot across any piece of ground in this section. Henry and me led out forty Barrier hands and we come on those fellows sleep. It was bushwhack, change horses, boil coffee, ride, and bushwhack. Hell, it was open war. They came at us one night where the schoolhouse stands. It was pretty rough for a while. where we found 'em. I recall three days of ridin' without But we drove Brean's outfit clean off Barrier. He never was able to get the crooks organized like that again. From that time on till the day Henry was killed he held the whip over Ed Brean."

"Jim," said Sebastian, "what did those two originally quarrel over?"

"I never rightly knew," mused Jim Kern. The man's tone was soft and evasive. "But," he added, "this thing comin' up is just a part of the old scrap never finished. Nothin' changes much."

"You feel it coming, Jim?"

Jim Kern's eyes were at once bright and hard. "Barrier's a great ranch and the coyotes will always be tryin' to hamstring it. All Sebastians have to fight. Your son will, and his son will. This section's got less people on it now than thirty years ago. It'll always be wild and half empty—a place where the tough ones come to roam. That's why you'll always be fightin', like you always been."

They were across the meadow and traveling single file up the trail. Shadows slowly swirled through the trees. Sebastian said: "Start back to the outfit as soon as it gets dark. I'm going to swing through the hills. I'll see you tomorrow."

Any other Barrier hand would have spoken his doubt. But Kern only inclined his head. Drawing into the deeper timber he watched Sebastian file along a corridor of the forest and vanish behind a blind angle.

Sebastian traveled no more than five hundred yards on the trail, for he strongly suspected his passage of the meadow had been observed. There was in him, as in Jim Kern, the registered impact of collecting trouble. At the first break in the trail he swung away and followed a lesser path; and presently abandoned this to strike into the trackless and fairly open heart of the forest, his course taking him upward toward the backbone of the Moonstones. On his right stood that canyon he had crossed previously in pursuit of Star Humboldt, but he avoided it now, not wishing to expose himself. Ten minutes later he arrived at a small crest from which certain darkling alleys of this broken land could be commanded. Here he paused.

Somewhere in the heart of these hills was Galt's camp, which he now sought. But his mind wasn't unreservedly on the job. It kept returning to Jay Stuart who had said: "Some things you ought to consider carefully before you pull Lily into your life." Stuart thought what everybody else thought, that Tommy was his son and Charm his natural wife. Lying like a foreign growth in his head, this problem colored and conditioned all his thoughts. It grew; it increasingly disturbed all other thinking. Now and then a rare moment of peace came to him, but the intervals never lasted long. In the greatest moments of his life—when he had held Lily in his arms and sensed the overpowering richness the future might hold for them—this bitter remembrance rose to destroy the glory of the moment and to leave him defeated and full of regret. He had known in the beginning that Lily and he would come to this tangled, sorry pass. Now he could no longer delay his decision. Whatever he decided, somebody would be hurt; but he had to decide. . . .

He pulled his horse back into the trees. Below him and to the north a rider appeared from the brush, rode down one of the open corridors and vanished around a bend. Sebastian considered this thoughtfully for one short interval and then turned to follow.

A Galt rider out on patrol. The man would be returning to Galt's camp, for all the shadows were thick cobalt now and the light of day was about gone. There was danger in this sort of pursuit, of course. But the time had come to press his luck and so he went on, coasted around the bend and got one final sight of the fellow sliding into the northern trees.

In that direction the terrain of the Moonstones turned extraordinarily rugged, breaking into a hundred ravines and ridges. To guess the Galt man's exact trail was to guess the course of a needle through a haystack. Knowing that, Sebastian veered to the east and toiled up the side of a ridge so that he might again command a bird's eye view. Four hundred feet higher he paused and thought he sighted the Galt man in the distance. But it was past the time for seeing anyone clearly and the best he could do now was to continue to the spine of this ridge and go north with it.

He was, he judged, approximately five miles from Camp Four, or a third of the way into these hills which ran another ten miles to Huggins Point before dropping into the desert like the prow of a gigantic ship cutting the sea. About three miles to the right, and three miles to the left, the sides of the Moonstones dropped likewise into the desert. Thus he sought a single spot somewhere in an area ninety miles square, though he suspected Galt's camp was more nearly within a five-mile circle which covered the secretive heart of these hills.

It was full dark when he arrived before a crosscutting canyon. He descended into it and rose out of it, laboring again to the high points. A quarter moon hung very low and very pale in the sky, accenting the brilliant black of the sky; wind roved the pine tops and rugged scarps softly. All this country he knew and had searched many times by night. There would be a fire to betray Galt's location, but he had never seen a fire.

Ahead of him was a blur of motion. He had come upon another break in the forward march of the ridge. There was a bare and sloping surface ahead, its yellow color glowing faintly; and a man was crossing it at a canter, bound away in a northwesterly direction. Stopped, Sebastian listened to the pony tracks fade out in the lower regions. Then he went on, traveling rather recklessly across the open ground. At the bottom of the grade he was in timber again.

This was slower going, for the way was sightless and led from tree to tree. Once he strayed from the trail into the brush and left a rattling wake behind him. The sound struck abnormally loud through a stillness that seemed to have no bottom; and such was its tricky influence that he felt as though he and he alone was abroad in the night.

At that point something as tangible as a stone wall barred his further progress. He stopped, not knowing why.

Puzzled deeply, all his senses abnormally sensitive to the impact of this fathomless world, he raked his surroundings and could see only the vague bulk of trees standing near. He could smell nothing but the aromatic dryness of the hillside. He could hear nothing. Then at once he knew what had stopped him. So far the wind had been a soft breath against his face, coming from the exact north. At this point it hauled around and became a strong draft from west to east, quite cold and quite definite on his left cheek.

He went on a hundred feet, and was out of that draft. He returned and was in it again. Some fault in the ridge above him was creating the suction, of course; but as he stared at the ridge he could see no flaw in it, no canyon breaking down its slope. Definitely aroused, he began to identify a trail cutting at right angles across the one he was on and running toward the ridge.

An actual feeling repelled him from that trail. Obeying the warning, he continued north for a matter of two hundred yards and wheeled eastward. The foot of the ridge marched out of the black; he got to it and began rising with it. There was no open route, there was no even ground. Some ancient eruption in the earth's bowels had torn the surface soil, leaving it pocked and pitted. Trees and brush rose irregularly; windfalls blocked him. He twined patiently about all this, climbing a yard at a time in thorough sightlessness, and not for a space of ten full minutes was he able to see his horse's ears. But when at last he worked his way out of this, and broke unexpectedly through the trees, he bought his pony to an instant halt.

He stood on the edge of a wall which dropped a full eighty feet to a ravine's rather level floor. Over across the darkness two other walls butted into this high transverse ridge running along the Moonstones. Some sort of an ancient disturbance had sheered the dirt away and left smooth rock faces there. On the fourth side—which was the exit to the forest—there seemed to be a narrow passageway hidden in a jumble of fallen stones. A fire burned at the bottom of the ravine, its red glow pulsing along the black side walls. Around the fire men lay idly, their horses standing over against the edge of light.

He started to turn away. But a voice said, with the finality of a gunbolt sliding home in its breech: "Stay there."

He had no alternative. The speaking man was directly behind him. At once a second man appeared at his right side and let out a soft, sliding question. "Who're you?"

"Never mind."

The man moved one pace backward. He was excited. He said: "Hear that, Breck? It's Sebastian." His body weaved across the dark. "I'm coverin' you, friend. I'm comin' to lift your gun. Be a little careful."

"Take it," grunted Sebastian.

The man slapped his palm against Sebastian's holster. He

got Sebastian's gun and reared back. "Turn around. Breck, call down to the boys."

Breck had come up to take the reins of Sebastian's pony. He didn't like it. He said, dryly: "Go on, Lonzo. Let's get out of here."

They turned into a trail Sebastian hadn't found and followed it downward, Lonzo leading the horse, Breck coming behind. Sebastian let the reins drop and locked both his hands around the saddle horn. He put a heavy pressure against them, all his body muscles flattening with the sudden impulse to jump. Breck stumbled and slapped the horse's rump as he recovered. He said to Sebastian: "Be a little careful, friend."

Sebastian thought coldly to himself, "Not now," and relaxed. They were back in the heavy timber, moving south. The cold current of air struck Sebastian again. The fellow called Lonzo turned here and marched straight for the black shadow of the ridge. It was a deceptive thing. They marched against it and into it, Sebastian's knees scraping the margins of a narrow defile; he felt a dampness. One winding turn brought them through the entry and then they were in the ravine, approaching the shining light of the fire. A man rose to block their progress. Lonzo said: "Never mind, Alec," and went on.

Another man walked forward. Somebody lifted a quick call, and dark figures rose from the far shadows and closed in. The pony stopped. Sitting soberly in the saddle, Sebastian watched that ring of eyes reach out and pin him. Somebody kicked the fire and light strengthened measurably. He turned his head. Buffalo Galt stood a pace away. Buffalo was grinning.

"Get down, friend Tom."

Duke DePard walked from the shadows and stood silently by. Looking into that thin, straight face, Sebastian could read nothing.

Chapter 10

Sebastian stood quietly in front of the fire, struck by a steady stream of air that scoured through the ravine and lifted and curled the ragged flame points against the back wall of rock. The liquid spraying of water sounded across the night. Galt said: "You didn't think I'd leave the trails around here unguarded, friend Tom?"

The full blood of this man heavily filled his cheeks; pride swelled him and swayed his yellow head like drink. Duke De-Pard remained in the background, face revealing nothing. The rest of the crew had drawn back to the edges of the light. Galt laughed outright, the sound of it beating flatly against the surrounding walls.

"Tom," he said, "you're a fool. I've had my boys riding back and forth all day, hopin' to catch your eye. So you saw one of 'em finally and followed him—which was what I hoped you'd do—and here you are."

"Very clever," agreed Sebastian dryly. But it was Duke De-Pard he watched; it was Duke DePard's eyes he stared into.

"Not just clever," said Buffalo Galt. "I can be pretty patient when I've got to."

"What of it?" grunted Sebastian.

Buffalo ceased to smile. "You don't see it?"

Sebastian said nothing. Galt's glance burned into him. "Maybe Jim Kern will get back to the outfit. Maybe he won't. I've got men tailing him. But if he gets back it will do him no good. At noon today I sat in a tree with a pair of glasses and watched your crew rounding up beef in the desert at Huggins Point. Your boys don't know it, but they'll never get any beef out of the Moonstones. When daylight comes that beef will be scattered fifty miles. So will your crew. They might stick together if you was there. They might make a fight of it. But you won't be there."

Sebastian's cheeks were smooth. He said, outwardly indifferent. "You always talked too much, Buffalo. I've knocked fool ideas out of your head before and I will again."

"What with?" Buffalo said. He raised his arm, his lips crushed together. But he controlled himself and spoke calmly again. "You made a mistake battering me with your fists. I'm no hand to forget. Well, we'll have some fun tonight."

Sebastian said coolly: "You're a jumping jack on a stick, Buffalo, with Ed Brean pulling the strings. He bought your breeches long ago. But when you've done what he wants he'll break all of you. No power under the sun will protect you and your crowd from that. You're thinking you'll trick him when the time comes. Other men thought they could. Where are those men now, Buffalo?"

Galt's neck cords ripped white streaks against the florid skin; his forehead glistened with sweat. Suddenly he stepped backward, thus bringing DePard and Sebastian face to face. He said:

"Duke, here's the fellow that killed Ben."

The glow of the fire flickered across DePard's cheeks. He bent his narrow body forward, saying nothing. His black eyes clung to Sebastian.

"Duke," murmured Sebastian coldly, "don't you hear the crack of your master's whip? Humboldt heard it. And it should be a source of deep satisfaction to you to realize your brother died in a scrap that Buffalo trumped up to feather his own pockets."

"Duke," breathed Galt.

Duke DePard twisted his head slowly, as though to relieve some cramp in his neck. He turned his queer glance on Buffalo; he jammed his hands into his pockets.

"Never mind, Buffalo. Never mind."

"You're no good any more," grunted Buffalo.

"That's right," said DePard gently. "I've lost Ben."

"I don't trust you," Buffalo lashed out.

"You'd be a fool if you did."

"What's that?"

DePard said: "Lower your voice on me, Buffalo. I have lost my respect for you entirely. I will take no more orders from a man who turns his friends into chopping blocks."

"We'll see," said Buffalo Galt.

DePard muttered, "Fine," and drew his hands from his pockets and let them hang straight down. "What'll we see, Buffalo?"

"I'll run this outfit—and you'll mind me."

DePard turned and presented himself squarely to Galt. DePard said: "I've made too many mistakes to care what happens to me now, Buffalo. I've got that edge on you. But try what you figure to try—if it's your decision."

Looking on as an absorbed spectator, Sebastian suddenly knew there was no fear in either man. DePard was all ice and iron—a fighting mechanism stripped of the ordinary cautions of men; and now the fatalism in him made him utterly indifferent. Sebastian guessed that Buffalo was thinking the same thought, for the chunky blond's scheming glance tracked through DePard and read him carefully. He had the instincts of an animal and a sly knowledge of people. But it wasn't fear that stopped him. At bottom Buffalo was pure gambler who played the odds as he saw them. It was some far scheming in his brain that suddenly made him shrug his burly shoulders and smile.

"All right, kid. Have it your own way. We've got other eggs to fry and this is no time for quarrelin'."

"I thought so," grunted DePard.

"You may be thinkin' wrong," stated Buffalo. "Which is something you and I'll consider later."

DePard took three backward steps, placing the fire between himself and Galt. He had no faith, and not until the shadows partially obscured him did he turn his back to Galt. He went straight ahead then, toward the ravine's entrance. Sebastian vaguely saw him swing up to a saddle and start away. Galt's voice struck instantly out.

"Where you going?"

"I'll be back," said DePard and was beyond sight. Buffalo Galt turned calmly to Sebastian. "You've got nerve, friend Tom, and your luck held to the last drop. It always has."

"DePard never was a cold killer," retorted Sebastian. "I knew that."

"But you don't know me, friend Tom. And your luck's all out now. Sit down and rest yourself. We've got some time to waste."

Matt Strang knew only one way to quell the restless devil inside of him—which was to ride until he was ready to drop from the saddle. So when he turned his jaded pony into Tumpah at three o'clock of the afternoon he ended a solitary circling of the desert that had gone on for almost forty-eight hours. He had ridden and slept a little and ridden again, without sense of time or direction. Disheveled, sockets black with fatigue, the light of his eyes heavy and dull from the strange thoughts that had ripped like storm through him, he looked utterly spent as he dropped off at the stable. The hostler was audibly shocked.

"What in hell's happened to you, Matt?"

"This horse is tired. Don't water him too much and don't feed him too soon."

"Yeah, I know, but what—"

Strang turned for Belle Gilson's, with the effort of lifting his feet out of the deep dust taxing his little remaining energy. But the sense of personal danger which had been with him all his life made him cast quick glances to left and right as he passed Tumpah's buildings. There was nothing to be seen. Tumpah, always seemingly asleep under the sun, now appeared more than usually tenantless. No ponies stood in front of the Madame's, yet habit made him touch the butt of the gun tucked inside his trouser top as he swung through the door. Inside Madame's man of all work, Nick the Greek, sat half asleep in a chair, keeping himself lonely company.

"I'll have a drink, Nick. Then fry me some supper."

Nick looked at him carefully and lowered his eyes without speaking. He went behind the counter, set out a bottle and glass, and ambled back to the kitchen. Matt threw a slug of whisky into himself quickly. He hooked his elbows on the bar for support and cradled his bent head between his hands, waiting for the liquor to pull him out of that deep hole into which he had dropped. He moved his head gently from side to side, rubbing off the dust and dried sweat. Afterwards he had a second drink and stared at his dulled image in the back bar's glass. It wasn't clear and it wasn't pleasant.

But if he was without hope he was nevertheless himself again and could be humbly thankful for having avoided the one thing he had always dreaded might happen, which was an open fight with Sebastian. This man had been the greatest of all his friends.

He was through with Barrier; he was free to ride. Yet he scowled into the glass and felt dismally lost. Barrier had raised him, as it had raised Tom, as it had raised Charm. All of them had come up from childhood on the ranch—to reach this bitter end. They had been, he recalled, kids full of laughter; and now the laughter was gone. He had no pride in his conduct the last three years. Neither had he any apologies. If in all those grinding months of alternate faith and discouragement he had often doubted his own sanity it had been because he loved those two people in a way that left room for little else. Because this was so he had been willing to bury his own hopes—if Charm and Tom had been open and honest and had gotten married. People made mistakes. People were human. But to stand by and watch Tom refuse to correct the mistake was to feel a misery that never would leave his bones. He had found the goodness of Tom Sebastian less than he had thought—and it made everything else in the world pretty grimy. His faith had been absolute. Now it wasn't. He had wanted these two people to be square. If they weren't square, nothing was square.

"Supper's ready," called Nick.

Matt went into the room back of the bar and sat down at a long table. Nick came out of the kitchen with a platter of ham and eggs and a cup of coffee. Matt said, without looking up: "Where's everybody?"

"Ain't nobody been here since yesterday night."

"Why?"

"Just gone somewhere, I guess."

"Buffalo's bunch?"

Nick returned to the kitchen, shoes squeaking. He hadn't answered. Strang ate his meal rapidly, hunger a live thing in him. He drank his coffee. "More coffee, Nick," he called. When Nick came in again, he repeated: "Buffalo's bunch?"

Nick stood at his shoulders, not speaking until Strang stared up at him. "Buffalo's boys wouldn't be comin' back here in a hurry, would they?" said Nick reluctantly.

"Why not?"

"Don't you know why?"

Matt Strang scowled. "If I knew I wouldn't ask."

Nick shifted weight. "You don't know?" he intoned. "You don't know what happened here Tuesday morning?"

"What in God's name you pussy footin' around for?" demanded Matt, full of irritation.

Nick said: "Sebastian walked in here for a drink of water and ran into Ben DePard, Dode Cramp, and Whitey the lunger. Ten minutes later he walked out leavin' Ben dead on the floor, Whitey in poor shape—and Dode foggin' the breeze down the street. Jesus, it was a scrap!"

Matt said, "What?" in a grinding voice and got up.

"You come here," grunted Nick and swung into the barroom. He went to the wall where Whitey the lunger had stood and pointed at the two bullet holes in the wall. "Tom's shots. Now come here," he said, and went down the length of the bar. "See that scratch across the mahogany: Whitey's bullet, which didn't miss Tom far. Right there in the corner's where Ben dropped. Cramp was out in the middle of the room."

"Tom was all alone?" growled Matt.

"He didn't need any help, did he?"

Matt Strang rested against the bar, face tipped downward to the spot where Ben DePard had fallen. The boards there were splintered from slanting gunfire. His old loyalty pumped through his veins; it was something he couldn't help. Nick went softly back into the dining room and left Matt alone. But Madame came down the stairs and saw Matt and challenged him.

"What you doing here?"

"Madame, where's Galt bunch?"

"Gone from Tumpah. You've got no business here, Strang. Don't get drunk tonight. Go back to Barrier. Ride back there now. Where's Tom?"

"In the Moonstones."

"Find him. Find him and tell him there isn't a Galt rider around Tumpah and hasn't been since last night."

"Madame," he said wearily, "I don't ride for Barrier any more."

Belle Gilson said, "You've quit?" And she stared at him a long while, reading the burned-in despair of his face. Madame knew men; she knew them thoroughly.

"You're a fool, Matt. You always were. And you're blind as a bat. In all your life you never stopped long enough to think."

"Madame," he said with a desperate swing of his manner, "what should I think?"

"Tom Sebastian's a better man than you'll ever be, Matt."

He said: "What do you know, Madame?"

"You get back to Tom and let him know Buffalo's in the Moonstones."

One strange, commiserating thought came to Strang then and he looked at Belle Gilson and shook his head. "Buffalo's your son—and it must be hell for you to see this going on."

"Matt," she called out harshly, "don't give me any pity. Get out of here and do what you're supposed to do."

He watched her climb the stairs and noticed the labor she made of it. Afterwards he left the place and walked back through the heavy dust of Tumpah's street. The sun had dropped over the hills. Here and there a lamp began to shine from the houses and here and there a man stirred abroad. But it was a dying town, its pulse faint and slow. He stopped at the stable door and called in.

"Got a fresh horse?"

"I'll lend you Benzen's mare. I'm buyin' it from him."

"Be back in a minute," Matt went on. At Blagg's place he halted; but the window was dark and the door locked. He stood here a while, a remnant of the old fury warming him. He twisted the knob and kicked on the panel and swung away. At the corner where the Winnemucca road turned in he placed his back against a locust tree. His mind was clear again. It bit into this trouble. "Galt gone since last night. So he must have discovered Tom was sending a crew into the Moonstones. It's where he'd strike for. Tom wouldn't know about that." He straightened against the tree, his instinct to protect Barrier alive in him. This was something he couldn't change. He groaned, half aloud, "I have wasted twenty-four hours," and pushed away from the tree, long legs carrying him back to the stable. Benzen's horse stood saddled.

"Where'd Galt go?" he asked the roustabout.

"Don't know."

"Where's Blagg?"

"Blagg got his face mashed in by Duke DePard. He left the country yesterday. That's a good horse, Matt."

Matt hauled himself into the saddle and went rapidly out of Tumpah. Barrier headquarters lay ten miles westward; up in the north stood the low outline of the Moonstones, a good twenty-five miles lying between Tumpah and that trail which entered the middle part of the hills. He let the horse canter for a little distance, pulled it to a walk, and presently resumed the canter. Thus nursing the strength of Benzen's mare he traversed the desert. Wind ran gently out of the north, out of Oregon. The moon was very pale and the stars thick and brilliant in the sky, though they shed little light upon the earth. Stray junipers hovered obscurely in the cloaking shadows. Ten miles from Tumpah he reached a Barrier water tank and let the horse wet its nose.

He went on. There was a little piece of land lying along the way that didn't belong to Barrier and when he reached it he felt its alien qualities come up through the legs of the pony. And he was surer of himself after he had passed it and touched Barrier range again. The quality of home soil was that real to Matt Strang. He had been born on that soil and nourished by it, and though he might ride far from it the pull was there, stronger than any other element in his life. He was not a narrow man; in his fashion he was as civilized as any tourist walking the streets of Reno. Yet there was in him the primitive allegiance which nothing could shake. A clan loyalty, a clan obedience. He had cast off Barrier's authority two days ago—and now he was riding back because he couldn't help it.

He wasn't given to reflection; he wasn't articulate. But this thing he felt in the marrow of his bones. And because he did feel it a self-blaming anger made him miserable. He was tired at a time when he shouldn't be. He was far from Tom when Tom needed him most. He let the horse stretch, the heavy outline of the Moonstones beginning to reach toward him. He wasn't far from the hill trail; and the darkness of the night got quite thick. More and more alert, he began sweeping the prairie with his eyes.

Later, when he reached the footslopes of the Moonstones he swung and paralleled its darkling mass. He had, he discovered, undershot the trail; it lay a mile or more to the north. He went that way at a quieter gait, knowing he still had a long trip through the hills to Huggins Point. He had talked about the roundup with Sebastian several days ago and therefore knew the Point would be the base of operations.

He was more and more tired; and unexpectedly his eyes began to trick him. A foreign object floated across the film of his pupil, passing from left to right. Bending in the saddle he watched the object vanish. He closed his eyes and opened them—and saw a rider break out of the blackness, coming straight on. It wasn't an illusion.

He stopped and in the stillness received the curt echo of a hoof striking rock. The man was maneuvering off there, not more than a hundred feet away. Matt swung his horse broadside and dropped his hand to the gun beneath his coat. He gripped its butt. He said quietly:

"Who's that?"

The man came on steadily, lifting a voice that bothered Matt Strang. It was familiar but he couldn't place it. "That's all right. No trouble here."

"Stop there," Matt said. "And sound off."

"DePard," murmured the man.

"Well, I'm Strang," said Matt wickedly, and waited no longer. DePard was bending in the saddle. Strang aimed his gun deliberately. DePard said, "Strang—" and the rest of it was knocked away by the crash of Strang's gun. He fired in cool and deliberate fury and wondered at the lack of reply. DePard continued to bend until Strang no longer saw him. DePard's horse galloped on into the prairie and stopped and whistled out its fear. DePard was down on the obscure earth, the breath audibly sweeping in and out of his lungs. It was, Matt reminded himself vigilantly, a trap. There was no mercy in DePard or in any of Galt's roving crew. These men were enemies of Barrier and he hated them all with an impartial, unconditional hatred. Duke was lying there, playing possum. Matt raised his gun again and sighted it carefully at the blurred figure. But he held his fire; some kindness he didn't know was in him prevented the shot. He said:

"Duke, get up and come this way."

DePard's voice was very thin. "I never drew on you, Matt. Don't stand over there. You put two holes in me—and I got to tell you something. Come here, quick."

"Yes?" said Matt, unbelieving.

"Come here," repeated DePard, and sounded desperate. "This is something you got to know."

"All I want to know is that you're dyin'," growled Matt.

"Come here—please," muttered Duke DePard weakly.

Strang turned his horse and walked a circle around De-

Pard, coming up behind the man. DePard didn't move. Strang got out of the saddle, his gun clinging to DePard, and stepped forward with a cat-like caution. He saw DePard lying on the ground as a man might lie when about to sleep, rolled forward on one shoulder, head down. Something told Matt then DePard was actually dying, for DePard's breathing was fainter and more irregular—and the sense of death was here. Matt stopped a yard away. "Where'd I hit you?"

"Never mind. You know where the trail goes into the hills? Ride three miles on it, till you pass the summit and start downgrade. You reach the Twin Rocks and pass between 'em. Bear sharp to the right. It brings you against a stand of pines and you don't see no more trail. But push through the trees and you hit a clear space. Get off you horse there and walk soft. Cross the clear space and climb the rocks you find—straight up to the top. You're looking over the rim of a ravine. That's the hideout."

"Why tell me?"

"I got to tell you."

"I've circled the spot a dozen times," said Matt curiously, "and never saw it."

DePard's breath broke and grew labored. His knees writhed slowly on the ground. Matt bent and let his hands fall on DePard's holster. The gun was there. It hadn't been fired. It hadn't been lifted.

"Kid," he said, "I'm sorry for you."

"What for?" grunted DePard. "This is a good way out before livin' gets any worse. Be careful when you climb the rocks, because Buffalo will have his men scattered around the hole. You'll be looking straight down on top of the outfit. They're all waitin' for two o'clock to come. Then they go for Huggins Point to knock the Barrier crew loose from the beef it's rounded up. I'm squealin' on the boys. I can't help it. I've got to tell you something which I want you to tell Sebastian."

"The hideout can wait," said Matt Strang. "I'll hit for Huggins Point."

"I'm tellin' you about the hole," breathed DePard, "because Sebastian's there. Buffalo caught him this afternoon."

"What—" sighed Strang. He bent down. He thought the man was dead then, for he could hear no breathing and he could feel no life. He said: "Duke—"

DePard murmured: "This is the best I can do. Tell Tom it's been the big regret of my life—" His voice dropped and almost ceased. Matt was on his hands and knees and his ear was against Duke's face to catch the continuing words which kept sinking farther back into the man's throat. There was a little more talk, a very little followed by final silence. Matt felt DePard's body relax.

Matt got up and cleared his throat. He fumbled around his pockets for a cigarette, forgetting the dangerous quality of this night; and the subsequent match light showed his raw red cheeks to be badly broken. He whipped the light out, dragged deeply on the cigarette smoke. He said, "That's too bad, kid," and dropped the cigarette. He climbed into the saddle and for a moment remained still, disturbed by feelings he could not understand.

Why should he feel sympathy for this man whom he despised? He didn't know. Black was black and white was white and there should be a clean answer to everything. Yet something was wrong here and it knocked the ground from beneath his feet. There was something here about life and about death he didn't know, that he never would know.

He never would know; that was what suddenly slapped Matt Strang in the face. He was twenty-six years old and hating and working and sleeping had been enough, and anger and laughter had been enough. And now some dark thing brushed across his mind and left him stunned by a sense of the incompleteness, the tragedy, the blindness of existence. For one instant and one instant only his straining imagination caught a climpse of cloudy mists lying great distance away. He recoiled from the image, and the image vanished; yet in that moment the common doubt of man came to him. It rushed through him and destroyed all his sureness. He drew a lung-sweeping breath, badly shaken. He said aloud, "Maybe I've been a sucker," and pulled himself together. The passing time warned him; he wheeled and raced toward the mouth of that trail which led back into the Moonstones.

He reached the foot of the hills and passed up the turning trail without much caution. Not until he felt the shadows of the Twin Rocks envelop him did he slacken the pace. At that point he swung to the right as Duke DePard had directed and drifted along a lesser trail. Brush caught at his stirrups, slashing clean alarms through the night. The sound of his traveling horse made an undue racket. He thought grimly, "I'll never get there," and reached the pines.

He saw no trail, but he drove directly into pure, dripping blackness of the timber and found the way easier than it appeared. There was little brush here. The big-bodied pines, one and another, swelled out of the general night and fell by. When he saw lighter color break across the foreground he knew he had reached the designated clearing. At its edge he dismounted, left the horse on dropped reins and moved carefully out of the trees. Left and right he saw nothing. Ahead of him was the rock mass announcing the rim of the hole. Beyond the rock mass a somber crimson glow alternately brightened and deepened the darkness; that would be Galt's fire at the bottom of the ravine.

He went down on his belly and crawled across the open strip. Sensitive as he was to the minutest reaction of sound or motion, he received no particular impact of trouble from his surroundings. It allowed him to move faster. At the rocks he lifted himself from one ragged elevation to another and suddenly found himself hanging on the edge of the ravine wall. Eighty feet below a fire burned freely and freshly, its strong light illuminating all the ravine's floor.

But the place was empty. Galt and Galt's riders were gone; and Sebastian was gone as well.

Sitting on his heels in front of the fire, Sebastian looked at his watch and found it close to one in the morning. He had been here three hours. Buffalo Galt's outfit lay beyond the circle of light, intermittently resting. Galt, who roved the ravine with a caged restlessness, came suddenly back from the shadows and stood over Sebastian. There was a tremendous impatience in him; his nerves jerked at his muscles and put a brighter flash in his big eyes.

Sebastian said dryly: "This business is harder on you than on me."

"You were born cold," grumbled Buffalo. "It's the thing I have held against you since I was old enough to hang on a horse. I have filed my teeth against the stubborn Sebastian manner and I've busted my knuckles against the luck you've always had."

Sebastian spoke distinctly. "Like all crooks, Buffalo, you've got a greasy streak in you. Now you're trying to pin the reason for it on somebody else. I'd like you better if you quit whimpering for sympathy."

It rasped across Galt's ego; it stung him and made him yell: "Sympathy!" A hard, heavy breath sighed out of him and he swayed on his short legs.

"You've got a brain and it's not a bad one," murmured Sebastian. "You've got imagination—more than I have. You're husky and able. You could be honest, but somewhere you jumped the trolley and I'm puzzled to know why and where."

"Honest? Not as long as a Sebastian's alive."

"Barrier is an obsession with you. To my knowledge it never did you a wrong and never lifted its arm against you till you got too greedy with its beef."

"It's been ground into my face since I was old enough to think," said Buffalo. His round temper-strained eyes clung to Sebastian. "I was born in a filthy place. I grew up like a weed in Tumpah, kicked aside by every drunk that went by. Whichever way I looked all I saw was Barrier range. Barrier men rode through the town—mighty proud and overbearin'. When you began to ride with the bunch you were just as proud and overbearin'. What right do you have to the ranch? it was handed to you. All the talk I ever heard was about Barrier. Men rode from the saloon and never came back. Barrier buried 'em somewhere in the hills. Barrier laid down the rules and us damned sinners had to do what we were told. You were born to do the rulin', friend Tom, and I was born to do the jumpin'. I said to myself, 'To hell with that—I'll do the rulin' when my day comes.' Well, my day's here. I never had a doubt of it since I got the notion ten years ago."

"There's something in your blood," reflected Sebastian. "I wish I knew what it was."

Buffalo shook his solid shoulders and removed his coat and threw it on the ground. He unbuckled his gunbelt casually, dropping it on the coat. He said, "I'm going to wash up," and walked into the shadows beyond the fire.

Squatted by the flame, feeling the surcharged hostility swirling within this pit, Sebastian's mind revolved around his narrow chances and found them no good. The gun encased in the holster was at one corner of his vision; he had only to stretch out his arm to seize it. But he sat still and his lips flattened to a long tough line and nothing broke the engraved taciturnity of his face. The gun was a snare. If he reached for it he was dead. They couldn't quite kill him cold—they wanted him to furnish the excuse. He bowed his head and let the long minutes drag by, never stirring.

Buffalo came back and stood with his boot points touching the gun. Then he reached abruptly down, pulled it from the holster and tossed it at Sebastian's feet. He said:

"An even break. Take it and get up. I'll walk to one side of the hole. You walk to the other. I'll take the gamble."

Sebastian's answer was balanced and dry. "It's no gamble for you."

There was a creeping stillness—a long, shaking interval of doubt and suspense. At last Buffalo said indifferently: "Have it your own way. Hand me the gun back."

"You do the reaching," advised Sebastian. "I know better than to touch it."

Buffalo took a step onward and bent and swept the gun into his thick paw. "You're smart," he said, but his voice shook a little.

"I'll wait my time," answered Sebastian. The strain was drying him out, sucking away his vitality.

Buffalo snapped: "I've heard that one time too many."

His continuing stare widened and a kind of scheming, hungry thoughtfulness froze the ruddy lines of his face. Afterward—a long moment afterward—he abruptly laughed. "You're smart," he repeated. Then he lifted his head and shouted into the shadows. "All right, boys. We're ready to go. Breck and Lonzo—you're stayin' here with Sebastian."

"Thanks for the rest," murmured Sebastian.

Buffalo said coolly: "This is going to be easy, friend Tom. Your gang at Huggins Point will be bedded down for the night. They might make a scrap of it, if you were there. But you ain't there. We surround 'em and there won't be any fight. By tomorrow night your beef will be over in Oregon somewhere." He was full of amusement then; he was hugely grinning. "I'll keep the Barrier boys a few days and send 'em back to you afoot."

He went off at a rolling stride, calling impatiently to his outfit. "Shake it up—shake it up!" Crouched in his spurious attitude of meditation, Sebastian heard Galt's men mount and ride away. The narrow entrance threw back the hollow strike of departing pony hoofs and presently this sound and the faint rattling of brush beyond died out entirely in the night. Breck and Lonzo moved up to the fire. Squatting across the flame, they watched Sebastian with a strict, reserved attention.

When Galt's outfit went away, Sebastian's hopes and fears went with it. He was helpless, he was trapped. But his mind raced to Huggins Point and visualized that scene of sleeping men just beyond the trees. A few of the boys would be riding circle, but they could not stop the disaster that would creep so unexpectedly down the dark hillside. He kept his head lowered so that the two men across the fire might not see his face. His hat brim protected his eyes, but he watched them greedily as they sat so woodenly side by side and never allowed their attention to leave him. It brought him a saving satisfaction to discover they were uneasy and a little afraid.

The fire was dying away and the circle of light crept inward, leaving the rest of the ravine in blacker mystery. Wind freshened through the entrance passageway; high above an owl hooted. Sebastian heard it and paid no attention to it. But after the sound had quite died he thought of something, and listened alertly. When it came again he brought up his head and stared toward the rim of the ravine; and he turned his head deliberately and looked aside to the shadow-hidden entrance.

Both men pinned their suspecting glances on his slightest move. They read something into his changing interest.

The soft, curt hoot of the owl echoed into the pit again. Lonzo drew his long legs beneath him. He stood up. He said:

"Get some wood for the fire, Breck. It's too damned dark around here."

"Let me stamp my feet," said Sebastian.

"Stand up—but don't ramble," agreed Lonzo, grudging the approval.

Sebastian rose. Breck started off to the lower end of the ravine. Lonzo suddenly thought of something. "Wait a minute," he called, and stopped Breck dead in his tracks. "That don't sound like no owl to me."

Sebastian kicked his boot heels on the ground and crouched down again, feeling both men's eyes tear suspectingly into each of his gestures. Lonzo spoke more strongly. "If this is a trick, Sebastian, it'll do you no good. Who's up there?"

"No trick, Lonzo."

Lonzo said: "It ain't smart for both of us to be spotted in this light, Breck. Wait a minute."

He stepped backward. Sebastian counted the strike of each retreating step. He counted eighteen. Lonzo stopped beyond sight. "Go ahead for the wood, Breck," he ordered.

"That makes me the fall guy," grumbled Breck; but he went on.

Sebastian folded his big hands together, finger laced between finger. Strength hardened his arms. He had waited. He could always wait, and this might be the time he waited for. He didn't know yet. He bowed his head and locked his jaws. All he wanted was one slim chance. Maybe these two fellows, so cagey and suspecting, would accidentally give it to him. Not by design, but by the clumsiness of their caution. He lifted his head half an inch and stared beneath the shelter of his hat brim, sweeping the shadows with a sharp attention; he put pressure into his right knee and inched his foot surreptitiously behind him, steadying his body. Eighteen boot steps was fifty feet; so Lonzo was fifty feet away.

Breck came back into the circle of light, limping a little, his arms hooked around half a dozen sticks of pine wood. Sebastian watched him hesitate and veer and approach the fire on the far side. He stopped beside the fire and tipped his body backward, preparing to throw the wood into the dying flames. He was like that, still off balance, when Sebastian struck him.

Sebastian threw himself forward from the cocked crouch, across the flames and against Breck. He smashed Breck's wide, alarmed face with his fist and his chest cracked into the wood and he went on over with Breck, falling on top of the man. Lonzo yelled from the bottom of his lungs and started out of the shadows. Sebastian heard him coming. The wood—which Breck had not been able to drop—fell on top of Breck's belly and Sebastian fell on top of the wood.

The wind was out of Breck. He drew up his legs and tried to roll. Sebastian dropped a short, battering blow on the man's temple and reached down toward Breck's gun. The man was lying on it and Sebastian had to haul him around to get his fingers on the butt of the piece. It was like wrestling with a corpse. Breck was unconscious but his weight was loose and awkward and he trapped Sebastian's arm as he settled on his side. Lonzo was racing up and he would, Sebastian knew, risk a shot in another three paces. The wood made it no better, for it pressed Breck down as Sebastian tried to pull the man up. He kicked at the wood with his nearest foot, got the revolver free, slung the man against him, holding him thus as a shield.

The racing Lonzo was literally on top of Sebastian. He saw he couldn't fire, broke his stride, and tried to circle around. Sebastian laid his gun on top of Breck's head for a steady aim and his bullet caught Lonzo with both feet in the air. Lonzo came crashing down, his legs useless, and fell in a long, forward dive that carried him over and over, beyond the fire.

Sebastian dropped Breck and sprang backward to his feet. He rushed forward. Lonzo was breathing fast. The bullet had hit him casually and he was trying to lift his gun again. He was on his side, trying for another shot when Sebastian went over his body at a long jump and kicked the gun out of his fist. Still running, he came to the corner of the pit where his own horse and the horses belonging to Lonzo and Breck stood. He got into his saddle, grasped the reins of the other ponies and passed down the tunnel.

The led horses kept dragging into the brush beside the trail, slowing up his pace. Deeper in the hills, Sebastian rode a little way from the trail, tied the extra ponies to a sapling and went on at a faster gait. The trail fell definitely downgrade. Half a mile on it swung into a road and at that point Sebastian oriented himself. This was a woodchopper's wagon road leading into the very heart of the Moonstones. A mile and a half directly west it joined the main north and south trail running from Camp Four to Huggins Point. Toward the junction Sebastian turned.

The fight in the pit flickered along his brain like a series of badly jumbled pictures, the heat of his own energies had dried him out and made him inordinately thirsty, and he knew that only the harsh anxiety riding with him kept a long overdue weariness from softening him up.

But he had not fired a second shot at Lonzo. In that fractional flash of time when thinking had given way to pure action he had avoided plunging a certain shot into the prone outlaw. It was the one comfortable thought in this long, brutal night.

He reached the junction of the woodcutter's road with the north and south trail and he stopped to make a quick decision. He had a choice of two routes—one via the timber, the other by way of the prairie. Galt was perhaps half an hour ahead of him, and Galt would be sticking to the timber so that he might preserve the element of secrecy all the way to Huggins Point. The hills would slow Galt's advance; it would take the men somewhat more than an hour to reach the camped Barrier men.

Sebastian doubted if he could overtake Galt by sticking to the hills; and he stood some risk of running into Galt. But if he dropped into the near-by prairie and raced for the Point by the slightly longer route it was an even bet that he might reach his men before Galt struck.

Considering it, Sebastian continued westward down the grade. Five minutes brought him to the open bench; he filed through an arroyo, reached the flat land and swung north, keeping under the deep lee shadows of the Moonstones as he traveled.

For the first twenty minutes of that ride Sebastian alternately walked and trotted; afterwards he put his pony to a slow canter and held it till he felt the wind of the beast lift and fall heavily. He went back to a walk, nursing that wind with a jealous regard. And in this manner he traveled. The straight up-and-down silhouette of the Roosters marked the halfway point. All the prairie floor threw off a faint silver shining. The soft wind came out of Oregon, bringing along the savor of that wild distance.

He passed the section line tank, and the pony scented the water and tried to pull in there. Dead to the fore lay the high, sheer shadow of Cape Horn—where the Moonstones met the prairie as a solid cliff meets the sea. He ran against it and slowly turned the circle it made. When he was quite around he saw Barrier's campfire gleaming at the foot of Huggins Point two miles away.

To the left of the fire was a low shadow which would be the beef held by a pair of Barrier men while the rest of the crew slept. To the right the Moonstones thrust a long descending toe into the desert toward the fire. Down that incline at any moment now Galt and Galt's men would be crawling. Sebastian steadied the horse into a run.

Long and patiently waiting, Lot McGinnis at last rose from the log and stepped into the trail, listening to the soft rumor of a rider rapidly drawing up from the south. Behind Lot, a matter of a mile, was the end of the Moonstones, where lay Huggins Point. He put his arm out to touch the solid body of a tree beside the trail. There was a faint patch of sky above him, its blackness pointed by the crystal-like glitter of stars; but down here none of that faint radiance intruded upon the dense, layered shadows. He shook his head faintly and was disturbed. "One man only," he said to himself. "How could that be?"

He considered it, not quite certain, while the horse came on at a full gallop. One man, traveling fast and not caring much about the noise he made. It was that last consideration which decided Lot. He put himself partially behind the tree, calling out:

"Wait a minute."

The rider's rein jerk whipped a hard grunt out of the pony. It plunged into the brush at the side of the trail and stopped. Dust rolled up against the sheriff's face, he heard saddle leather squeal. He said, calmly: "That's all right. I know you've pulled your gun. I haven't. What's your name, friend?"

A vigilant voice said: "I don't get this. Talk again."

"I make out your voice, Matt. This is Lot McGinnis."

"What are you doin' here, sheriff? You know what's up?"

"I know," said McGinnis. But he quit speaking. His head turned and he got the impact of advancing riders. It was what he had waited for, and a sudden urgency came into his voice. "Either ride by, or get your horse off the trail."

"Sure," grunted Matt Strang. "I hear 'em. That's Galt's bunch. Who else would be rammin' through here? You know what's up, Sheriff?"

"Certainly—certainly. You better bust on to the Barrier camp."

"You're stayin'?" breathed Matt Strang. He shifted in the saddle, waiting for an answer that never came. He said softly, "Lot, you're a tough old snooser," and put his pony farther into the brush.

McGinnis spoke anxiously. "You better get on, Matt."

The reverberations rolled forward more strongly from the oncoming party. A bland, cool breeze drifted along the forest corridors and Lot McGinnis tipped his face to it and let the weight of his body rest against the tree. He lifted a hand and pinched the corners of his mustache. Years ago, he recalled, Jack McKelton had turned to bay at almost this exact spot, a big-bodied outlaw who had laughed even in his last breath. He was trying to remember McKelton's features, but the image was indistinct and far away. Time did that; time went on and all things faded behind the mists and then a man was left alone with nothing but vague memories. Well, there was an end—there always was an end. Matt Strang stood beside him, speaking again. "I think I'll stick around, Lot."

The sound of the advancing column was quite distinct. "You're young, Matt," murmured Lot McGinnis, "and a fool, like all young men. Get over behind that tree. Stay there and keep your mouth shut. Never mind anything else—keep your mouth shut." The head of the coming party was a blurred shadow just ahead. A faint jingle of metal gear ran forward; a horse sneezed. They were advancing at a slow walk. Lot McGinnis made a quarter turn, facing them directly. His hand made an involuntary swipe at his mustache again. He straightened and let his cool suggestion slide across the utter dark.

"Stop a minute, Buffalo."

The call lifted and floated and died; and afterwards motion ceased in this narrow trail and silence pulsed like the heavy slugging of a man's burdened heart. The column had frozen. Lot McGinnis waited until further waiting was dangerous. He said then: "No harm meant, Buffalo. I want to talk to you."

Buffalo's inexpressibly aroused voice said: "Who's that?"

"Lot McGinnis."

The pondering silence came once more and remained for a

longer interval. Buffalo, the sheriff knew, was smelling this obscure spot for trouble. His animal senses were reaching out in discovery. He said afterwards, in a surer, easier voice: "You alone, Lot?"

"That's right. Turn back, Buffalo."

"What?"

Lot McGinnis said with an even, painstaking distinctness: "This is the end of your picket rope, Buffalo. You've got a bright idea, but it won't work. One more killing will bring the State of Nevada down on your neck. The minute you drop another Barrier man you and your boys are going to be hunted out of the country. I propose to see that done, unless you turn back."

"And you're alone," remarked Buffalo in a sliding, sibilant calculation.

The old man read Galt's thought. "I'd be a bad man for you to shoot, Buffalo. There'd be more posses on your neck than you ever saw in this country. I have let you run too long. Turn back and pay off your crowd. A little humbler life is the prescription, my boy. As long as you were a private nuisance you didn't make anybody mad. But you're comin' to be a public nuisance—which is fatal. I have chased a lot of men through these hills who found that out too late."

"Lot," said Buffalo, all at once rash and impatient, "what the hell's this milk and honey advice for? I don't get it."

"Maybe I'm a sort of friend of yours, son."

Galt's horse moved. Galt was coming ahead. He said: "Step aside, Lot. There's no law against ridin' this trail."

But Galt's horse had to stop, for the sheriff stood in his tracks, barring the way. Galt swore out his sudden anger. "You damned relic, get out of the road."

Lot McGinnis said: "I think you're entitled to know why I'm warnin' you. It is the regret of my life you weren't told many years ago. It happens, Buffalo, that I'm your dad."

Buffalo Galt's heels audibly thumped the flanks of the pony. It sprang against Lot McGinnis. The sheriff's body vaguely stumbled backward, but Galt had wheeled and he had drawn his gun. He said something, low and fast and half-strangled, and then the flat report of his shot beat and broke against the heavy night. He fired again, all the horses of the column beginning to pitch into the brush. A man cursed at him. Another rider raced forward and knocked Galt's horse aside. "You maniac, that's your finish!" And into this boiling confusion Matt Strang laid his quick firing.

Galt's horse fell instantly and Galt was out of the saddle

withering the brush around Strang with his replying shots. But a second horse rushed between Matt and Galt and that horse threshed wickedly across this narrow interval. Somebody yelled a warning; the whole party went crashing off the trail. Galt had disappeared. There was a distant hallooing behind Matt. He heard it but his attention was violently occupied with the churning blackness around him.

Nothing definite showed up through this obscurity, yet he scraped the trail with four reckless bursts of fire and then held his peace. Flat against the tree he heard Galt's party recoil. There was a long calling through the brush, a high and angry passage of talk, and one man's insistently repeated yell: "A trap—a trap!" It kept fading backward; and another sound kept coming forward. Crouched low, Matt Strang got the nearing reports of another party. He rose then and ran into the trail. The hollow scuff of that advancing outfit rolled around a bend; he jumped off the trail and sent his sailing cry at the gray shadows scudding toward him. "Wait—Tom! Wait—wait!"

Barrier boiled around, deploying into the brush. Sebastian's calm voice said: "Who's calling?"

"Wait," ordered Matt. "Don't jump into that. Galt's been here. That's them you hear goin'. McGinnis is down on the trail. Goddammit, Galt shot him and I missed Galt!" He was back in the trail, bumping irregularly up and down the ruts. Sebastian's voice seemed to lay order and authority across the bitter confusion. "Stand fast—stand fast a minute." Burnt powder smell tainted the air. A little echo of Galt's men straggled back from the depths of this abysmal night, a faint confusion came up and a moment later the trail telegraphed a steady, dying drum. Matt stumbled over Galt's dead horse and fell forward, his skull sliding along the rough bark of a tree. He pulled himself to his knees and felt around and touched Lot McGinnis. "The man's dead," he said bitterly. Somebody came on and stood above him. Sebastian spoke. "This it?"

"Try a match."

Sebastian crouched. He said, "What are you doing here, Matt?" He struck a match and cupped it between his hands and lowered his hands until the flittering glow reached the face of Lot McGinnis, who lay there dead with his silver head rolled against the dust of the trail. One hand rested awkwardly across his chest, palm downward on a bullet hole. The light went out. Matt Strang swore from the middle of his throat and squirmed on his heels. Sebastian lighted another match, his glance going across to Matt Strang's sultry, outraged face. Matt Strang reached over and slapped out the match. He got up. He said: "I was comin' down the trail and ran into Lot. He was waitin' here for Galt. Well, he tried to stop Galt from goin' on. He said he was Galt's dad. Galt shot twice. I was slow."

Sebastian repeated quietly: "What are you doing here, Matt?"

Matt burst out: "The last two days have been hell! DePard's dead."

"You sure?"

Barrier was advancing through the brush, with Jim Kern speaking from somewhere near at hand. "That bunch has busted out of here. Why follow?" A colder breeze scoured the broken slopes; the big tree beside Matt Strang telegraphed down the straining squeal of its upper branches. Strang said, very quiet with his words: "Me and him shot it out at the base of the Moonstones. It was pretty dark and we bumped together. I wasted no time and I was lucky. I saw him die. He had a minute to tell me he was sorry for a certain thing. He wanted me to tell you—"

Sebastian broke in peremptorily. "Be quiet. I know the rest of it. I always did. Hear me, Strang. You heard nothing and you know nothing. Understand?"

Strang groaned out his words: "It's been hell, Tom! It's been hell!"

Sebastian cleared his throat. He didn't say anything but his arm lifted and dropped on the shoulder of this man who had been so deep a friend. Jim Kern was standing by. He said: "McGinnis? Well, he was one of the old ones. Like me. So that's one less. What do we do, Tom?"

"Leave a couple of men here until daylight. Rest of you go back to the beef. Put Lot on a horse and take him to Camp Four. I'll have a wagon come up from the ranch for him."

"Galt?" said Jim Kren.

"Galt?" Sebastian rose and stood there in the dark. He said, "It's all right, Jim. Galt's men are smart enough to know what will happen now. By noon tomorrow most of them will be out of Nevada." He joined Strang and they went single file down the trail. Three miles ahead they fell into the broader Camp Four road, followed it over the summit and so came upon the shanties and the waiting car. Striking a match to his watch then, Sebastian found it to be three o'clock. In another hour day would crack through the solid black wall eastward.

Chapter 11

They drove into Barrier plaza at breakfast time and found a rather lonely group clustered at the head of the long dining room table. The campaign in the Moonstones had taken away all but four of the ranch crew, Charm and Charm's son, and the Hollywood people.

"You look very pious and somewhat bored," observed Sebastian.

"This place was meant for a crowd," said Jay Stuart agreeably. "It's so empty now that even the echoes follow us around for company. However we haven't been bored. Timmy's been teaching us to read cattle brands."

Charm had instantly risen. Her dark still eyes clung to Sebastian, slowly reading him. "Have you had luck?" she asked, a deep and personal anxiety coloring the quietness of her talk.

"It's all right," he said, and glanced across her shoulder to Lily Tennant. Lily hadn't spoken; but her smile was waiting there for him. He should have felt the lifting power of that smile. But he didn't. Utterly weary, he went around the table and sat down beside her. Matt Strang followed suit. Gath, who was an old man and privileged with his tongue, spoke sarcastically to Strang:

"What you doin' here? I thought you'd—"

"Gath," said Charm Michelet, her voice peremptorily ordering him to be still. But her attention divided itself intently between Strang and Sebastian a moment, seeking the story. Afterwards she went out to the kitchen and returned with a plate of hot biscuits and freshly crisped bacon, and placed it in front of Sebastian.

"Any news?" said Kit, who thus far had remained silent.

"Nothing much," responded Sebastian. But then he looked around him, at the rest of the crew, at Charm. He spoke evenly, without emphasis. "I hate to tell you this. Lot McGinnis was killed early this morning."

The silence came on, full and speculative. They were all watching Sebastian. Lily Tennant's head turned and she explored his enigmatic features with a thoughtful attention. A telltale smokiness again laid a cloud across his brow line. She had known him only a week, but she knew him thoroughly—and this expression was a warning.

Some aimless conversation ended the meal. Standing beside the door to let the others pass through, Sebastian dropped his arms around Tommy rushing by and pulled the youngster up to his chest. He said: "Son, it's high time you were learning to ride. I'm going to buy you a pony. You want a pony?"

Tommy laughed from the bottom of his chest and yelled, "Yuh—pony!" And began to kick his way down Sebastian's long frame. He pushed his way around the big people and ran across the living room, awkward on his unsteady legs. He tripped on a rug, fell soundly, and laughed again. Sebastian watched him a moment and then turned up the stairs to his room.

Weariness slowed him down. He pulled off his shirt and filled the wash basin with hot water, doggedly lathered his face, and watched the gaunt and dried-out features of a stranger appear behind the stroke of the razor. He was, he thought somberly, growing old. Well, he never had been young. The responsibilities of Barrier had fallen upon him at eighteen and the wildness of early manhood had died then.

It was something he would always regret—that little interval when nothing much mattered and the hours of the day were to be spent carelessly, without calculation. He had passed that by. He had seen it go. Now and then deep rebellion punished him and now and then some perception of the happiness life ought to hold stormed through him and made the routine of the ranch empty and dismal. There had been such a moment as this in Bill Fell's cabin. And when he had held Lily in his arms, the fragrance and richness and desirability of the girl had swept him up to the highest peak of living.

He scrubbed the soap from his face and walked stolidly back to his shirt. He tucked it in. There had been that one moment. But that was all. He was looking back at something that wouldn't come again. He was seeing the last of his hope die. In a few years he would be like his father—a man turning grayer with the seasons, not particularly afraid of the future but seeing no personal happiness in it, living only for Barrier. The events of the last twelve hours had laid upon him a duty and in the ride from the scene of the fight to the ranch house he had made up his mind to accept it—because he could honestly do nothing else.

He was standing in the middle of his room, scowling down

at the floor, when Charm quietly entered. She closed the door and stood against it.

"What happened?"

"It might have been pretty bad. Galt was riding for Huggins Point with his boys. But Lot stopped him on the way. He killed Lot. That was Buffalo's fatal mistake. He won't hold his men. They'll skip out."

"So you're through with them?"

"Not yet, Charm. Galt is still here."

She put up her hands in a protesting way. "Tom, I don't want you to go through any more of it."

"Steady."

She looked at him and he saw the blackness of her fear; then she dropped her head and said in a soft, submissive voice: "I will say no more. You must do what you wish."

"Not what I wish, but what is necessary."

She put her hands together. They trembled perceptibly from the pressure she squeezed into them. Sebastian drew a long breath. His tone was very slow, very deliberate.

"Charm, do you want me?"

Her head lifted swiftly and shock raced across her face. Her lips parted, but she didn't speak. The rising glow of her eyes spoke for her. It turned all her features soft, it made her at the moment beautiful. He had always known the depths of this girl and the strong tide of feeling behind her reticence; only, this was something more powerful than he had imagined.

He said quietly: "You are a fine woman, Charm. Any man ought to be proud to have you. I would be. I think I've been cheating you these last years. You've never asked for anything. If my name means anything to you I'd like you and Tommy to have it."

She came forward, still without voice. She reached up and placed her arms on his shoulders and slid her hands behind his neck, lacing them tightly together. Her glance passed slowly across his face, from feature to feature, as though she were storing what she saw unforgettably in her mind. The pressure of her hands drew him down. He put his big palms behind her back, to steady her as she came upward on her toes; and when he kissed her he felt the primitive and fierce surrender of her body. She was giving herself to him as an outright gift, without a single thought of reserve. He knew that. He knew that whatever he did to this girl in the years to come, she would never change and never regret. It was a fidelity that had no limits.

It shamed him to know he was receiving more than he could give; to know that part of his feelings would be locked away from her. But he was thinking, as he kissed her, that she would never know that lack in him and never have cause to grieve. It was his decision. He released her and stepped back, and he was humbled at the quality of beauty in her eyes then. He said: "I'm going to Tumpah. I should be back in two hours. Tomorrow, if it suits you, we'll run in to Reno and have Judge Sillavan marry us."

He waited for her answer. But she didn't speak; she only nodded—that radiance which was deeper than smiling turning all her faintly olive features supple and eager. He went across the room and out to the balcony; and because she had stirred in him a tenderness not far from tragic he closed the door quite softly behind.

The Hollywood people were scattered in the big chairs around the fireplace, talking in brief and enigmatic phrases. The ranch, he saw, had relaxed them. The impatience and the wore edge they had brought to Barrier a few days before was quite gone. He went down the stairs and over to the phone. He rang Carson City and called for Mark Haley, who was the governor's political adviser. He waited there, slouched against the wall, listening to the melody in Lily Tennant's voice as she talked. Mark Haley came on the wire.

"This is Tom Sebastian, Mark. I'm at the ranch. You know the situation up here—you remember what I told you last week?"

"Yeah. So now what?"

"Buffalo Galt shot and killed Lot McGinnis this morning about two o'clock. This was up in the Moonstones. You get hold of the governor, Mark, and have him send a couple of special deputies up here. No, not tomorrow. Today." He didn't say any more. He hung up and turned to his guests.

"I've been a poor host," he said. "As soon as I come back from Tumpah I hope to be a better one."

Kit rolled her dark head on the leather back of the chair in which she was deeply settled. She watched him in the dark, odd way which made him somehow uncomfortable. She said: "You have let us alone. You haven't put us through the jumps. So you've been a perfect host, Tom."

"If the visit has rested you I'm mighty happy. You all needed a rest."

Her hands lifted from the arms of the chair and made an expressive gesture. "You knew the desert would get us, didn't you? I told you when we came that it was an insidious influence. I was right."

He grinned. She was trying to resent the influence of the ranch but couldn't. He turned to meet Lily's quiet glance, and the humor left him. It fell instantly out of him. "I'll see you in a couple hours," he told her and went across the living room. Out in the plaza, beside her car, he heard her voice come after him; and he turned and watched her walk forward with that slow, purely unconscious grace that was something like music. The swing of her supple body and the tilt of her head sent strange, rough currents of feeling through him. She stopped in front of him, the first brilliant sunlight shining across her smooth brown hair. He could not escape the infinitely direct and candid curiosity of her eyes. She was puzzled; she was disturbed.

"You've changed, Tom," she told him.

He had to do something with his hands. So he pulled out his pipe and slowly packed it, keeping his eyes on the chore. "I guess I'm a little tired, Lily."

"You're not being altogether honest with me. Are you thinking of—of what may be between Jay Stuart and me?"

"No," he said, very brief.

"Would it make a difference?"

"No. You're an honest woman, whatever you have done. You couldn't be otherwise."

"Have I been too bold, Tom? Perhaps I have. You mustn't judge me by the ordinary rules of womanly reticence. Hollywood teaches us to speak for what we want. I had hoped you'd understand that the other day by the water tank. I have to go where my heart goes. I can't help it."

"It is the finest thing in you—and I'll never forget it."

Her voice came to him so slow and so subdued that he brought up his head. "That sounds as though you are saying good-bye, Tom."

He could not help but see the hurt—the deep hurt—lying on her grave cheeks. And that was like a knife turning in him. He put his pipe back into his pocket and drew a long breath. "Lily," he said, and stopped. He couldn't bring himself to tell her what he had to say. He couldn't bring himself to it at this moment. He added lamely, "I want to talk something out with you, when I come back."

She looked steadily at him; and then she was quite pale. She murmured, "All right," and turned away and walked back to the house. Sebastian crawled into the car and kicked on the engine. Matt Strang, meanwhile standing discreetly outside this scene, came rapidly forward. He put a hand on the car door.

"Where you going?"

"Tumpah."

"Then I'll go."

"No," said Sebastian. He looked at Matt Strang. He said, "I'm gald you're back here, kid," and sent the car across the plaza, ripping up the dust recklessly. Straightening into the Tumpah road, he said bitterly to himself: "I ruin whatever I touch. There never was a chance for Lily and me. I knew it in the beginning. There will be ten minutes' misery for her, and that's all my fault. God damn you, Sebastian!"

After Sebastian had left the room Charm listened to the footfalls die down the stairs, a queer dreaming expression along her faintly flushed cheeks. She head the murmur of talk in the living room and the subsequent sound of the car starting. Going to the bedroom window she watched Sebastian drive around the house and point for Tumpah, and then her calm manner turned shaded and fearful. Wheeling about, she went to the door and opened it and started out. But she stopped on the threshold, drew back and closed the door again. Lily Tennant was coming up the stairs.

She stood with one hand on the knob, her lips faintly parted, her breathing quickened. Happiness was a thing that swelled through her and filled her with a kind of glory. There was a feeling in her of richness, of fullness. To her eyes the room was beautiful and every object in it touched by grace and a kind of melody, nameless and tuneless, was in her mind. But because she was so overflowing with this happiness, because it sharpened her imagination and made her so responsive to the emotions of life, a sudden and sharp sadness came to her at the thought of what this meant for Lily Tennant. From the wild heights of her own mood she saw the darkness of loving and not being loved. Her lips trembled and came tightly together. She opened the door in dread, just as Lily reached the balcony.

"Might I see you a moment?"

Lily said, "Certainly," with a small show of surprise and came into the room. Charm didn't close the door; she held her hand on its knob and studied the other girl's unusual soberness. She had envied Lily Tennant, but that was gone now. She dropped her eyes, speaking almost humbly.

"Has Tom spoken to you?"

"No," said Lily. "About what?"

Charm's words were sad and a little puzzled. "He was in such a hurry I thought he hadn't. It is strange to me that men can be strong sometimes and at other times run from their strength. This is a cruel thing and maybe you will hate me. There have been days when I hated you, and I'm ashamed of that meanness now. But I don't want you to hate me."

"If it is something you two have discussed," suggested Lily gently, "perhaps you may tell me."

Charm straightened her slim body. A native dignity composed her face. She said: "We are to be married."

There was a wonder in her then that a woman could be so stoical, so resolute in pain. Lily Tennant's mouth reshaped itself slowly, the full, soft curve disappearing; and Lily Tennant's eyes changed. The white, compressed calm was something Charm could not understand. The silence clung to the room a moment. Then Lily spoke slowly and without emotion. Her lips scarcely moved. "You are getting a very fine gentleman, Charm. I congratulate you."

"Yes," said Charm. "I know that." Lily Tennant's pride left in this girl a deeper humbleness. But her happiness kept thrusting itself forward and she could not help saying what she did. "Why shouldn't I know it? I have lived beside him many years. I know what makes him happy and I know what makes him sad. You see, I have trained myself for him. I will not be a burden, I will never be silly or bold."

Lily lifted a hand faintly. Her tone remained rigidly even. "Is there another auto on the ranch? I should like to get back to Reno rather soon."

Charm said, with a simplicity that mirrored the fatalism of long-gone ancestors: "It is best. If I did not think so I should have let him tell you. To see him again would be sadness for you. It would be worse than it is now. This is why I have told you, before he came back. Gath will bring a car around, and drive you to town."

"Thank you," said Lily. Then she added: "You're a lovely girl, Charm," and wheeled swiftly from the room.

Charm put her hands to the house keys at her belt—the symbols of her life. She was trying not to cry.

Sebastian reached Tumpah an hour after leaving the ranch, having used up most of this time in a detour of the desert that carried him back and forth several times across the trail between Tumpah and the Moonstones. When he passed Madame Gilson's place he saw no ponies standing outside. He didn't stop there; nor at the garage, though the garage hand waved at him. He was operating on a guess but he didn't want to question any of the Tumpah people who had enough grief living between two fires without being dragged into further trouble. Beyond town he took the small road climbing past the graveyard, passed into the thin pines and ran the machine straight abreast the porch of Buffalo Galt's shanty.

He cut the engine. He called out: "Buffalo," and raked the empty yard and the adjacent barn with one rapid glance. After a little silence he called again, got out of the machine and walked across the porch. This was asking for trouble. Yet the impulse in him was so strong that he turned the knob, kicked the door open with his foot and swayed aside from the opening. He waited a moment, hand on the butt of his gun, then stepped fully into the doorway. The room was quite empty.

He went back to the kitchen, explored it visually, and crossed to the bedroom; and he stood there a while with his back indifferently to the porch and speculated on the suit of neat black laid out on the bed. A drawer of the bureau was pulled open, but it hadn't been emptied. A suitcase lay on a chair, partially filled. Presently he swung into the front room, sat down in a chair and soberly packed his pipe. He was facing the porch, with his ears cocked to any sound traveling up the near-by road.

His guess, he told himself, was working out right. Galt had returned to Tumpah because nothing on earth could keep the man away from his headquarters. But Galt had returned alone. A scrutiny of the desert trail between Tumpah and the Moonstones had revealed a broad tide of tracks leading into the hills—which was Galt's outfit heading for Huggins Point. There was no such definite print of riders returning. It was as his father had long ago told him: Outlaws would follow a leader as long as the leader was lucky. But there was no loyalty among crooks. They were like animals, forever keening the wind. When scent came into the wind they faded back into the brush. Galt's men had followed Galt as long as he had avoided a showdown; but the killing of Lot McGinnis was a bad omen, for he was a part of the law—and the law would strike back. They would travel to other ranges.

Sebastian lifted his chin, listening into the morning's stillness. The sludge in the bottom of his pipe fried sibilantly. He sat there, his black bare head bowed doggedly, teeth clenching the pipestem. This one incident had broken Galt's hold, it had dispersed Galt's guerrilla army. But Galt was still here.

He remained still and contemplative, reflecting on the man's uncanny luck. It had pulled Buffalo through many a narrow place; in all this fighting he had never been touched. He seemed to have a savage prescience of trouble which warned him when and where to move, and it might be that this wild instinct would guide him in the last maneuver of the long-drawn game. There was no certainty when men took to the killing trade. Somebody had to die and nobody could guess the answer before the smoke cleared. One thing remained certain: Galt's incredible ambition and his deep cunning would never let him be still. He would never stop fighting Barrier till his breath stopped.

Sebastian tapped his pipe stolidly on the edge of the table; he refilled it and stuck it back between his teeth and got up. He no longer had any choice in the matter; nor was his mind doubtful. In the long ride from Huggins Point to the ranch house he had squared his mind of two inevitable decisions. One related to Charm, the other to Buffalo. In both things he had let himself drift too long, hoping for an easy end. But there was no easy end. He had committed one mistake in allowing himself to love Lily Tennant. He had been soft about that, hoping for the impossible to happen; and he had let her in for grief. He would not be soft with Buffalo and allow other people to suffer that mistake.

He looked at his watch, put on his hat and went back to the car, scanning the surrounding yard with a long, sharp glance; and he drove back into the town and stopped at the garage pump. He got out and waited till the garage hand came from the back of the shop.

"Fill the tank, Lee." He bent his body against the machine indolently and watched Lee. He didn't want to ask the man any questions; he tried to get his information without it. Lee Bond stood with his hand on the pump, not making any effort to lift down the hose suspended by the pump. He stared at Sebastian.

"Tom," he said, and cleared his throat.

"What's that?"

"When you pull out of town—"

"I'm not asking you anything, Lee. Don't get yourself in a jackpot. You've got to live here."

Lee said, "Well, don't drive past that shed down there at the street-end." He unhooked the hose and walked to the rear of the car. He added another word that Sebastian didn't hear. Sebastian put his palms flat on the car's hot hood, thinking of the warning. He stared at his fingers and mentally surrounded the shed Lee had mentioned.

It stood halfway between Madame Gilson's and the last building on the right side of the street. There was a front door, a single front window and a back door. Once upon a time it had been a saddle shop. But it was a silly place for a man to use for an ambush because it had two blind sides. The thing to do was to cross the street to the north walk, go down the walk to the last building, cut away from the walk and approach the shed by one of its blind sides. He knew what would happen if Buffalo was inside. Buffalo would come swarming out, because Buffalo couldn't stand a waiting game. But it didn't sound right to Sebastian. Buffalo had too much guts and too much pride to hide and shoot a man driving past. There was something haywire. . . .

He pushed himself back casually from the hood and made a slow turn, intending to cross the street to the northern walk. He took three slow steps in that direction and then stopped. Buffalo Galt walked out the yonder shed as though bent on business of no particular importance, reached the exact middle of the road and turned and came marching on.

Drawing all his senses inward, Sebastian watched Galt advance in that exact measured stride with a cold flash of admiration. Buffalo had reasoned out his attack and he was putting pure will into it, suppressing that unreasoning anger which so often jerked him around. There was a gaunt nakedness of purpose here—a strict obedience to a lifelong obsession. It was a gamble that Buffalo didn't need to make. He could be retreating to the hills like the rest of the party. But here he was, out in the middle of the street, under the hot sunlight, playing his stack down to the last white chip; trying to make that last white chip good. His confidence in his own luck was unshakable.

One part of Sebastian's mind was engaged in this remote thinking; the rest of his head registered every detail of the street and of the oncoming man. The distance between the shed and his position by the car was approximately four hundred feet, far beyond the limits of accurate revolver play. Buffalo knew it as well, for he made no attempt to draw. He came unerrantly on, a broad and chunky figure swaying a little from side to side as he marched, but cleaving a straight line out of the dust. He was in his shirtsleeves and the yellow hair of his hatless head picked up the sunlight and heightened the ruddy color of his face. And he wore a gun strapped on either thigh—the first time Sebastian had ever seen such double armament on the range.

Sebastian's attention centered on those two guns and tried to fathom the reason for them. A man moved along the right side of his vision sidling from one building door to another; on the same side of the town another man put his head and shoulders through a second story window and remained there. Sebastian heard Lee drop the gas hose and say, "Good God," in a swift, shocked way, and retreat for shelter. The sun burned on his wrists and the smell of fear freshened across the dead morning air.

Sebastian spoke into the utter stillness. "Buffalo," he called out, "stop right there." But he quit talking, understanding the uselessness of it. Buffalo had covered half the distance without a sound, nor did he bother to speak afterwards. Sebastian's straight-hanging right arm swung gently and touched the gunbutt held in the holster there; but he didn't draw and he wasn't worried about that. It wasn't a question of speed. It was a question of nerves. The man who broke before another hundred feet of that distance had been closed up was simply punching his lead through so much space—simply emptying his gun. The sun was behind him, over his left shoulder; his shadow ran off at a right angle, straight and rigid.

At a hundred and fifty feet—or with better than half the distance covered—Buffalo reached down, pulled his left gun, transferred it to his right hand, and began firing. At the same time his stride lengthened out and he broke into a run.

Sebastian swung and put his left shoulder point toward Buffalo, decreasing the target he made for the man; and remained so, without drawing. All the echoes of the town came crashing down on his head. The first shot smashed through the windshield of his car and pieces went flanking and jangling across the hood. The second shot laced the dust at his feet; of the other four from that gun he had no record. The breath of them touched him and died—that was all he knew. He kept his eyes pinned to Buffalo's changing face. Stone-cold, he watched a red blood congest it. The man's will was inflexibly bent to the chore but his aim wasn't true enough and the knowledge of it seemed to kick a fiercer insanity out of him.

He had covered another fifty feet at the end of the sixth shot. When that sixth shot tore through the undulating noise of this street, Sebastian's mind changed. The report was still rushing through the town when he moved into the fight. His eyes registered Buffalo's subsequent actions. Buffalo flung the empty gun aside and dropped his right hand to the remaining weapon lying at his right thigh. At the same time he came to a full stop.

Sebastian's bullet caught him thus poised in his tracks, with his fresh gun lifting for a more deliberate aim. Sebastian fired once, and then a second time and slowly lowered his gun.

That second shot struck Buffalo in the pot of the stomach and knocked a long, hollow grunt out of him. He broke at the knees, at the hips and at the neck and he fell in an awkward wheeling motion, with his arms feebly seeking to break the shock of his collapse. He rolled once and tried to support himself on his elbows, but strength poured fast out of him and he fell again, face deep in the dust. One final effort turned him over on a shoulder. There he rested.

Sebastian's voice tonelessly crossed the thick, descending silence. "Are you through, Buffalo?"

Buffalo didn't answer. Sebastian walked forward, the squeal of his boots quite loud in his own ears. He circled Buffalo and looked down. Buffalo's eyes rolled up at him, and it startled Sebastian inexpressibly to see the gray calmness of death settling across that face which but one moment before had been so crowded with life and passion.

"Are you through?" he repeated quietly.

There was a disturbance on the farther edge of Sebastian's vision and he looked up to see Madame Gilson running out of her saloon. The loud bawling of her voice shattered the stillness. "Buffalo—Buffalo!" People were standing on the walks, staring out upon this scene; but they weren't coming forward. Sebastian lowered his head.

"Buffalo—what was all the extra shooting for?"

Buffalo's tone was controlled by that same remote, fatal calm which lay in his eyes. He said, articulating his words distinctly: "I was trying to break your nerve, friend Tom. To break your nerve before I got within good range."

"I waited you out, Buffalo."

"Yes," said Buffalo. And then some last flash of the old rage warmed his veins: "You always bragged about that. Jesus, it's a bitter thing to see you standin' there sound and hearty on your feet, with me here. I spent my life fightin' Barrier and I've broke my heart against it, friend Tom, and I've found out you can't whip a Sebastian. God damn you, I've found that out!"

Sebastian heard his name gasped out; and lifted his head. Madame Belle Gilson was running up, the loose flesh of her shoulders jouncing at each step, the gray hair streaming its frowsy way across her beet-red cheeks. She had thrown her head back from exertion and her mouth was a wide unlovely smear out of which came a weird lowing cry. She dropped on her knees and crawled toward Buffalo; and she lifted him up and cradled his head into her capacious bosom.

"Buffalo—my boy!"

Buffalo's face was faintly ironical. He said faintly: "This is a late date to remember it, Madame."

"My boy," she repeated, voice high and strangling.

"Madame, I'm cashing in. It's been a rotten game all along. But I hold nothing against anybody for that."

Madame's red eyes peered through the screen of disheveled hair to Sebastian. She didn't seem to see him. She looked down again at Galt.

"Who was my father?" muttered Buffalo. "Be quick about it, Madame. I've got one foot across the line right now."

"Louis, my son—" said Madame.

"What's that?" asked Buffalo, very drowsy.

"Louis is your name. But I'm the only one that ever called you that."

"I'd forgotten," murmured Buffalo. "It's been such a hell of a long while ago. Madame, your shoulder's comfortable and I don't mind dyin' on it. It's straight that Lot McGinnis was my father?"

"Lot McGinnis."

Galt let out a long, low groan. "What a hell of a joke." He tried to rise and fell back, head rolling across the Madame's lap. Sebastian abruptly removed his hat and walked away.

He put his hands on the car door. He said to the garage hand, "Fill the tank, Lee," and bent his head downward until it rested on his knuckles. He was incredibly tired. Lee said presently, "It's full, Tom." Sebastian crawled behind the wheel and kicked on the engine. He explored his pockets for his pipe and couldn't find it; and then he turned the car wide around Madame Gilson, who sat there in the dusty street and held the dead Buffalo's shoulders in her arms and slowly rocked him. He left Tumpah immediately.

Chapter 12

Tom Sebastian left Barrier for Tumpah at eight o'clock. The Hollywood people pulled away fifteen minutes later in the extra ranch machine piloted by Gath. Standing on the porch, Matt Strang watched them go and couldn't understand why. They had all been kind enough to say good-bye to him, but they had explained nothing and he was too taciturn a man to ask. Charm had not appeared. Reflecting on this, Matt turned into the living room and found the girl halfway down the stairs, waiting, listening.

"What'd they go for, Charm?"

She didn't answer. Matt saw the unhappiness of her face and drove another question at her.

"You never cared much for those folks. Did you say something disagreeable that made 'em leave?"

She said, very quietly, "It is terrible not to be loved, Matt. My heart aches for her."

He didn't understand; he stared at her. "What's that?"

"It was best," she said.

He said roughly: "Come down here, Charm." And he waited, darkly scowling at the girl, until she had descended the last steps and stopped in front of him. "What was it you told her, Charm?"

"That Tom was marrying me."

He said loudly: "You lied."

Her eyes widened. "No, Matt, it is true. This morning he asked me."

He took off his hat and threw it into a chair. He plunged his fists deep into his pockets and held them stiffly there. He was a harassed and bitter looking man then, with his feelings scoured brutally by what he had to say. "Kid," he said, "I love you—I can't help it. It doesn't do me any good to have to tell you this. But I guess it's my chore."

Some of the light faded out of her eyes. They became startled and fearing. Her breath quickened. "What, Matt?" she asked him in a weak voice.

There was a clear misery in this man. He didn't look at her directly. "Charm, the daddy of your boy is Duke DePard.

And how in God's name did you ever get mixed up with him? I don't understand."

"How do you know?"she whispered.

"I know."

Her shoulders were slack. She said dispiritedly: "I'm sorry you know."

He repeated his question more gently. "How'd you ever mix with Duke, Charm?"

She made a slow, tired gesture with her arms. "I was very silly four years ago, Matt. I met him a few times at the dances—I believed the things he told me. Afterwards—" and the words came out in a long downsweep of tone. "Afterwards I knew better. For he never met me again. He forgot about me. Go ahead, Matt. Go ahead and hate me."

"No," said Matt, "it was a mistake anybody could make. I don't hold it against you."

"Tom told me that once."

"Look," he said, "we've got to straighten out this mess. Sit down, Charm. This is tough, but I got to tell you."

She made no effort to sit down until he pushed her gently back to the divan. He turned away from her, scowling at the room, his raw and homely cheeks thinly drawn. She said in a rapid, fearing voice: "Matt—what—" That whipped him around. He drew a long breath. He said:

"Duke DePard's dead. We collided out on the desert last night and there wasn't any other way. Just before he cashed in he said he wanted you to know he regretted what he'd done. He was sorry he hadn't gone through with the bargain. And he was sorry he'd never seen his boy."

Still and slack, her eyes showed no forgiveness. She remembered, but not with pity. "I have no sympathy for him."

Well, when Tom came here this morning and proposed to you, he knew DePard was dead and that Tommy had no father. As long as DePard was alive there was just a chance that something might happen to make the situation straight. That chance is gone, DePard bein' dead. So Tom did what he felt was the thing he had to do. I read that man like a book. He wouldn't let you and the kid down. He wouldn't dodge a chore. Not ever. But to fix things straight he had to say so-long to whatever hopes he had with the Tennant girl. Good God, Charm, couldn't you see how he looked at her?"

She said, brokenly: "No. He asked me—and he meant it!"

Matt pointed his long finger at her. "Listen," he said. "Listen to me."

But she was crying. She didn't hear.

Sebastian drove into the Barrier plaza at ten o'clock and got out, so weary he didn't see Matt Strang sitting on the steps until his boot struck Matt's boot. He stepped back and scrubbed his big hand across his eyes, and found Matt looking curiously at him. Matt didn't get up. He said in an indolent, summery voice:

"A little trouble, Mr. Sebastian? You look like hell."

"Matt, I'm going to sleep the clock around."

"It would be swell if you could. Your eyes are fit to burn holes in something. But you ain't sleepin' yet. You're about to drive into Reno. And I wouldn't delay it much."

"What?"

"Sit down," suggested Matt, "before you fall down. I got to make a speech. I don't like it, so don't interrupt. But sit down."

Sebastian obeyed. He propped his elbows on his knees, and cradled his head in his broad palms. He said, irritably: "I'll listen to it."

"Sure you will, Mr. Sebastian," said Matt Strang, dry and humorless. "It was a large gesture you made, but it won't work. If there is any marryin' to be done, I'll do it. That's been decided between Charm and me already. It's a date."

Sebastian reared back. "Matt—" he said.

"Don't interrupt. This is tough enough as it is. I come out of the bunkhouse and I see your guests driving for Reno. I don't know why, so I asked Charm who tells me she's informed the Tennant girl you've decided to marry her. Charm, I mean. I don't get that, for I've got eyes enough to see where your appetite is as regards the two women. Well, your guests leave after that."

"Matt," said Sebastian, heavy and displeased, "why did you interfere?"

Matt Strang narrowed his eyes against the sunlight. He looked far out into the desert. His lips came thinly together. He said: "Don't be noble, kid. This mess is bad enough. I got it straight and straight it stays. Everybody can't get what they want, but that's no reason for cheating somebody else out of a break. Like I said, Charm and I are going to be the first and second parties to this particular marriage. Get to Reno and see what you can do about the rest of it."

"Where's Charm?"

"In her room. Let her alone."

But Sebastian got up and went inside. He climbed the

stairs and went to Charm's door and tapped his knuckles against it. He said, "Charm, I want to see you," and tried the knob. It didn't give; it was locked. Standing there, lips making a solemn, tough line across his sun-darkened face, he listened carefully and heard nothing. The silence inside was stubborn and absolute. He said, more persuasively, "Charm," and knocked again. The skin on his forehead wrinkled up, the smokiness deepened in his eyes. She was in there, but she wouldn't speak. And at once he knew what the whole answer was. He turned back down the stairs and crossed to the porch. Matt Strang still sat on the steps, staring narrowly at the far horizon.

"She's hurt, Matt," muttered Sebastian.

"Wouldn't you be if you'd had the bottom of things knocked out from under your feet?"

"You damn fool—"

Strang got up abruptly. "No, it wouldn't work the other way. She thought you liked her best, when you proposed. She believed it, all right—until I stepped in with the truth. But even if I hadn't said anything, she'd found out soon enough. A man can't keep his heart hid from a woman very long. She'd discover the truth and you'd keep rememberin' Lily and both of you'd end up miserable. This is the best way out. She knows it now. As for me, I'm happy for what luck I've got. Go on, get in the car."

Sebastian put his arm on Strang's shoulders and stared somberly at the man's taciturn cheeks. "Kid," he said. "Kid—"

Matt Strang's laconic manner was only a forgery. It fell apart now and some of the emotion he hated to show got into his talk. "You're the only damned man in the world I'd play second-fiddle to, Tom. But I'm satisfied. We got to take the breaks we get and make 'em do. No use cryin' for somethin' that can't be had—or all of us would be cryin' till the world turned to water." He stopped talking and dragged out his handkerchief; and he blew his nose soundly. "There's one thing I wish you'd do for Charm and me. We can't live in the ranch house—"

"You'll never leave Barrier," broke in Sebastian.

"No, Barrier's all we've got. Anyhow, Tommy's your kid as well as mine. So we want to build a house up at Camp Four, on the edge of that meadow—"

"Yes," said Sebastian.

Matt suddenly thought of something. "I never asked you how you came out in Tumpah."

"I met Buffalo on the street."

"So that's over?"

"That's over."

"Tough," muttered Matt. "But it's the end of scrappin'."

Sebastian looked carefully at his foreman. "Matt, you've changed."

"Yeah," said Matt, "I guess I have. Watchin' DePard die last night got me. He wasn't any good, but he died with nothing but regret for his mistakes and it didn't make sense—and nothing made sense. It's tough. It's—" He tried to catch some solid word for the intangible emotions in him. But there were no proper words. "It's a hell of a thing to have the disposition of a man's life on your conscience. I can't be sorry for what's happened. But I don't feel so eager to lift a gun again."

"I have felt that way since the day my father died, Matt."

"Just so. Therefore get in that buggy and bust for Reno. I don't know if you can fix it up or not. It's a pretty bad mess. But go after it, kid."

Sebastian crawled under the wheel. Matt slammed the car door and swung away, embarrassed over all that he had had to say. Sebastian drove out of the plaza and straightened for Reno, one hundred and forty miles away. The brassy glare of another hot day lay across the land.

A little past one o'clock Sebastian entered Reno, cruised down Center Street and slid in to the curb. Haste had driven him recklessly all the way from the ranch and a fear of finding Lily gone was very real in him. But there was one prior chore that he had to get done—one logical step to take that wound up all his difficulties. Leaving the car, he walked around a corner, went up a flight of steps and entered a plain office ante-room. The sign on the door said: "Ed Brean—Land and Mining Investments." A young man stood at a window, reading a paper. He looked over the top of the paper carelessly. When he saw Sebastian he lowered it at once.

"Brean in?"

"I'll see," said the young man.

"Never mind," countered Sebastian. He went to an inner door and pushed it before him. The young man said, "Just a minute," but Sebastian, entering Brean's private office, closed the door behind him, definitely keeping the young man out. Brean turned suddenly in his swivel chair.

"Ed," said Sebastian, inexpressibly cool with his words. "You're a very cagey man and you never leave any tracks behind you. I have nothing to prove against you. But it doesn't matter."

Brean's bland face tightened preceptibly. His eyes revealed a wary interest; they clung to Sebastian. "All Sebastians," he murmured, "run true to form."

"You're all through up my way," said Sebastian. "Maybe you already know it, but if you don't I'll supply you with some elementary information. Buffalo Galt is dead and Duke DePard is dead. This morning you haven't got a man left in that country who'll run errands for you."

"The news," murmured Brean, "has already reached me." He put his fat arms on the edge of his chair and adjusted his overflowing body in it. He took a cold cigar from the table and clamped it between his solid jaws. The gray hard surface of his already inscrutable face became more pronounced. He was a poker player, looking on now at the uncertain fall of the cards. He had spent his life fighting Sebastians. But there was nothing to indicate his inward feelings. "All Sebastians are alike," he repeated.

"Just so," agreed Sebastian. He reached into his pocket and took out two empty cartridge shells. He laid them on the desk, in front of Brean. Brean's glance whipped down to them.

"There," indicated Sebastian, "is the sum and substance of my argument with Buffalo this morning. I can prove nothing against you. But it makes no difference. You're completely through with Barrier. I don't want you or any man working for you to cross my soil again or enter Tumpah again. Should you be inclined to question that, just look again at the shells. That's my answer, now, or at any future time."

"I seem to hear Henry Sebastian talking," murmured Brean and raised his round, fat countenance. Then he said: "Nothing changes much in this world. I wish I was thirty years younger. I would throw those shells back in your face and personally do what I can find no man to do for me. If I only had a son—"

"You're through," broke in Sebastian in a still, definite voice.

Brean only looked at him. A small reflection of the ancient hostility was working its way through the gross tissues of his cheeks and making some small disturbance around his heavy lips. But it died soon and left him as he was before, uncommunicative and obscure. Sebastian turned on his heels without further talk and went down to his car. He backed out of the parking space, circled to Virginia Street, crossed the

Truckee and drove to the little bungalow behind the locust trees. He stopped and sat still a moment, staring straight ahead of him, some anxiety and excitement pumping through him; and a sudden deep recklessness reached all along his muscles, to make him forgetful of his extraordinary weariness.

He got out and walked up the bungalow steps. There were four trunks standing on the porch and some handbags, and the door of the house was open. Looking through it, he saw all the Hollywood people standing around. When he went in they turned toward him and he could not tell just then whether they hated him or scorned him. In any event they had no words for him. His attention swung to Lily who had placed her hands on the center table as though to steady her body. The whiteness along her clear cheeks was distinct; and then he saw resentment appear on her lips and in the tilt of her head. The silence was very strong, very cold.

He said: "I'd like to say something on my own account, Lily." He wasn't asking the others to leave the room. He was really ordering them to go. He knew no other way to handle it; he had to be intolerant and arbitrary because the fear inside him was pretty real. He had to smash his way through opposition again. It was the only thing he had any faith in now.

Jay Stuart said, inhospitably, "This is a little bit thick, Sebastian," and showed his anger. Kit had moved away to a wall; her back was placed against it and she stared at him with an aloofness and reserve that would not admit recognition. Even Timmy Akin seemed to have no sympathy for him. He was, Sebastian thought, in the enemy's camp. They would show him no mercy. They had Lily back in her old life and they wouldn't let her go.

But Lily said unexpectedly: "All right."

"Lily," protested Jay.

"Run along—all of you," Lily Tennant told them. Her manner was unbreakable. Timmy walked out to the porch immediately; Kit Christopher crossed to the more stubborn Jay and took his arm and they went down the kitchen hall, closing the door behind them.

"I don't know why I should hear you, Tom," said Lily Tennant. "The whole thing is over."

He rubbed one heavy palm across his hand and felt no hope. He was tired to the marrow, he was discouraged. Now that he was here he had nothing much to say for himself. That suddenly did his recklessness leave him—the sight of Lily had wrecked his nerve this soon. She stood behind the table, straight and supple and proud. She was actually a beautiful woman, with all the richess of the world waiting for her. He had no hope. The slender vigor of her body, the grace and fire of it, couldn't be for him. He hadn't luck enough to possess it; and never would.

"Well, Tom?"

He said: "Tommy's father was a man by the name of DePard, who was killed last night in the fighting. He was a common crook in Buffalo's gang. I had known this all along. It is true, as Charm told you, that this morning I asked her to marry me. If it seems strange to you, Lily, I can't explain it. Only I'd like you to remember that when we were in Bill Fell's cabin and I kissed you, I meant it. That's all."

He saw whiteness grow more pronounced on her cheeks; it deepened the shadows along her smooth brow. There wasn't any sureness in her voice. It fell, it lost strength and was colorless.

"You don't need to explain, Tom. You're marrying her because—" She checked the rest of it. "No, I won't say something unkind. You're just marrying her. That's all there is to it."

He said bluntly and badly, with no attempt to make it seem favorable: "Charm's marrying Matt Strang, not me. I was turned down."

There was an almost absolute stillness in the room. He could not understand the change he saw. The rose-tints ran swiftly across her face. Her expressive lips stirred; and at once she was openly angered.

"Why did you come here?"

"I don't know," he said wearily. "I don't know."

"Yes, you do!" She came around the table, walking toward him with that stirring grace that was like melody. She stopped in front of him and looked up at his blackened, fatigue-etched cheeks. Her darkly blue eyes were full of storm. "I can tell you, Tom Sebastian! And I have a right to say it. You proposed to Charm because you felt it was your duty to give her and Tommy a name. According to your own thinking that came first—to recognize your obligation—and everything else came afterwards."

"Lily—" he said.

"But she wouldn't have it that way—and so you have made your bow to your duty, and now you are here." The thought of it made her more intense, more openly scornful. "You know how I felt. I'd thrown myself at you. But you pushed me back because I didn't fit into the scheme of things.

But you are quite free again and you want me. I am second choice. I am what is left after everything else has been fixed up and everybody else satisfied. You want me to throw away all my own hopes and wipe away whatever tears I've had and come smiling back—and feel happy to be second choice."

"Yes," he said, drearily, "I suppose that's it."

She checked her talk and stared at him. She said, more calmly: "I came back to Reno with my mind made up, Tom. Do you think I'd change it again? I have my tickets bought for Hollywood. Do you think, after all that's happened I'd throw them away? I said good-bye to my career once. Do you think I would give it up again?"

"Lily—" he said, very humble, very sad.

But she lifted one small doubled fist and struck him full in the chest; and then she put both arms around his neck and dropped her face against his coat. He felt the releasing emotion race through her. He thought she was silently crying. He put his arms around her, hungrily, not understanding this strange moment. But when he felt the weight of her body against him he knew he would never let her again get outside his possession. Then he heard her say:

"Of course, I would! I always knew I'd come back—if you wanted it so! I can't help that, Tom. I can't help it! But don't hurt me so desperately again, Tom! Please!"

She lifted her head and he bent his solemn face downward; and all that he felt was in that long, crushing kiss. And it was strange that when she stepped back from him she was smiling.

"On that table are nine telegrams from Hollywood. It doesn't matter now, my dear. They never mattered since the night you walked into this room and scowled at me."

"Lily," he said, "you're doing most of the giving. Is it worth it?"

"Who knows? We can only do what we must do. And this is what I must do. I've never asked life to make me happy. All I want is to love—to be loved. That's what I told you in the beginning. You are a strange man and your will seldom bends. Maybe we shall have our regrets. But I think you love me—and if you do I know you'll never change. You are the rock hills of your country. That is all I ask. It is enough."

Timmy was in the doorway. He cleared his throat and spoke brusquely. "If this is a rehearsal it's very good. But there's a train leaving."

Lily said, soft and smiling and tender: "Here is my man, Timmy."

"I envy you," said Timmy, very slowly. "For you are two full people and there won't be any dull days for either of you, as long as you live."

Sebastian pulled up his heavy head and he smiled his slow, rare smile. Faint recklessness returned to his glance and some of that sharp, keen sense of living came back to his features and erased the weariness on them. He put an arm around Lily. He said:

"That will be a long time, Timmy. Old soldiers never die. They merely fade away."

SIGNET and SIGNET CLASSIC Books of Special Interest

- ☐ **SIGNET DOUBLE WESTERN—SMOKE OF THE GUN by John S. Daniels and WILD RIDERS by Lee Hoffman.** (#J8667—$1.95)
- ☐ **SIGNET DOUBLE WESTERN—WAR PARTY by John S. Daniels and THE CROSSING by John S. Daniels.** (#J8761—$1.95)
- ☐ **SIGNET DOUBLE WESTERN—THE MAN FROM YESTERDAY by John S. Daniels and THE GUNFIGHTERS by John S. Daniels.** (#E8932—$1.95)
- ☐ **CONQUERING HORSE by Frederick Manfred.** (#W8739—$1.50)
- ☐ **LORD GRIZZLY by Frederick Manfred.** (#E8311—$1.75)
- ☐ **THE VIRGINIAN by Owen Wister. Afterword by Max Westbrook.** (#CJ1247—$1.95)
- ☐ **THE GREAT GUNFIGHTERS OF THE WEST by Carl W. Breihan.** (#W7434—$1.50)
- ☐ **CROW KILLER by Raymond W. Thorp and Robert Bunker.** (#Y7316—$1.25)
- ☐ **THE WESTERN WRITINGS OF STEPHEN CRANE edited by Frank Bergon.** (#CJ1189—$1.95)
- ☐ **BOUND FOR THE PROMISED LAND by Marius Richard.** (#E7459—$2.25)
- ☐ **THE PIONEERS by James Fenimore Cooper. Afterword by Robert E. Spiller.** (#CJ1156—$1.95)

* Price slightly higher in Canada

Buy them at your local bookstore or use this convenient coupon for ordering.

THE NEW AMERICAN LIBRARY, INC.
P.O. Box 999, Bergenfield, New Jersey 07621

Please send me the SIGNET and SIGNET CLASSIC BOOKS I have checked above. I am enclosing $__________ (please add 50¢ to this order to cover postage and handling). Send check or money order — no cash or C.O.D.'s. Prices and numbers are subject to change without notice.

Name ______________________________

Address ______________________________

City __________ **State** __________ **Zip Code** __________

Allow 4-6 weeks for delivery.
This offer is subject to withdrawal without notice.

Chapter 1

Driving from Carson to Reno, Lily Tennant saw the sullen banner of dust boil up in the valley and cross the highway like smoke from a grass fire. When she came nearer, pressing a slim foot on the brake pedal, its yellow cloud billowed against her and dimmed the burning brilliance of the Nevada sun. Squarely blocking the highway, a man sat in the saddle of a true palomino pony and presented her with a long broad back. Cattle filed out of the desert on the left, crossed the road and went bawling and fretful into the desert on the right, lumbering hooves churning up the bitter alkali. Lily Tennant came to a full stop and sounded her horn.

The horseman, seeming to count the passing stock, didn't bother to move. Settling back on a leather seat that stung her with its soaked-in heat, Lily knew then she had made a mistake in pulling the top of the roadster down at Carson. As long as the car was in motion there was some breeze to cut the furnace-like temperature of the afternoon; but trapped here in the desolate open the sun instantly scorched her exposed skin. She laid her arm on the edge of the door and drew it sharply back; the enamel was that hot. The car's chromium trim threw off a thousand slivers of sulky light—and her wrist watch told her she had been waiting five minutes. She tried the horn again.

A young steer bolted from the stream of beef, whereupon a second rider appeared from the obscure haze and turned it back into line. A heavier billow of this acrid dust rolled down upon Lily Tennant and she bowed her head against such insistent misery and saw her dress turning to a grimy drab. When she looked up again the rear vision mirror showed her a still, slim face flushed and faintly damp. Actually, her makeup—as little as there was of it—was dissolving, and the ivory smoothness of her forehead was really dirty. She was, she thought with growing outrage, a complete wreck and nothing but immersion in ice water and a change from the skin out would ever make her the same woman again.

And there the man sat, another strong and dumb character of the wide open spaces, ignoring her torture. Lily Tennant, whom Hollywood knew as a marvel of self-discipline, had a temper as well and now she suddenly let it go and banged the horn button with a violence she hoped would express the pure venom of her feelings.

The tall man wheeled his horse reluctantly and rode back to her car with a deliberation that was unutterably wicked. All she saw of him as he bent slightly from his saddle was a steel-gray glance and sun-bleached brows above a bandanna covering the rest of his face. The hair showing beneath his hat was black as ink, the exposed surface of his face was deeply tanned.

"After all," said Lily Tennant, acidly quiet, "this is a state highway."

"That's right."

"So—haven't I been punished enough?"

He hooked a leg around the saddle horn; and that indolent gesture, too, served to feed her just anger. Nor did it help to know that his glance, solidly steady, saw her at her cooked and wilted worst. He said: "Why?"

"For daring to honk at you when I came up here ten minutes ago."

"Wrong guess," he said, and afterwards thought to pull the bandanna down from his face. Yellow dust puffed up when he brushed it aside. He had long, solid lips and the rest of his features were smooth and taciturn and indifferent, matching the inscrutable gray of his eyes. "I am only trying to get my cattle across the road," he added.

"I am only trying to get to Reno."

"You'll have plenty of time to waste after you get there," he observed quietly.

"If that could possibly be any of your business," Lily Tennant retorted.

Instantly she regretted the open anger of her words, recalling the shrewd observation of Sam Wein in Hollywood who had done so much for her. "You got a temper," he had said. "It's the electricity that pushes you on. But don't never waste your temper on the wrong things, Lily. Save it for the times when an explosion will blast something that's got to be blasted."

"Sorry," said the man on the horse. His tipped-down f[illegible] was young, but as masculine as any she had ever se[illegible]